Drop Dead Gorgeous

ALSO BY RACHEL GIBSON AND GALLERY BOOKS

How Lulu Lost Her Mind

Drop Dead Gorgeous

A NOVEL

Rachel Gibson

G

GALLERY BOOKS

NEW YORK   LONDON   TORONTO   SYDNEY   NEW DELHI

Gallery Books
An Imprint of Simon & Schuster, Inc.
1230 Avenue of the Americas
New York, NY 10020

First Gallery Books trade paperback edition April 2022

GALLERY BOOKS and colophon are registered
trademarks of Simon & Schuster, Inc.

For information about special discounts for bulk purchases,
please contact Simon & Schuster Special Sales at 1-866-506-1949
or business@simonandschuster.com.

The Simon & Schuster Speakers Bureau can bring authors to your live event.
For more information or to book an event, contact the Simon & Schuster Speakers
Bureau at 1-866-248-3049 or visit our website at www.simonspeakers.com.

Interior design by Michelle Marchese

Manufactured in the United States of America

1   3   5   7   9   10   8   6   4   2

Library of Congress Cataloging-in-Publication Data
Names: Gibson, Rachel, author.
Title: Drop dead gorgeous : a novel / Rachel Gibson.
Description: First Gallery Books trade paperback edition. | New York :
Gallery Books, 2022.
Identifiers: LCCN 2021025564 (print) | LCCN 2021025565 (ebook) | ISBN
9781982118150 (trade paperback) | ISBN 9781982118167 | ISBN
9781982118174 (ebook)
Classification: LCC PS3557.I2216 D76 2022 (print) | LCC PS3557.I2216
(ebook) | DDC 813/.54—dc23
LC record available at https://lccn.loc.gov/2021025564
LC ebook record available at https://lccn.loc.gov/2021025565

ISBN 978-1-9821-1815-0
ISBN 978-1-9821-1817-4 (ebook)

For Mary and Texas transplants everywhere.
If you measure driving distance in hours and know that Coke
usually means Dr Pepper—well, bless your heart,
you were raised by a Texan.

Glorious Way Evangelical is the center of my momma's life. She looks forward to church worship like an alcoholic looks forward to happy hour at Woody's Watering Hole.

Sundays are the Lord's day, and I've spent most of mine praising God and singing in the Glorious Way choir, listening to Reverend Johnny J. Jackson, and wishing my behind wasn't getting numb.

If I was any good at figuring sums in my head, I'd add up how much of my life has been spent sitting on hard pews. I mostly rely on the calculator on my phone, but if I had to take a guess at the number . . . there's four Sundays in a month, multiplied by twelve months in a year, times twenty-five years . . . subtract the times I faked a head cold or period cramps, and that equals . . . a whole heck of a lot.

The phone in my dress pocket lights up and I slide it out far enough to see who's texting. I glance up at Johnny J. preaching his usual fire and brimstone, then open the text from HotGuyNate. I bite my lower lip to keep from grinning like a cat full of canary. I type *Yes* and hit send. I've never driven more than twenty miles for a hookup or a coffee date, but Nate is the kind of guy worth driving two hundred miles to meet. "Brittany Lynn!" Momma says under her breath. "Jesus is watchin' you."

I try not to roll my eyes as I slide the phone back into my pocket. If that's true, Jesus is interfering in my love life. Don't get me wrong: I love Jesus—but I've spent so much time in devotion, I reckon I've earned bonus points that I can use here on earth or in heaven.

"Evil demons whisper temptations into the ears of man. These demons are liars! Do not listen or you will burn in hell when our Lord returns!" Johnny J. is yelling about Satan and scaring the sinners clear in the back row. "Lord, deliver us from wickedness!"

"Lord, deliver us from wickedness," Momma repeats, clutching a Bible to her big breasts. When it comes to the good book, I don't know anyone who knows more than Momma. You could say she's an expert on the rapture, and she dreams of the day that she floats to heaven on a fluffy cloud and gets to wave goodbye to the sinners left behind. In particular, Daddy and his second wife, "Floozy Face."

I've never liked Floozy, and she's never liked me. She thinks constructive criticism is her way of being helpful. I think constructive criticism is her way of being a bitch. She says I need to grow up. I say, "You need Jesus." She tells Daddy I'm immature for my age. I tell her she's vertically challenged. It goes without saying that we're never in the same place for long.

I was ten when Daddy moved out of our house and in with Floozy Face, aka Mona Lisa Calhoun, and Momma has hardly spoken to him since. At my high school graduation Momma refused to be in the same picture with Daddy and me no matter how much I begged.

After all these years she's still as bitter as ever. I tell her that good Christians don't dream of riding off on a big, fluffy cloud, hooting and hollering and acting holier-than-thou. I tell her to get bigger dreams for herself, but Momma never listens to one thing that she doesn't want to hear. I inherited that from her, I'm told.

I glance at my phone twice more, and by the time Johnny J. is done sermonizing, my behind is so numb that I have a hard time standing up. Momma has a harder time than me, but she walks with me out to our old minivan. Momma is staying for Bible study, and someone in the group will give her a ride home afterward. She has plans to quote scripture, and I have plans of my own.

"Why are you drivin' all the way to Alpine to see Lida Haynes?"

Lida has been my best friend since second grade at Marfa Elementary, but I quit speaking to her last week when she said some very hurtful things. "Alpine is only twenty-six miles from here," I tell Momma, even though she knows this. "See you later. I'll call if I'm spendin' the night." I give her a hug, then hop in the van and head out of the church parking lot. I sing along with Jason Aldean on the radio and stick my arm out of the window to wave goodbye. Singing has always played a part in my life. When I was young, I dreamed of being a country-and-western singer. Momma used to drive me to competitions when we could afford it. I even won first place a time or two.

I drive past the turn to Alpine and head in the opposite direction toward El Paso, two hundred miles northwest of Marfa. Momma used to make my outfits. The best was a leopard-print coat made so I could look like Shania Twain at the Texas Shooting Stars singing competition. I was nine and belted out "That Don't Impress Me Much." Momma still has the video. The next year I became obsessed with *Hannah Montana* and changed my stage name to Wittany so that when I got famous I could switch back to Brittany and not get mobbed by fans. When I was seventeen I tried out for *American Idol* in Austin. I thought for sure the panel would love "Wittany," but Simon said I should come back after I lost weight. Paula agreed—and she was supposed to be the nice one. Wittany died that day, and the only singing I do these days is at church.

Even though I've given up on that dream, I do write lyrics. My most creative time is when I'm in bed at night. I have notebooks full of songs and my latest is called "Big Dreams in a Small Town." I keep the notebooks under my mattress and I've never shown them to anyone.

I pull my phone out of my pocket and slide it into the holder next to Momma's dashboard Jesus. I have a text message from my Visa but nothing from HotGuyNate since he texted me in church.

I met Nate on Tinder this past Thursday. He's driving from somewhere in New Mexico and we're meeting at the Kitty Cat Lounge. If we like each other and things are looking good, I plan to pounce on him like he's a bag of catnip.

Nate isn't my first Tinder date. I've been on the site for a few years. I'm also on Match.com, OkCupid, and Plenty of Fish. I want to fall in love and get married, but the closest I've ever come to it was a six-month relationship with Ricky Nunez when I was twenty-two. Ricky had a snaggletooth and acne and lived in a beat-down double-wide.

He broke my heart.

Nate is a lot better looking than Ricky, and that's an understatement. He's the kind of good-looking that I've always dreamed of finding. He has dark hair and blue eyes and a flashy white smile, and he swiped right when he saw me. I've been walking around for days feeling sassy and filled with glow. Lida is the only person I told about Nate, but she wasn't supportive at all. Instead she reminded me of Pete Parras, a superhot guy who used to hook up with me until he found a superhot girl-friend. Lida said she could tell by Nate's bio and photos that he was a user like Pete and she couldn't be happy for me. I had to remind *her* that she moved to Alpine for smooth-talking Bubba Crum and lived with him for a year before she found out that he had a wife in Van Horn and a baby momma in Fort Davis. She said she learned from Bubba how to spot a liar but that I didn't learn anything from Pete. I got aggravated with Lida and said some things I shouldn't have. She got aggravated with me and said things she shouldn't have, and we haven't spoken since. We've never gone this long without talking, and I don't know if we can ever get back to the way things were before we got ugly with each other.

An hour outside El Paso, I pull into a truck stop for gas, grab my suitcase from the back seat, and head for the bathroom. I change out of my church clothes and into a pair of jeans and a "Don't Mess with a Texas Girl" T-shirt with rhinestone embel-lishments, of course.

Right after I graduated from beauty school, I took profes-sional online cosmetics courses. Since then, I take refresher classes to keep up on the latest trends and techniques. I might not be the thinnest or best-looking girl around, but I do the best I can with what I've got.

I open my cosmetics bag and apply makeup to complement my latest look. Last week I covered my brown hair with a dark blue balayage. I did it all by myself and I'm really happy with how it turned out. I coordinated the color with my nails and had Lorna give me a deluxe pedicure.

Lorna is the owner of the Do or Dye, where Momma and me work five days a week, back-combing hair halfway to heaven and spraying it down with enough extreme hold to survive a cat-five hurricane. It's okay for now, but I don't want to work there all my life like Momma.

I find my teasing comb, lift the hair on the crown of my head with one hand, and shake a can of Helmet Head with the other. Most people make the mistake of spraying the hair directly, but the trick is to create a nice fog and let it settle.

I brush my teeth real quick, pay for my gas, then hit the road again.

Blake Shelton is on the radio and I crank it up to sing along with him and Gwen. Out of all the men singing country these days, I'd have to say that Trace Adkins still has the best voice (sorry, Blake), but Sam Hunt is smoking hot. If I ever saw him in person, I don't know if I could control myself.

My phone dings with a text, but I can't see it for the sun pouring through the windshield. I pull it from the holder and put it in the shade of my lap. I glance from the highway to the message, then back again.

It's from HotGuyNate: *Are you there?*

I push the talk-to-text icon and say, "I'm about sixty miles away," then tap send. The closer I get to El Paso, the more my nerves tingle and my stomach gets tight.

The text dings. I pull it up. HotGuyNate: *I can't make it.*

I blink several times and read it ten more. I can't believe it and I glance back and forth from the highway to the text. My heart drops and pounds at the same time. "Is this a joke?" I say, and tap send.

He came up with the plan to meet in El Paso and picked out the Kitty Cat Lounge. I jumped at the chance, but it wasn't my idea.

HotGuyNate: *Sorry.*

Sorry? That's it? I lied to Momma, fought with Lida, and wasted my time, effort, and gas money. Worse than all of that, a man's let me down—again.

I raise my phone and ask, "Why?" then hit send. I blink back tears of hurt and disappointment. Why can't anything ever work out for me?

HotGuyNate: *My wife found out.*

Wife? He has a wife? My phone slips from my hand and disappears between the seats. He's married? His Tinder profile says he's single and the only pictures are of him. Lida was right and I told her she wasn't a good friend.

Now I'm aggravated and shove my hand between the seats. Tears burn my eyes and roll down my cheeks. I feel around and touch a corner of my phone. Momma says I have a quick temper. I say she's right. She says I need to control it. I say not right now. I'm going to give HotGuyNate a *hot* piece of my mind first

I lean toward the passenger side for a better grip on my phone, but I keep my eyes on the highway. I don't have a lot of rules when it comes to dating. You could say I have low standards, but I do draw the line at married men. I know firsthand what cheating does to a family.

I inch my phone toward me with my fingers and peer between the seats. My daddy cheated and none of our lives were ever the same. I love him, but he was a skirt-chasing liar.

A loud scrape drowns out Blake and Gwen on the radio. The van leans sideways and I sit all the way up. Dirt and scrub hit the windshield and I slam on the brakes. More dirt. More scrub. I can't see a thing. Everything is happening fast and my brain can't keep up. The van tips this way and that. I'm upside down and right-side up. I'm rolling. Momma's dashboard Jesus flies past my head. Everything goes black.

I always heard that when it's your time to die, there's a warm light that leads you straight up to heaven. You're surrounded by so much beauty, it hurts your eyes. Your dead relatives are there and y'all fall on each other's neck and weep. Angels sing and blow trumpets, and you're filled with so much love that you just know you've landed smack-dab in heaven.

It's not like that. At least, not for me. There's no warm light and certainly no beauty. There's blood everywhere and I'm assuming it's mine. I don't know a single soul in the room, and instead of singing angels I just hear the solid *beeeep* of a heart monitor. A doctor stands on a little step stool and pumps up and down on my chest with the palms of his hands. I only know that's my body on that gurney because there's no mistaking my blue balayage. A steady red stream runs down my arm that's hanging off the bed and blood drips from my middle finger to a puddle on the floor.

Wait, if that's me on the bed—who am I? Are there two of me? *Am I going to die?*

People rush past, tying yellow surgical scrubs behind their backs and white masks around their heads. They snap on gloves and shout to each other. Someone cuts the jeans and the "Don't Mess with a Texas Girl" T-shirt from my body while someone wheels in one of those defibrillators like on TV. I look down, but my clothes aren't bloody or cut.

The doctor puts two paddles on my chest and everyone backs away and lifts their faces to the flat screen above the bed. The doctor shocks my heart and my body jerks so hard I raise a hand to my chest, but I feel nothing. No jolt of pain or fluttering heartbeat, but the green line on the monitor bounces and beeps across the screen. I reckon that's good.

No one sees me standing at the foot of the gurney, but I don't think I'm dead. Not yet, anyway. I should be freaking out right about now, but I'm not. Mostly I'm just confused about what in the heck is going on. I figure that I'm outside my body, watching someone shove a tube down my throat. I figure I'm in a hospital emergency room, but I can't figure out how I got here or why I'm such a mess. The last thing I remember is sitting in church and something about Momma's dashboard Jesus.

I look around. Is my momma here, too?

My heart monitor flatlines again, filling the room with the steady *beeep*, and a blinding flash draws my attention to the ceiling. I look up at a bolt of brilliant lightning above me. It wavers and flickers like it's made of pieces of shattered mirror. One of my arms lifts as some unseen force pulls the rest of me upward. I guess this is the light everyone talks about. The one that will take me to the family reunion in the sky. I am sucked through the ceiling and placed on a white circle of light. I'm by myself but I don't feel alone. I don't have time to sort things out in my brain before flashes of silver and blue soar past my head and the circle beneath my feet stretches in both directions and forms a path that looks like it's been bedazzled with pink rhinestones just for me. It sparkles and glows and fills me with warmth from the inside out. At the end there's brilliant gold light that I'm assuming leads to God, not the Wizard of Oz.

My pathway to heaven is in front of me, and my life is behind. I'm not overcome with joy like the Reverend Johnny J. preaches. I'm not angry, but I am not exactly thrilled, either. I have plans for my life. I want to get married and have children. I want to go to a RaeLynn concert and belt out "Queens Don't" at the top of my lungs. I want to go to Paris and see the Eiffel Tower and eat macarons at Ladurée.

None of those things will happen now. It doesn't seem fair. I want to go back home. The backs of my eyes sting but tears don't fill them.

I'll miss out on all that. I'll miss my momma most of all, but I try to take comfort in the hope that I'll see my grandparents again. I love and miss them. Well, except for Daddy's side. Papaw Snider died before I was born, but I heard he and the devil drank from the same straw. The same could be said for Mamaw Rose, too. She used to call me "Pudge's girl" and pinch me really hard for no good reason other than she hated Momma. She was horrible, and if evil people get what's coming to them, she's roasting in hell. At least I hope so.

As if God heard my unkind thoughts, I am thrown back into the emergency room like a bad penny. The ceiling slams shut, sending down bits of shattered mirror throughout the room. The same doctors and nurses are still working on my lifeless body, but they don't seem to have noticed the bolt of lightning or the glitter falling all around like polished rain.

What the heck is happening?

"I thought you were a goner."

I turn toward an older Hispanic man standing in the doorway. He's wearing a red polo shirt buttoned up to his throat, horrible red-white-and-blue plaid pants, and shiny white golf shoes. He has a huge salt-and-pepper mustache like Pancho Villa and he's looking straight at me.

"What?"

The man lifts a golf club and motions toward the monitor on the wall. "You almost checked out for good."

The green line bumps up and down with my heartbeat and I point to myself. "Are you talkin' to me, sir?"

"Of course."

"You can see me?"

"You have hair like a peacock." Well, I wasn't going for peacock, but I like the comparison. I almost thank him, when he pushes his hands out at his sides. "And *grande*."

Yeah, I could stand to lose a few, but he looks like the only exercise he gets is combing that bushy mustache. I keep my opinion behind my teeth because there are more important issues facing me right now. "Am I dead?"

"Not yet."

"Was my momma in the accident?"

"There was no one else. You came in alone."

I didn't kill Momma or anyone else. That's a relief, and hopefully a good sign for the whole heaven thing. "Am I goin' to die?"

"Questions of life or death are not for me to know." He shrugs. "But it's not lookin' good for you."

"That's what I thought." I move toward him. "Are you a ghost?" His outline is fuzzier than mine.

"Not exactly."

"An angel?"

"Not yet."

"A demon?"

"*¡Dios me libre!*"

"Are you dead?"

"Most definitely." His smile lifts the corners of his mustache. "I died on a beautiful June mornin', the kind you only see if you're lucky enough to live in Texas. Not a cloud in all that endless blue." He stares past me, all dreamy-eyed, like he doesn't see or hear the chaos in the room behind me. "I double-eagled on the eighth. Do you know the odds of hittin' a shot like that?"

Like I care. I glance over my shoulder at the people working on my body. I have a lot of questions and he's talking about golf.

"Six million to one," he answers anyway, and I return my attention to him. "Ten seconds later I was struck by lightnin' and died before I hit the ground."

I don't know anything about golf, but I know a lie when I hear one. I was raised on Texas *bool-sheet*. I love a good whopper same as anyone else, but this one is so bad, it insults my intelligence, and if there is one thing in this world that gets me riled up, it's being mistaken for stupid. "Well, don't that beat all you ever stepped in," I say, shaking my head like I'm impressed. "What are the odds of hittin' a six-million-to-one shot, then gettin' hit by lightnin' on a sunny day in June?"

"That's not for me to know."

I roll my eyes. Of course not.

"I am just a concierge, is all."

"A concierge?" That's a new one on me. "Isn't this an emergency room? In a *hospital*?"

"Most certainly." Before he can clear things up, another bolt of brilliant lightning splinters the ceiling and blasts glitter all over the place. I hear the beep of my heart flatlining and I am pulled upward again. "Go with peace in God's light," the old golfer tells me.

"Am I dyin' again?" I've heard of people dying and coming back, but I've never heard of them dying, coming back, and dying again. Maybe it's one of God's mysterious ways.

"Don't get off the path."

"What? Why?" That sounds like an important piece of information, and I push a hand against the ceiling in an effort to stop. "What will happen if I get off the path?" My hand passes through the tile and I yell down at him, "You should have talked about that instead of your dumb golf game!" I am yanked through the crack and it slams shut behind me with such force that sparks scatter beneath my feet. Just like before, flashes of silver and blue arc past my head, but this time they quickly dissipate into nothing. A pitch-blackness presses into me so completely that I see nothing. Where's the white circle like last time? The glittery path?

Am I in hell?

"Whatever I did, I ask God's forgiveness," I call out, my voice shaking, but I've never committed sins that deserve hell. Maybe I've fornicated a time or two . . . or fifteen . . . but finding love in all the wrong places is not a big sin. Not like murder or devil worship or drinking on Sunday.

As if on cue, the glittery pink path lights up beneath my feet and stretches toward heaven. This time I am moved along like I'm standing on one of those walkways in an airport. I'm still confused about everything that's happened to me, but a few things are sorted out in my head now. I'm fairly sure I've died twice. I think I wrecked Momma's minivan and lost her dashboard Jesus. She can buy another bobblehead doll, but she doesn't have the money for another car. I don't know what she'll do without her van.

I don't know what she'll do without me, either.

The last time I tried moving out of my momma's house, she pitched a fit and fell in it. "I can't stand the thought of you leavin' me, Brittany Lynn. You're all I got," she cried. She kept it up until I couldn't take it anymore and gave in, and that was just me wanting to move across town. Dead is a little further than Russell Street.

I'm only twenty-five. I have dreams for myself that don't include dying. I want to open my own salon someday. One that smells like a spa treatment—eucalyptus and steam—instead of perm solution and Aqua Net. I already have a name picked out and everything: Shear Elegance Salon and Spa. I saw it on Pinterest and think it sounds real classy. I have my plans all figured out . . . except for how I'm going to afford it and how I'm going to get Momma out of Marfa.

The Do or Dye isn't what I consider a high-paying career, and Marfa isn't exactly what you'd call cosmopolitan. We do get tourists on the weekends, coming to gaze at stars or see where *No Country for Old Men* was filmed. They come to Marfa to view the ghost lights or look at Donald Judd's art installation, but no one's going to rush to Marfa for a cut and color or a deluxe pedicure.

I wish I was rich and Momma wasn't so stubborn. I wish life was fair, but it doesn't matter now. If life was fair, God would do something about famine, mass murder, and period cramps. If God was fair, bad people would die at twenty-five and good people could live out their dreams.

Wait, I hope God didn't hear me complain about how he runs things, because everyone knows that God doesn't like ingrates and whiners.

The walkway stops. Did God hear me? I clutch my chest

above where my heart used to be. Am I going to get tossed out again? I guess I wouldn't be mad about that. My path is still sparkly, but the brilliant gold light at the end seems to be fading.

The golfer said not to get off the path, but he didn't mention anything about the path stalling on the way to God's light. I don't know if I should start walking or stay put. Should I hoot and holler like Momma on her cloud? I'm not sure, but if there is one thing that's a calcified fact, it's that if the path starts to reverse, I'm running like hell in heaven's direction.

I look around for a sign or a signal or something. The harder I look, the more I think I can see outlines of other paths. Those paths aren't as bright as mine, maybe because I can also make out the outlines of people. A lot of people. Those paths are crowded and I'm all alone on mine. "Can y'all hear me?" I call out, but I don't get an answer. There's one more big difference, too. Those paths are moving and mine is not.

Why? Did God change his plan for me? If that's the case, he should take into consideration that I've been a good Christian all my life. Maybe I don't get all hypnotic and speak in tongues. Maybe I don't raise my arms in church and beg God to take me up right then and there. I'm just not that kind of person. I'm more the kind who watches it all and thinks that praying to get plucked up like a carrot is just plain stupid. And as everyone knows, you can fix just about anything but stupid.

Wait. Was that unkind? Did I just think that out loud? Did God hear me? Why is this happening to me?

Does he know about the bonus points?

3

I'm thrown out like a bad penny again. That's twice now. The ceiling slams shut and that glittery stuff floats downward like before. I don't know what happened. I was just standing on the path, waiting around for it to restart, and now I'm back at the hospital, but not in the emergency room like before. There are only two nurses with me now and the room is less chaotic. The only sounds are the beeping monitors and the rhythmic swish of a ventilator.

I stand at the end of a bed and watch as one nurse adjusts tubes sewn into my chest and taped to my skin. Another checks the web of wires attached to my body from the equipment keeping me alive. They talk about the hours I've been in surgery and how many times I died on the table. If that isn't scary enough, looking at my body is terrifying. I want to curl into a ball and tell myself this is all a nightmare.

The blue balayage is gone and my head is shaved. There's some sort of probe sticking out of my skull, which I don't think is ever a good sign. My eyes and nose are so swollen and purple that I hardly recognize myself. Just the tips of my blue fingernails show beyond the splint on my left arm and hand. Sutures close a horrific incision that runs from my sternum to mid-stomach. It looks like it hurts, but I don't feel any pain. A white sheet covers me from navel to the tips of my toes, and the sight of my exposed belly and breasts upsets me more than anything else. I have struggled with my weight my entire life, and now this. My chest has been cut apart and sewn back together again. I am so broken that I hardly recognize myself. The least the nurses could do is cover me and give me some dignity.

"Welcome back."

It's the golfer, and I move to stand in front of him. "Get out of here. I'm practically nekked."

"I've seen worse." A smile lifts one corner of his thick mustache. "I've seen better, too."

"Does the Welcome Wagon know you're a perv?"

His mustache falls. "I have no control over a patient's nekked state. It's my duty to greet new arrivals and explain their circumstances. I keep track of all incomin' and outgoin', calm fears and answer questions."

Great. I have a few of those, but before I can ask, a nurse moves from the side of my bed and walks straight through me. It's a bump and whoosh and charges the air with little snaps of static electricity. She doesn't seem to notice and continues down a hall past closed doors as tiny gold and blue pops follow behind in her wake. "That was—"

"Shh," he whispers, leaning forward in anticipation. "Wait for it."

I don't know why he's whispering. No one can hear us. "What?" I whisper.

"Shh. Wait for it. . . ."

The nurse turns toward a room and all the tiny pops catch up, pass through, and snap her fingers when she touches the door handle. She yelps and jumps back, shaking her hand.

"Woo-ee, it never gets old." The golfer laughs. "That made my day."

If that makes his day, then he must lead a very dull life, but it does get me to thinking that maybe carpet isn't really to blame for static shocks after all.

"The bigger the spirit, the bigger the snap, crackle, and pop, and you got her good. Last month a doctor's hair stood straight up after he passed through a three-hundred-pound football player." He clears his throat and straightens. "But physical contact with the livin' is discouraged. For obvious reasons and such."

I'm a cosmetologist and can carry on polite conversation with just about anyone, but this guy says a lot about nothing, and I have important things to get to the bottom of. "Where was I?"

He turns to me and answers, "The in-between."

"In between what?"

"Life and death. You were revived several times, so your path was put on suspension until your destination was determined either way." He squares his shoulders. "Our trauma doctors stubbornly fight for every life. We are the best trauma hospital in the state, and that includes Parkland, no matter what Ingrid claims. She was concierge at Parkland the day President John F. Kennedy died, after all."

"Well, all I—"

"All hell broke loose that day, I can tell you," he says over top of me. "How she got promoted to director of Southwest Thirty-One is still a mystery."

"That in-between place was scary as all git-out," I say, stopping his tangent before I get real aggravated with him. "I don't

ever want to get stuck there again." He looks like he's not going
to give up on his Ingrid rant, but I can talk water uphill if I have
to. "I didn't know what was goin' on or where I was headed. You
said I was dead and now I'm not. I was there and now I'm back
here. You didn't explain anythin' before I got sucked up again."

"There wasn't time. I told you to stay on the path. I did
my job."

Well, he sucks at his "job," if you ask me. "Isn't there a manual or guidebook or somethin' on what to expect when you die?"

"No. There are no *Dyin' for Dummies* books."

I think he just implied I'm a dummy. I think he's getting back
at me for calling him a perv. I tell myself not to get worked up,
but I can't keep my eyes from narrowing.

"What happened to you is uncommon, but I'm sure you've
heard of folks dyin', then comin' back. With you dyin' several
times on the operatin' table, and with the Pacific Rim catastrophe, you're lucky you got back here as quick as you did."

Pardon me if I don't feel all that lucky. "There's been a
catastrophe?"

"Yessiree. Catastrophes tend to gum up the works. When
tens of thousands of folks pass in a big earthquake, and a hundred thousand more with the tsunami . . ." He shakes his head.
"It'll get sorted out eventually."

That might explain the crowded paths I saw, but . . . "This
isn't the first disaster since God created the world, and you're
sayin' he hasn't come up with a catastrophe plan in all that time?
What's he been doin'?"

"That's not for me to know."

Of course not.

"I'm just a concierge is all."

He's just a wing nut is all.

"Now that it's clear you will be with us until the time you pass, wake, or are moved to a different facility, you will need to know how to proceed and what to expect while in a comatose state." He points his golf club at me. "From the time of birth, your spirit creates energy to fuel your physical body. When you die, your spirit leaves the earth plane, and without fuel, your physical body is returned to the elements."

He drops the head of his club and continues. "In cases such as coma, your body goes dormant but your spirit does not and keeps creatin' energy as always. When all that energy is no longer used as fuel, the spirit may leave the physical body for periods of time. However, while you are free to leave your physical body, you are not free to wander the hospital. You must remain here or in the Limbo Lounge. There are no exceptions," he says, like he's reading from *Dying for Dummies*. "Like all energy, yours will eventually drain from use. You will feel tired and need to reenter your physical body in order to recharge both."

Oh. I don't like the sound of returning to my body. The stitches holding me together look painful, not to mention the probe in my head. "Is there another way? Maybe a chargin' station like in the airport?" Last year when Momma and me flew from Midland to Amarillo to visit Aunt Bonnie Bell, cell charging stations were all over the place.

"You're not a cell phone."

Duh. "How long does it take to recharge?"

"That depends on your activity. Strong emotions from you, or the livin' around you, will accelerate the drain. And if you have family visitors, we prefer you remain in your room with them."

"Why?"

"That's not for me to know. I don't make the rules."

Uh-huh. I get the feeling he's playing dumb. Either that or he's lazy.

"Is this our new guest?"

I look to my left at a middle-aged man moving toward me. I'm so shocked to see anyone else that it takes a second or two for me to notice the solid outline of his tuxedo and ten-gallon hat. His edges aren't fuzzy like the golfer's. He looks more solid, like me.

"Yes. This is Marfa." The golfer turns to include the other gentleman. "Marfa, this is Clint."

"Howdy, Miss Marfa. That's some hair."

"Thank you, sir." I think. "Who's Marfa?"

"You."

"Me?" I put a hand on my chest. "My name isn't Marfa. I'm Brittany Lynn Snider."

"We already have a Brittany in this unit. That name has been claimed, so to avoid confusion, the incomin' party shall be referred to by their hometown," the golfer says, sounding like he's reading out of *Dying for Dummies* again.

"That's right, Miss Marfa." Clint continues down the hall and we walk with him. "My real name is Tom but there was a Tom, a Thomas, and a Tommy before I got here. Clint is my hometown."

Who cares? "Marfa's ugly. I don't want to be called Marfa! Why can't I go by Brittany Lynn or Lynn or by my last name?"

"I don't make the rules, and you have bigger concerns than a name, Marfa."

Wing nut. I let the name stew because I *do* have bigger concerns. "How long has it been since my accident?"

"On the earthly plane, you arrived four hours ago."

Four hours? It feels more like thirty minutes. "Has my momma come to see me yet?" I ask as we pass a room. I try to look inside but all I can see is the foot of a bed and a maroon curtain.

"No. I haven't seen anyone."

I wrecked the van and broke her Jesus, but she should be here by now. "Really? Her name is Carla Jean Snider."

"Does she live in El Paso? The traffic gets mighty backed up at the Spaghetti Bowl this time of day."

"No. She lives in Marfa." El Paso? What's the Spaghetti Bowl?

"That's three hours away, Miss Marfa."

I stop again. "What?" My memory is fuzzy, and just when I think it's going to clear up, it doesn't. "This is Big Bend hospital, right?"

"No."

"Pecos?"

"Wrong direction," the golfer says over his shoulder as he continues. "This is UMC El Paso."

"What?" I pass rooms on each side of the hall as I hurry to catch up with them. "How did I get here?"

"An ambulance brought you in."

"All the way from Marfa?"

"No. We don't send our ambulances that far away."

"I'm in El Paso," I say more to myself than anyone. "Are you sure?"

"Sure as can be, Miss Marfa."

"Why am I in El Paso?"

"Maybe one of those geo tours," Clint suggests, as if I look like the kind of girl who'd pass on a mountain of Buc-ee's Beaver Nuggets in favor of a mountain bike. He stops and tips his hat to a woman with fried blonde hair and skintight Wranglers. "Miss Kodiak."

"Clint. Concierge." Her outline is as solid as mine and Clint's, but she looks through me like I'm invisible. I recognize the look. I've seen it many times from snooty women like Kodiak. If she was nicer, and if I didn't have better things to do, I might give her a professional consultation and recommend a deep-conditioning hair mask for those thirsty roots growing from her center part.

"She's a long way from home," I say as she moves down the hall.

"That's her birth name," the golfer tells me. "They're about to bring Kodiak out of her coma, and she best shake her tail feathers and get there before she's marked as unresponsive and gets shipped off to Vista Hills for long-term care." He raises his voice. "She's not goin' to like the concierge at Vista Hills. Connie's from Terlingua and was left in the sun too long."

Kodiak runs down the hall and disappears into a room. "When a patient is comin' out of a coma, it's best if both body and soul are together for obvious reasons," the golfer tells me.

We continue down the hall, getting farther from my body, and I ask if the same holds true for when a person passes on. That seems like important information. "We prefer a soul raise from their physical being. Unfortunately, there are occasions when it doesn't occur that way."

Unfortunately? That sounds scary. "What happens?"

"Shit happens, Marfa. That's what." One minute he says, "That's not for me to know," and in the next he says "we" as if he was in on the planning. Now it's "shit happens" like he's Forrest Gump. He sighs and explains, "Sometimes a soul can't make it back to their body before their portal opens, and they are raised up from wherever they happen to be at that moment, be it in deep conversation or playin' bingo. Some patients witnessin' the passin' are reassured by the splendor and warmth of God's light while others screech like caged monkeys."

Bingo? I shake my head but don't ask. I'm confused and nothing about this day makes a lick of sense. The last thing I remember is sitting in church next to Momma. The night before, I remember I was writing lyrics like I always do. *Real Housewives* reruns were on the television, and I was texting . . . someone. "Why did I drive all the way to El Paso?" I wonder out loud.

"Do you have relatives in the area?" Clint asks.

"No."

"Visitin' a nice young fella?"

HotGuyNate. I was texting HotGuyNate from Tinder. I had plans to meet him in El Paso. I don't think I made it.

"Here we are."

We turn right and the hall opens to a room filled with sofas and wooden tables and chairs. It's like a common area in a retirement home, complete with people watching *Highway to Heaven* reruns on a large television or staring into a fish aquarium as a hologram of Noah's Ark battles choppy waves in the big tank. I take a step back. "Are we still in the hospital?"

"Yes and no. This is a part of the hospital that dwells on the spirit plane. It cannot be seen or accessed by humans. We call it the Limbo Lounge."

I take another step back. "Can I get stuck here like the in-between?"

"No. This is not a path to heaven. This is a place to relax and socialize while you wait."

The room looks to be filled with eight people, give or take. "And these people are . . . ?"

"Like you. In a comatose state, whether from traumatic injury or illness or other unfortunate events. Which, as you know, is a stressful and confusin' time. Patients come here to put their feet up—as the sayin' goes."

Most of the people in the room are in street clothes. Two cowgirls and an older woman wearing a housecoat and slippers are playing bingo. There's a blonde sitting alone at a card table, wearing a light blue slip, with her head down on her crossed arms, like she's so relaxed, she's zenned out. All of them look so normal that I can't begin to guess why they're here.

"It was a pleasure, Miss Marfa," Clint says as he moves to a small table and joins the women playing cards. The cowgirls stand to greet him, and from the height of their hair and size of their belt buckles, it looks like they ran afoul at a rodeo. Or maybe they were at a backyard barbecue and fighting words were exchanged, like when Aunt Sissy opened a can of whup-ass on Cousin Jr.'s wife for saying Aunt Sissy's old dog looked like roadkill and smelled worse. It happens to be true, but no one gets away with insulting Aunt Sissy's dog—or the Aggies or her Frito pie, come to think of it.

If I die, I don't know how much I'll miss family barbecues, but I am going to miss Frito pie, Texas sheet cake, Little Debbie Nutty Bars, Dr Pepper, and such.

"Television viewin' is provided by Paradise Inc. and includes such favorites as *7th Heaven*, *Heaven Help Us*, *Made in Heaven*, and *Beetlejuice*. Schedulin' is listed in the drop-down menu." The golfer points his club at the aquarium. "The reflectin' pool is strictly first come, first serve and offers hologram imagery from religious scenes throughout history."

I look at the television and the aquarium and ask, "What if you're an atheist?"

"You're in for a shock, I can tell you."

I reckon that makes sense. "Why are some people in regular clothes and some have on hospital gowns?"

"That is determined by what a patient was wearin' when they arrived." The golfer thumps his club on the floor. "I need all y'all's attention. This is our newest guest, Miss Marfa," he announces.

The other "guests" smile, greet me with a welcoming howdy, or give a little wave. They all seem friendly enough, except for the blonde in the blue slip, who sits straight up and outright laughs. I guess she's not zenned out after all. Strands of ash- and honey-colored hair slide across her face and chin. The kind of ash and honey blonde that doesn't come from a box, Supercuts, or the Do or Dye. I don't need to see her face to know she is beautiful. The kind of beautiful that comes from genetics and money. Her long fingers and pink nails rake through her hair and she says, all hoity-toity, "Good God, that's a hideous name," and I wish I could argue with her.

An elderly woman with a white pouf of hair touches my arm. "Don't pay her any mind, Miss Marfa. Some people are just cracky and notional." She's wearing a hospital gown and orthopedic socks, and she tells me her name is Miz Pearl. I follow her to a baby-blue couch across the room, and I'm quickly surrounded by her friends. Most have old-lady names like Pearl, and all want to know what happened to me. They ask the names of the doctors who've worked on me and about my coma and Glasgow score. I can't answer because I don't even know.

"I'm a three," Pearl tells me. "Stroke. It won't be long now."

I meet Brittany Larson (four-wheeler accident), who looks like she's my age and the reason I got stuck with Marfa. Then there's Valentina (fell off a pyramid at cheer camp), who's missing one purple ribbon from her brown ponytails; Tommy (skateboard accident and the reason Clint is Clint); and Portland (allergic reaction to a rattlesnake bite while hiking Lost Dog Trail). And me, Brittany Lynn Snider, a.k.a. Marfa (rolled her momma's minivan), almost died on her way to a Tinder date.

4

The title *90 Minutes in Heaven* sounds like a porno flick, but Tommy and I seem to be the only two of the same mind.

"Ninety minutes? I can get it done in ten or under," he says with a smile. "Then what am I gonna do for the next eighty? Talk about feelin's?"

I'm the only one who laughs, and I figure the older folks don't get it and the others are afraid of committing blasphemy.

The golfer shows up to tell me Momma's arrived, and I meet her in my room. She's pale and her cheeks are flushed, and she takes one look at my body and bursts into raw tears that flood me with sorrow and guilt.

My momma cries about everything. It doesn't matter if she feels sad or happy or proud. It doesn't matter if she's feeling heartache over an ASPCA commercial or bad like when she fries someone's hair.

No matter what, I hate to see her cry, but more than that, I hate to be the cause of her tears. Normally, I'd hug her and promise anything to make it stop, but I can't. All I can do is lightly put my hand on her shoulder and hope I don't zap her like I did with the nurse earlier. I wait a few seconds, but there are no gold and blue pops, and the only whoosh comes from the ventilator pushing oxygen into my lungs.

"My baby," she cries, carefully touching the scratches on the back of my free hand.

I rub my palm across her back and wish I could feel the warmth of her touch. I wish she could feel the comfort of mine. "Don't cry, Momma," I whisper, but she doesn't hear me.

We've never had much, but she always went out of her way to make me feel special. When I graduated sixth grade, we marked the occasion at the Dairy Queen with chili dogs and Dr Pepper floats. DQ has always been our place to celebrate, even when I only received a green ribbon at cheer tryouts in the tenth grade. We celebrated with chili fries and Buster Bars when I passed my boards and got my cosmetology license, too.

Momma always makes me Texas-shaped waffles on my birthday and a flag cake on the Fourth of July. She's a strong believer in God and that Texans are just a bit better than other people. She believes in the Marfa ghost lights, and that Yardley English Rose perfume covers the stink of Aqua Net.

Tears drip from her cheeks, and she bows her head to pray. "Oh Holy Lord, my maker and my protector. You reign on high above me and are worthy of praise." The golfer was right about strong emotions draining my energy. It flows out of me in visible waves, and I lay my cheek on her shoulder. She tells God that she accepts his higher plan for me—but then she bargains like a horse trader. "Heal my Brittany and I'll spend more time at the Agave Festival this year, sharin' my faith story and handin' out Bibles to sinners," she says. "I know I have to work on forgivin' and forgettin' and with Jesus's help, I'll be real civil to

Pudge the next time I see him." She pauses a moment before she adds, "And Floozy Face." If I wasn't so tired, I'd smile. I sit on the edge of the bed to rest and feel myself waver between earth and the spirit realm. Like the golfer said, I simply start to drift.

"I'll give up chili Cheetos with Frank's RedHot. Lil' Debbie Oatmeal Cremes, too."

Wow, she must be serious.

"And fornication with Jorge Espinoza."

What did she say? I'm almost gone now.

"I know it's wrong to sin in the back of his taco truck. Especially on Sunday."

She always said that she went to Espinoza's Especiales for flautas. My soul relaxes into my body and I feel a familiar sense of being, of rest and comfort. I let go of the stress of living and dying, and I dream I order Jorge Espinoza's tacos at the Dairy Queen. I dream of Daddy and his black Lab, Scooter, and I hear muffled voices like I'm underwater.

When I wake again, I know where I am. I know I'm in the hospital and I remember how I got here. I remember Nate the Tinder date; I remember I lied to Momma and fought with Lida, but I don't remember much beyond leaving church.

I recognize the beeping monitors and whooshing respirator, and I recognize Momma . . . and Daddy. My instinct to mediate before things get ugly kicks in, and I sit up and swing my legs over the side of the bed. They're standing just inside the door, and Daddy has his arm around Momma. She's crying into his chest as he talks with a doctor over the top of her head.

When my folks were married, I can't recall them hugging each other very much. It's uncomfortable to see them show affection to each other. I don't like it, and I wish they'd go back to normal. I look around for Floozy Face to run interference but she's not here.

I can't hear what the doctor is saying, but I don't need to. It's written all over Daddy's face. His eyes are red and pinched with sadness. He clears his throat and gives a sharp nod. "Thank you," he tells the doctor. "I know you're doin' what you can for my girl."

If you look up "good ol' boy" in the dictionary, you'll likely see a picture of my daddy. He loves cold beer, smoke billowing from the barbecue, and talking about the time he killed a wild boar with nothing but his pocketknife.

He's a deputy at the courthouse and makes good money, which, according to Momma, always made him a target for floozies. He drives a pickup and follows the unwritten pickup rules: his truck has monster tires so no one will think he's a wimp. There's a hunting rifle in the rear-window gun rack, no matter the season, and he always travels with his dog and a toolbox in the back.

His belt has a rodeo buckle the size of a dessert plate and the leather says "Pudge" on the back. He moseys through life and nothing much gets him worked up. This is the first time I've ever seen him like this. He looks sad and tired and old.

Momma and Daddy move out into the hall as an X-ray machine is wheeled into the room. I follow them. Daddy steps aside and drops his arm from Momma's shoulders. "What in the heck was my girl doin' in El Paso?" he asks.

Momma shakes her head. "I have no idea. She said she was headin' to Lida's."

"Did you get her cell phone? Maybe she called somebody."

"Won't do any good unless you got her passcode."

It's 5233. Same as my Visa pin number.

A tiny sparkle drifts downward and is followed by several more. I know what that means. Heaven is looking to take me up again. I don't want to die in front of my parents. Please, Lord and baby Jesus, I pray, not right now. Momma will never get over seeing me die.

"Lida said she ain't heard from Brittany in a few days," Momma continues, grabbing a tissue from her purse. "She might be lyin'. She's a Haynes and never got above her raisin'." There are those who say the same thing about Momma's people.

The sparkles stop; my prayer was answered. "Don't matter now. Brit can tell us when she wakes up." *If* I wake up. That's what they're both thinking but are too afraid to say out loud.

"Let's find the cafeteria while all this is goin' on." Daddy motions down the hall. "When was the last time I bought you supper, Carla Jean?"

Momma's brows lower and she opens her mouth to say something rude. Then she must remember her promise to God and says, "A while ago. I think the last time is when you drank too much and fell on your face at the Lost Horse."

Daddy, being Daddy, laughs. "Are you sure I wasn't on the ground kissin' your feet?"

"I'm sure, Pudge."

I don't recall a time when they ever talked and acted like regular people. Other than dying a couple of times, this is the weirdest thing that's happened today.

They walk away and I decide to stick around long enough to see my X-rays. It only takes a few moments for me to wish I hadn't. I'm not a doctor or nurse or even a hospital volunteer, but I don't need to be any of those to know that the cracks in my skull look bad and the tubes in my heart don't look too promising either.

I don't want to see any more and walk into the hall just as shards of silver and blue burst from the room a few doors down. I move toward the shattering sparks and take a peek inside at a small gathering of people weeping on each other's neck. Miz Pearl's frail body is laying on the bed, but her spirit is a few feet away, having a heated conversation with the woman in the blue slip who said Marfa was a hideous name. The blonde points to the opening in the ceiling while Pearl shakes her head. The blonde towers over Pearl but she doesn't look a bit intimidated by the younger woman's size or the anger in her voice. Pearl gestures to the door and I can see her say, "Out." The woman in blue looks like she wants to keep arguing, but she tosses her hair and storms past like she doesn't see me. As if I'm not even standing here.

The vital signs on Pearl's heart monitor crash and a shimmery hole opens above her head. She turns to her family and whispers something to an elderly gentleman; then her soul is gently lifted toward heaven. Sparkles rain down on her upturned face and I raise a hand to wave goodbye.

"Go with peace in God's light." The golfer materializes beside me like he's stepped through a gap in time and space.

The ceiling closes beneath Pearl's feet, and the last bit of glitter drifts from above. "How'd you do that?"

"I'm the concierge."

"You forgot to tell her to stay on the path."

He smooths his big mustache with his thumb and index finger. "Some folks heard the hoot owl's hoot."

I point to myself. "I hear the hoot owl's hoot. I hear it plenty."

He just shrugs and disappears as easily as he appeared.

"At least I'm wise enough to know your golf pants are an eyesore," I call after him. Maybe it's not so wise to antagonize the "concierge," but this is the second time he's implied that I'm a dummy. People think I have a quick temper, but that's not true. I'm just easily aggravated is all.

Several nurses join Miz Pearl's family, and I head in the direction of the Limbo Lounge, pausing to look into other patients' rooms as I pass.

The other Brittany's legs are in traction, and a guy with a man bun sits by her bed, holding her hand and talking to her. I can't hear what he's saying, but I can tell it's something real sweet. He picks up a cup of water and holds the straw to her lips. She's conscious. Groggy, but definitely awake. Which is not only good news for her, but for me, too. I can have my name back.

Skateboard Tommy is in the next room, and it looks like he's attached to about as many machines as I am. I see his spirit looking uncomfortable as two women cry over his comatose body. He glances over at me, and I give him a little wave because I know how he feels.

The blue-slip woman is in the room next to Skateboard Tommy. She doesn't have a breathing tube shoved down her throat and there isn't anything taped to her face. Her body isn't bruised or swollen or hooked up to pulleys like that of the other Brittany. She looks like she's peacefully napping and could wake up any second and hop out of bed. Well, maybe not. My attention is drawn to the restraints buckled around her wrists and ankles and hooked to the bed frame. If all the patients in this ward are in a coma, I wonder why she's the only one strapped down.

Up ahead I recognize the back of Cheer-Camp Valentina's purple Cougars cheer outfit, and I speed to catch up with her. She's chatty and tells me she's been in the hospital for a week, and that she can't stand to stay in her room while her momma and daddy are so emotional. She says it makes her sad and very tired. I can relate and try to lighten her mood with tales of my own disastrous cheer tryouts. By the time we enter the Limbo Lounge, she is showing a full mouth of braces as she laughs.

"I love your hair," she says as we take a seat on a yellow sofa. "How did you get it that color blue?"

"Practice," I answer as the concierge walks in with a beautiful woman wearing an orange-and-red Jalisco dress. She has bright tissue flowers in her black hair and looks like she just escaped from a Cinco de Mayo parade.

"Is it May fifth?" I ask anyone in hearing range, but things like time and dates don't matter here and no one seems to know for sure.

"I need all y'all's attention." The golfer thumps his club on the floor. "This is our newest guest, Señora Ana Marie Garcia Lopez." He turns to her and adds, *"Estoy a sus órdenes."*

Wait. "He didn't tell me he was at my service." I turn to look at Valentina. "Did he say that to you?"

She shakes her head. "What a creeper."

Clint heads across the room faster than I ever saw a guy his age move. He tips his hat and says, *"Buenas noches. Me llamo Clint."*

Valentina is probably ten years younger than me, but we look at each other and snicker because old guys making fools out of themselves is funny at any age.

Behind me I hear a sharp laugh that I recognize. I'd noticed the blue-slip lady when I walked into the lounge. She's sitting by herself again like she prefers her own company. I glance over my shoulder and into her icy blue eyes. She's so drop-dead gorgeous, she could be on the cover of a fashion magazine.

She raises a perfect brow and asks, "Can I help you, Marfa?"

"You can call me Brittany."

"I prefer Marfa."

"Marfa's ugly. I prefer Brittany." I pause and add, "With two *t*'s."

"Marfa suits you." Her lips turn upward but there's no joy in her smile. "Brittany with two *t*'s," she adds, all high-and-mighty.

Normally, I try to be a nice person, but this has been a crappy day and I'm all out of nice. "Why are you strapped to a bed even when you're in a coma? Are you whack-a-doodle?"

Her smile falters and her eyes look crazy. "You're a cretin."

Well, I'm not such a cretin that I don't know her meaning, but after the day I've had, "cretin" seems like a downright compliment. "And you're a triple-dipped psycho," I say, because it wouldn't be Christian to come right out and call her a crazy bitch.

Her smile flatlines and I turn away.

"Do you know her?" Valentina whispers.

I shake my head. "What's her name?"

"I don't know. She has evil eyes. If you look at her, she'll suck you into her evil vortex like Blair Waldorf from *Gossip Girl*."

"Only blonde like Serena."

"And old."

She doesn't look much older than me. "How long has she been here?"

"She got here not long before you. Maybe a day or so." Valentina dares a quick glance behind her. "I heard the doctors say she's goin' to wake up soon." Her shoulders droop and she looks down at her lap. "I wish the doctors said that about me."

"I don't think I'm goin' to wake up," I tell her. "I already floated through the ceilin' twice since I got here."

"I saw Durango float through the ceilin' when she was here. I bawled like a baby." Her shoulders droop a bit more. "Even if you don't have tears on the outside, you can fill them in your heart."

I learned that earlier.

She looks up from her lap. "What's it like up there?"

I don't want to scare her with my experience on the defective conveyor belt, so I say, "About what you expect. Bright light and a path and stuff."

Valentina's eyes grow wide with curiosity. "Did you see heaven?"

"I never got that far before I was spit back out." I take a deep breath and face facts. "I'm fairly certain I'm goin' to die soon."

"Maybe you won't. There's always hope."

I just smile like I'm optimistic, but I'm not. I saw my X-rays. I saw broken bones and all sorts of tubes inside me. I saw a lot of damage and not much hope.

"Jemma Jennie," the golfer calls out. "You've got visitors."

Valentina grabs my hand. "If he calls your name, don't go. Everyone around here is so boring. Durango was my bestie but now she's gone. Please stay and we'll be besties."

"Okay." I laugh.

The blonde squeezes between me and Valentina, forcing Valentina's hand to slip from mine. "Yes, please stay," the woman says, as if she's part of the conversation.

I look at her weird smile, then across her flat chest to Valentina, who's smashed against the arm of the couch. She and I seem to feel the same shock.

"Sorry we got off on the wrong foot, Brittany. I haven't been myself since I got here."

WTF? "Ah. Yeah."

Valentina squirms her way free and stands on her feet. "See ya," she says, and escapes the crazy, *rude* woman. So much for being besties.

"Let's start over." The woman shoves her bony hand at me. "I'm Detroit."

I don't ask if that's her real name because I'm busy staring at her perfect skin. I know we're not real, or in our real bodies, but she looks flawless, like she's never had a zit in her life. I give her hand a quick shake, but I don't say anything. Her eyes aren't crazy like they were before, but I still don't trust her.

"Why are you here? Car accident? Domestic dispute?"

Domestic dispute? "I rolled my momma's minivan."

"Ah . . . a minivan. What a shame." It's not what she says but how she says it that gets my back up, as if she doesn't even like the word *minivan* in her mouth.

"Yeah. It was a real turd-mobile, but it was paid for," I say, chuckling at her pained expression.

"Charming," she says, but not like it's a compliment. Then she seems to remember that she wants to "start over," and her smile returns. "'Paid for' is admirable in an intrinsically consumptive world. Your momma must be wise."

She might be trying to act like she's normal, but she's not right. "Why are you in the hospital?" I ask just to be polite.

"I had an accident in the bathtub." She waves the question away as if it's nothing. "Let's be friends, shall we?" Her teeth are really white and her posture is weirdly perfect. Women like Detroit don't get suddenly chummy for no reason.

I get a strange feeling like I'm back at Marfa Elementary and Andrea Dingell, aka The Dingleberry, is acting nice to set me up. Like when she wanted me to play jump rope with her and her friends, only I always had to hold one end of the rope and never actually got to jump. "Okay. Sure."

"I like your blue ombré."

"It's a cobalt balayage." I don't know that I believe her. "I did it myself. I'm a cosmetologist," I say with pride.

"Of course you are." She pats me like I'm a cute dog. "I didn't mean to eavesdrop, but you said something about dying soon."

I think I told Valentina I wasn't going to wake up.

"You're so young." She gives me a soft smile. "You have your whole life ahead of you. It's so unfair."

That's what I've been thinking, too. "I'll never get to all the things on my bucket list, that's for sure." Not that there's a lot on it.

"As in?"

"As in, I always wanted to see the Eiffel Tower."

"Très tragique, Mademoiselle Brittany," she says, and then starts talking to me in French like I have a clue what she's saying. She could be calling me all kinds of names, but it sure sounds pretty. "Parlez-vous français?"

"No. I speak English, Texas, and Spanglish." If you count the swear words I picked up from Mamaw Rose, a bit of German, too. This tall, sophisticated woman next to me actually laughs. Or at least seems like she's trying to laugh. If she's trying, it's only Christian that I try, too. "What's on your bucket list?"

"Nothing." Her smile falls and she stares off like she's looking at nothing, too.

"Not one thing?" I think we're around the same age, and she doesn't have anything on her bucket list? She looks like she comes from money, but she can't have done everything she's ever wanted or lived every dream.

"I guess I would go to Banff one last time."

Banff?

"Marfa!"

I turn my attention to the golfer and he motions to me with his club. "Your folks are in your room."

I don't think I'm ready for an emotional round two with my parents. I know that sounds bad, but it's such a heartache to see them so sad. My energy will drain, and I kind of wanted to hang out, flirt with Tommy, and watch family-friendly television. "See ya around, Detroit."

"Yes. You will." I can feel her gaze on my back as I cross the room. I think Pearl was right about her. She's cracky and notional, or, like Daddy always says, "half a bubble off plumb," but most folks have all sorts of issues. I've been known to pitch a hissy a time or two and live to regret it.

"You might want to watch yourself around Detroit," the golfer warns as I move past him.

"What's wrong with her?"

"That's not for me to say. But she's not from around here."

That's obvious, but not everyone's lucky enough to be from Texas.

5

I dream I'm a kid again and Andrea Dingleberry's bullying me into a corner. She calls me Tubby Toast and she and her friends laugh. Dingleberry was always the prettiest girl in school, and I could never figure out why she was so ugly to me. She was also the only kid who ever admitted to knowing a thing about *Teletubbies*, let alone the fact that Tinky Winky ate Tubby Toast. Talk like that was grade-school suicide. Dingleberry was never the sharpest Crayola in the crayon box, but what she lacked in smarts she made up for in mean, and no one ever crossed her.

"Rise and shine, Bestie."

I am startled awake and just about jump out of my body. Detroit is standing over me with that crazy smile on her face.

I sit up and swing my legs over the side of the bed. "What are you doin'?"

"Waiting for you."

She's creeping me out. "Why?"

"Why not? We're friends."

Well, the jury's still out on that.

"Friends look out for each other."

She's looking out for me? Like Lida? I feel horrible for thinking she has a crazy smile. Maybe she can't help it, like a person can't help hitchhiker thumb or wonk eye.

"Your heart rate fell and I thought you were going to die." She raises one hand toward me, then drops it at her side. "But here you are."

I think about Lida and how we left things. It was my fault. I got emotional and flew off the handle, and now I might never get the chance to say I'm sorry. Maybe Detroit isn't all bad. Maybe she was just having a bad day. "How long have you been standin' here?"

"Since your parents left." She shakes her head and says, "Wow. What a pair." Like earlier when she was talking about Momma's van, it isn't what she says but how she says it, like she's on her high horse looking down at cow patties. Just when I start to feel bad for her, she makes me think my first impression of her was right.

"What do you mean?"

"Oh." Her tone sweetens with her smile. "Just that they seem lovely."

I'm not buying it, but maybe she's trying.

"How does your mother get her hair that high?"

"Practice and a butt-load of super-hold."

"Charming."

"She's had the same hairdo since before I was born. Kind of a cross between a tumbleweed and an artsy installation."

Detroit smirks, looks like she's caught between shaking her head and nodding. "Artsy is always good."

"Yeah. If you wanna appear like you strapped a tumbleweed helmet on your head. And Daddy thinks that buckle hides his beer gut, God love 'em both."

Her quiet laughter softens her face and makes her even more beautiful. "Well, your parents are here and they love you." She goes from sounding snotty to sincere in less than a second. I wonder how she does that, and I wonder if I'm the crazy one.

"Are your folks here yet?"

She waves away my question. "My parents wouldn't dream of cutting their vacation short just because I'm in the hospital."

Wow. I can't even wrap my mind around that.

She blinks a couple of times and changes the subject. "I assume you're from Marfa. Home of the Prada installation."

"You've seen it?"

"Not in person. I studied interventionist art in college."

Inter what? "'Marfa Prada is a surrealist comment on Western consumerism.'" She looks kind of impressed, but I just shrug. "Art forms are serious business in Marfa." I don't think you get to graduate high school if you haven't written at least ten essays on each one. Lida forgot about the Stardust sign and almost didn't make it out of ninth grade.

Together we move from my room and walk toward the Limbo Lounge. "When I eavesdropped on you and the little cheerleader, you mentioned that you died and went to heaven." She crosses her arms over her chest and grabs her elbows.

My boobs always get in the way if I try to cross my arms. "I didn't go to heaven. I was on a path, but then I came back because I guess it wasn't quite my time."

"Talk to me about the path."

"It's about what you'd expect. Warm. Bright."

"Is it short? Long? Straight? Curved? Did you see heaven?"

"Yes, it's a brilliant gold light at the very end."

"Any place to hide?"

"In heaven?"

"On the path."

"Why would anyone hide?"

She shrugs. "Were you alone?"

"The first time, yes, and about halfway through the second time. Then I saw other paths in the distance with lots of people. The golfer said those were crowded on account of a catastrophe."

She motions toward the aquarium where Jesus is walking on water and the golfer is chatting with the rodeo girls. "The golfer is the man with the heinous mustache?"

I laugh. "That's him."

"What catastrophe?"

"A big earthquake and tsunami, and it's gummed up the works, I guess."

"Hmm . . ." She tilts her head to one side and looks off like she's thinking about something real serious. "I bet a person could blend into a crowd of victims rushing heaven," she says, more to herself than to me. "Would anyone notice that it's you and not someone else?"

That's a scary thought. I remember that Detroit's supposed to wake from her coma soon. Maybe Valentina was wrong about that. "Are you afraid of dyin'?"

"No."

We step into the Limbo Lounge and I wave to Valentina. "I was, but I'm not now. I guess 'cause I already kind of died twice. Third time will probably be the charm."

She turns her attention to me. "How much longer until you die for the third time?"

"I don't know."

"Guess?" She grabs my arm. "It's important."

"I don't *know*," I repeat, pulling my arm away.

"Think. Do you feel any different in the moments prior to the lightning striking and the threshold opening between heaven and earth?"

For someone who's not afraid of dying, she sure seems desperate to know all she can. "No, but there's always that glittery stuff fallin' from the ceilin'. That's about all." I give a little wave to Tommy. "Do you think he's good-lookin' for a skinny skater dude?"

"Who cares?" She grabs my arm again and pulls me to a small table like we've got something really important to talk about. We sit across from each other and she leans toward me. "If someone asked to take your place, would you do it?"

"What? In heaven?"

"Yes. Hypothetically, would you change places with someone so you could live out the rest of your life?"

I'm not one to use my brainpower in hypothetical conversations. I'm one for shootin' the shit and clever embellishment. The difference between the two is making up stuff for fun and games and making up stuff for no good reason. "You can't mess with God's plan."

"What if you were compensated?"

"How? Money?"

She nods. "If you could name any price, how much is your path worth to you?"

I think about Momma's van and play along *hypothetically*. If I could have anything, I'd buy Momma a new van with those captain's chairs that swivel and a dashboard Jesus made of real gold. I'd buy Daddy a new truck with the biggest tires he could find. While I'm at it, I'd get a truck, too. A big one with leather seats.

"Got a figure in your head?"

"I'm gettin' there." For me to sell my place at God's knee, I'd need enough money to make my dreams come true. Like seeing the Eiffel Tower and opening Shear Elegance. I'd get my song lyrics put together with a studio musician.

"How much?"

"Not so fast. If I sold my place in heaven, what would happen to my soul?"

She looks as if she hasn't given that a thought. "I guess you'd stay on earth with your body."

"Have you seen my body? Even if I live, I'll never be the same."

"You could buy all the special equipment you'd require. Invest in a home gym to suit your needs." She lifts a hand toward me. "You could buy your momma one of those special vans to haul you around." She drops her palm to the table and smiles. "Isn't that wonderful?"

"Home gym? For who?"

"Whom."

"That's what I asked you." This bizarre hypothetical conversation is making me realize it's better for me to die. "I don't want to be a burden to my momma. I don't want her feeding me and wiping my behind. I don't want to exist in a useless body until the day I die."

"On the bright side, you could go to Paris."

That's the bright side? "My plans never included Momma wheelin' me around the Eiffel Tower." I doubt Momma could make it half a lap.

"Get one of those motorized wheelchairs that can climb stairs."

"I don't want to live like that, not for me or for Momma."

"I'm sure she'd rather have you with her—no matter your disability—than gone."

The conversation makes me sad, and I feel heavy with emotion. If I stay or go, Momma's heart gets broken either way. "I don't want to talk about this anymore."

She leans back. "I need your path, Brittany."

"Hypothetically?"

"No. The next time the threshold is opened. You stay here and I'll take your path."

I know she's speaking English but I'm not sure what she's saying. "I don't think that's possible."

"How do you know?"

"It's not in the Bible. If it's not in the Bible, it can't happen." Her eyes are getting a little crazy and wild like before she decided to be my friend.

"The Bible is an outdated text. Only uneducated fools cling to their Bibles." She wraps her hand around my wrist. "I have more money than you can spend in two lifetimes. It's all yours."

I stand and look down at her. "No."

"Do it for Momma."

"You're goin' to hell on a scholarship," I say, and pull away.

"This isn't over, Brittany," she calls after me.

Valentina is on a green couch watching *7th Heaven* and I sit next to her. "You were right about Detroit. I talked to her and I got sucked into the evil vortex of Blair Waldorf."

Valentina glances across the room. "What'd she do?"

"Acted like she wanted to be friends." So she could buy my place in heaven and leave me to suffer here for all of eternity. "But she's rude and selfish and out of her pea-pickin' mind." And she never did get around to explaining how she was going to compensate me from heaven—if that's where she'd go.

I can feel Detroit's eyes on me, but I kick back and listen to Valentina's plans for her future.

"I'm gonna be a Dallas Cowboys cheerleader," she tells me.

Sadly, she might not be.

"When I'm eighteen, I'm goin' to the tryouts."

"I tried out for *American Idol* when I was a few years older than you," I tell her.

"Oh my gosh, did you make it?"

"No." I don't go into the brutal Wittany details, but I do tell her I still write lyrics.

"It's too bad you won't get to hear your songs on the radio." Valentina thinks for a moment and says, "But when you go to heaven, you'll get to meet people you never met before, like great-grandparents and Lindsay Lohan and . . . that boy who played Carlos on *Descendants*."

"Lindsay Lohan died?"

"Didn't she?"

"I don't think so."

"Oh well, you'll get to find out stuff like if alien abductions are real."

"Tommy, Valentina, and Marfa!" the golfer shouts out. "You got family visitin' your rooms."

I'm okay with leaving the lounge this time. My energy feels like it's draining faster than before, and I want to see my momma and daddy for as long as I got left.

6

"Rise and shine, Bestie."

Not again. Before I can even leave my body, I know Detroit's back.

"I've been waiting for you."

I stand in front of her, looking up at her face, glowing and beautiful. I'm not fooled this time, and I know why I've been thinking of Dingleberry lately. She and Detroit are opposite sides of the same mean-girl coin.

"Go away." I knew better than to trust her, but I gave her the benefit of the doubt. Like holding the end of Dingleberry's rope while she and her friends laughed and looked right through me.

"We're friends."

"No." I shake my head. "You don't care if I live a hard, empty life. You don't care if Momma has to break her back takin' care of me all her life. All you care about is gettin' what you want. That's not bein' a friend."

She turns up her smile. "Let's start over."

"No." I move past her and out into the hall. Last night was very emotional. After my parents got back from dinner, they got a diagnosis that kicked them in the gut. Watching them kicked me in the gut, too.

"We got off to a bad start. You didn't understand my proposal. That's my fault."

"I understood it."

"I just want what's best for you."

"Ha! Even if I believed your stupid, harebrained 'proposal' for one second, which I don't . . ." I stop and look up at her. "My parents got the news that even if by some miracle I don't die, I'll live in a persistent vegetative state for the rest of my life. I won't recognize them or even know they're in the room." I cover my face with my hand. "My daddy's a strong man, but his knees buckled and he cried like a baby. And Momma . . ." I shake my head. I know my real heart is beating in my body down the hall, but I feel the pain of seeing my parents deep in my soul. After I'm gone, I'm going to figure some way to come back and give them comfort. To watch out for them. To be their guardian angel until they join me in heaven.

"I'm certain things would carry on like they are now. Your spirit would escape your body again, and you'd make new friends at a new facility. My grandfather Chatsworth lived his final years at an excellent care facility in West Palm. He had a nice view of the lagoon from his window. You'd love it there." She shakes her head and gives a little laugh. "But West Palm isn't exactly Palm Beach, now is it?"

I look at her through the cracks in my fingers. "My parents live in Marfa," I say slowly, because she's clearly one taco short on three-fer night. "So no. Movin' to some special facility across the country isn't what's best for me or my folks."

She folds her arms across her chest and stares into my eyes, hard, like she can intimidate me. "They'll still have you."

For a while she's tried to act like she isn't crazy, but with her hard stare, and her talk of Palm Beach and lagoons, she's not even trying now.

"That should give you comfort. Think of Carla Jean and Pudge. Don't be so selfish."

I point to myself. "Me?" I drop my hand and continue down the hall. "It takes a real sick puppy to want someone else to have a bad life as long as you get what you want."

"It isn't like you've had a good life to begin with. You cut hair and paint toenails."

"I'm not ashamed of what I do for a livin'." I've never hit anyone in my life, but if I was to start now, I'd stomp her into a puddle of skinny bitch. "I'm a cosmetologist."

"Girls like you are always cosmetologists."

"You're nasty as all git-out."

"I've been called worse."

"I bet you have." I'd call her worse if I wasn't a good Christian. The faster I walk, the faster she talks, and I can't get to the Limbo Lounge fast enough.

"Your parents could hire around-the-clock care."

"Go away." I sprint down the hall to get away from her. It's been a long time since I've run anywhere, so "sprint" might be an embellishment.

She sticks to me like white on rice. "You're going to have a heart attack before we've reached an agreement. If I come out of my coma soon, it will be too late."

For one, I don't think a spirit can have a heart attack, and two, "That's not my problem." I'm not gasping for oxygen, which is a new experience for me.

"Let's talk it out," she says, as if there's still a chance.

"I'd rather sandpaper a bobcat's butt in a phone booth," I say over my shoulder.

"Charming."

"I wouldn't trade my place in heaven with you even if I could. So no. A thousand times no. With my dyin' breath I'll still be tellin' you no."

"Then die." She stops and calls out after me, "You have nothing to live for anyway."

I get one last glimpse of her as I rush into the lounge. She's stopped stalking me, and I hope she's drained her energy and has to recharge. That will give me a few hours (or however long it takes) of peace before I die.

Visiting hours are over, and I notice that most of the regulars are in the lounge. Clint is missing and the golfer has Señora Ana Marie Garcia Lopez all to himself. Tommy and the rodeo girls are watching *Angels in the Outfield*. Valentina is sitting alone with her clasped hands between her knees, looking dejected, and I sit next to her on the couch.

"I'm glad you're still here," she says. "Miz Jemma Jennie told me she saw your room light up, and I was afraid you'd gone to heaven."

"Jemma Jennie?"

"The rodeo woman in the pink shirt and ugly gold fringe."

Speaking for myself, I like the gold fringe and think the shirt would benefit from a few rhinestones. "No, but it won't be long now."

"How do you know?"

I shrug. "I just do."

"That sucks donkey balls."

"Yeah." I nod. "Big ones." I don't think it's quite my time yet, but I look up at the ceiling just to be sure. The tile shimmers, but there's no glitter falling on my head and no sign of lightning. The golfer laughs at something and I look over at him. He points his club to the big fish tank, where it looks like Daniel is stuck in the lion's den. Clint has joined him and Señora Ana Marie Garcia Lopez, and the three of them shake their heads at the same time.

I can't remember exactly what the golfer said about being near my body when it's time. I've had several false starts, placed on my path only to be kicked back off twice, and I'm confused. I need to ask him what will happen if I don't make it back to my room in time, but a familiar bolt of lightning shatters the ceiling above my head and I guess I'm about to find out. Bursts of glitter rain down, and I glance around the Limbo Lounge at the other patients. The cowgirls and Tommy look over from the TV, but the golfer and Clint are so wrapped up in their competition for Señora Ana Marie Garcia Lopez that they don't seem to notice.

"You're goin' to make a great Cowboys cheerleader," I tell Valentina as I slowly float upward.

"Maybe you'll get spit out again."

"Maybe," I say, but I'm ready to go this time. Heaven's got to be better than living like this the rest of my life.

I look at the golfer and shout across the room, "Adios, wing nut!" He glances up at me now. I'm tempted to flip him my middle finger, but I'm on my way to heaven and can't risk it. My feet are level with the top of Valentina's head when I give her a final wave. "If I don't get spit out, it was nice knowin' you."

Señora Ana Marie Garcia Lopez screeches like a caged monkey, Valentina waves, Tommy gives me a thumbs-up, and Detroit launches forward and grabs my ankles.

"Get back here."

For a few brief seconds Detroit plays tug-of-war with heaven. "Let go, you psycho."

"I tried to be nice." She pulls hard and manages to yank me to the ground. I land on top of her with a satisfying thump.

"Get off me, you fat hillbilly."

Fat hillbilly! I raise my fist to smack her a good one, but my wrist rises above my head and I float upward again. She stares at me with her loony-tunes eyes, and I think about kicking her in the head. Then I remember that I'm on my way to heaven. What would Jesus do? "I hope you get the help you need," I tell her. "You're not wrapped tight."

"I don't need help," she growls, getting to her knees. I'm being pulled up faster now, but she doesn't give up. She jumps on the couch next to a stunned Valentina and springs at me. One of her feet lands on my shoulder and the other kicks me in the chest as she climbs up my body—or my spirit, or my whatever—like a ladder. "I just need your path."

"You can't have it!" I wrap my arms around one of her legs, but she manages to slip through my grasp. She puts one foot on my face, the other on the top of my head, and kicks off as if I'm a springboard. I fall to the floor on my back and look up as her pink toenails disappear through the ceiling. Amid a dazzling spray of sparkles and brilliant light, the tiles slam shut. The last of the glitter rains down on me as the other patients gather around, and we all stare up at the ceiling in stunned silence. "Did that just happen?" I ask everyone and no one, because I'm not quite sure.

The golfer's face appears above me and he looks even pervier from this angle. "What's goin' on here?"

"Detroit pulled me down, then I floated back up, then she jumped on my head and dove through the ceilin'." I pause and add, "I think."

He turns his gaze to the others. "How?"

"Marfa was floatin' up, like she said," Valentina answers. "Then the evil woman grabbed her legs and pulled her down."

"I saw 'em both fall to the floor," Tommy adds.

"I saw that, too." Clint shakes his head and adds over the sound of Señora Ana Marie Garcia Lopez's wailing, "I thought for sure Marfa had squashed that lady flatter than a road toad."

"Flat as a fritter," Jemma Jennie says, and her cowgirl friend adds, "She ain't from around here."

The golfer looks up at the ceiling, then returns his attention to me. "How'd she manage that?"

"How should I know? You're the concierge." I get to my feet and pull down my "Don't Mess with a Texas Girl" T-shirt.

"She was spring-loaded."

"Maybe it wasn't Marfa's time," Jemma Jennie suggests. "Maybe the lightnin' made a mistake and struck in the wrong place."

"That's one of my big fears," the other cowgirl confesses. "I don't want to get sucked up by mistake."

Señora Ana Marie Garcia Lopez cries louder and Clint puts a comforting arm around her shoulders.

"The portal doesn't open in the wrong place. If Marfa was bein' taken up, it was her time," the golfer says. "No one gets 'sucked up by mistake.'"

"Then where's the skinny blonde?" Clint wants to know.

"She'll get sent back any moment now," the golfer answers, and we stare at the ceiling for more than a few moments. "I've never seen anything like that."

"Is she stuck in the 'in-between'?"

"I don't know."

Señora Ana Marie Garcia Lopez starts talking so fast that

I can't understand what she's saying. I don't think Clint can either, but he says, "Don't worry, darlin'."

Valentina glances at me, then returns her attention to the ceiling. "What if she doesn't come back?"

"That rarely happens," the golfer answers.

"Rarely?" I turn to him. If it was possible, I'd be hyperventilating just about now. As it is, I make a strangling sound like I can't breathe.

"You said you never seen anythin' like that," Tommy reminds him.

"I haven't. I've heard about it."

"Don't appear like she's comin' back," Jemma Jennie says.

What's going to happen to me now? Can I still go to heaven?

"Jemma Jennie's right," the other cowgirl points out. "That woman in the blue slip ain't comin' back."

She stole my path and didn't even pay me! "Now what?"

The golfer turns to me. "Come with me, Marfa."

*I*t actually worked. I wasn't sure it was even possible, but I climbed Brittany with two t's like she was Jacob's ladder and I'm here. On a sparkly pink path as gaudy as her "Don't Mess with a Texas Girl" T-shirt and just as ridiculous. I got over glitter headbands and rhinestone hair bows when I was shipped off to boarding school at the age of nine.

Not that any of that matters. The path is moving toward a golden light and that's all I really care about. I start to walk and peer through the darkness as I move. Brittany said there was no place to hide, and as far as I can tell, she's right. If I look hard to my left and right, I can see people on other paths that appear like conveyor belts and they're all leading to the same golden light.

Can they see me? I glance over my shoulder. Is anyone following me? Will I be discovered and tossed back into a life I can't bear? All the gossip and whispers and gloating. Not again. I fought a chubby Texan for this. I earned it. I outsmarted everyone in the hospital. I deserve this. Now I just have to outwit anyone and anything else standing between me and my perfect life with the Most Holy Trinity.

My pink path converges with the others and I pass a man with a white beard wearing a white linen suit and straw fedora like he's a field guard for Saint Peter. He isn't following me, but I run toward the light just in case. I don't know what I'm going to say to God once I'm standing before him, but I'm not all that concerned about it. My family has been granted private audiences with Popes Pius X, XII, and John Paul II.

I think he knows me.

The path becomes wider and more crowded, but we're not getting closer to the golden light. How long is this going to take, for Christ's sake? I shove my way past people in swimming suits, men and women in sarongs, and children in shorts and T-shirts. There's a man in a business suit and another wearing a Speedo and one flip-flop. Most are barefoot like me. No one is talking. We're moving, but heaven stays the same distance away.

I stop long enough to point to the golden light and ask a kid in a LeBron James jersey, "Is that heaven, do you suppose?"

He looks at me and says something that sounds like he's speaking Thai. I move on and find a woman in shorts and a cheap bikini top. "Why aren't we getting closer to heaven?"

She looks at me and her eyes are kind of fixed. "Where am I?"

I ask someone else and get a "What happened?" Others ask, "Why am I here?"

"Did I get washed away?"

"Where's Cheryl?"

"Is this a Disney cruise?"

These people are of no use, and I keep pushing through until I finally get to a set of golden turnstiles. Turnstiles? Is this some sort of checkpoint where illegal entries are discovered? I watch a man in a burgundy uniform move forward, and the process appears easy enough: a person walks through and the machine spits out a ticket on the other side. No one seems to be stopped or denied.

"Excuse me," I say, cutting between a girl in a gold sari and a man and woman in matching triple-XL "Phuket I'm Going to Bangkok" tank tops.

"Dan, she just shoved herself in front of me," says the fatty behind me.

"Line's in the back," Dan tells me.

I don't bother with a response as I watch the woman in the sari. She walks through without a problem, but the arms don't rotate when it's my turn. I'm reminded of the time Georgiana Aldridge and I decided to ride the Paris Metro like Parisiennes. Our cards didn't work, so we hopped over the arms with a group of boys. I remember a flashing red light as we scattered. Très audacieux.

I look around, lift myself up, and slide over. I'm scared a red light will flash this time, too, but it doesn't, and when the fat woman walks through, I grab her ticket. A commotion breaks out, and Dan yells, "Catch her, Doreen!," but she's no match for me. I work with a personal trainer five days a week and can jog circles around her without breaking a sweat. I side-plank and boomerang, SoulCycle and weight-lift. I'm lean and toned and the perfect size two.

I jog through wispy clouds that are kind of bouncy beneath my feet, and I think about who will attend my funeral. Mother will make sure it's beautiful, and everybody who's anybody will be there. Even those who didn't care for me will arrive in their latest Rolls or Maybach, looking très soignée, and pretend to cry. The easier question is who WON'T be at my funeral. The only name that comes to mind is Sarah Worthington. I went out of my way to help her navigate society, but she was pathetic. Her sense of style was an assault on fashion, and it wasn't my fault that she had her eyes on Freddy Chambers and Freddy only had eyes for me.

The mist thins a bit around my bare feet and ankles, and I stop near hundreds of dark windows, each blinking with a different red number.

"Serving number two-seven-three-three at window twenty-one," a tranquil voice announces from nowhere but is heard everywhere. The girl in the gold sari holds up her ticket and walks through the crowd to window twenty-one.

I smile like I did that time in Paris. I'm next and I got here because I'm quick and determined and brilliant. I make my way forward and look at the number on my ticket: 000,000,000. What? Why is my number different? Another window blinks and I fully expect nine 0s to be called.

"Serving number two-seven-three-four at window sixty-three."

Fat Doreen sticks up her hand. "Here I am," she says, and moves forward.

Wait. She entered the turnstile behind me. That should be my ticket. What in the hell is goin' on?

7

"Where are we goin'?" I ask the golfer as I follow him from the Limbo Lounge. He doesn't bother to answer, and instead of walking to my room, he opens a door and we step into a place filled with sunshine. The door closes and a platinum-blonde woman stands within rows of different-colored tulips that stretch back as far as the eye can see. She has fuzzy edges like the golfer and is dressed in all white. Her eyes are turquoise like the ocean in a Sandals Resorts commercial, and she glows from the inside out like she just descended from heaven.

"Ma'am, are you an angel?" I ask.

"*¡Dios me libre!*" the golfer says as if in pain.

The woman smiles and lights up even more. "Oh, honey, your lips to God's ears. I'm Ingrid, director of Southwest District Five, Area Thirty-One."

"Where am I?"

"You are in my office. I decorated it myself." She glances about and makes a sweeping gesture with her hands. "I created it from childhood memories. It's my little slice of paradise."

I've stood on my bedazzled path and I've seen God's light. I spin around within the tulips and take in all the vibrant color. "It's beautiful." But it isn't heaven, and I don't think it's hell.

As if reading my thoughts, she says, "My office is in neither heaven nor hell. For some of us, our path isn't as straightforward as others, but if we are judged redeemable, we are placed in holy service and given a second chance. I hope to earn my place in paradise soon."

The golfer gives a shout of laughter and swings his club in the air like he's hit a long shot.

"I died in a fire that consumed Madame Tilly's Dove Palace in 1890. I had not learned to control my jealous temper, and I took a kerosene lamp to Kitty Heaton's bed while she and my regular gentleman, Nelson Butts, enjoyed a two-dollar carnal act. Five people perished, including myself after kerosene splashed on my petticoat. I went up like a torch."

She's still smiling, and I wonder if it's required that a director or concierge explain how they died.

"I know this is confusing, but think of a celestial family tree with heaven at the top, various limbs of merited atonement for the transgressed in the middle, and hell at the roots. For those souls who deserve neither heaven nor hell, we are given a chance to earn a place in paradise through a branch of *Holy Services*. My office descends from the Progression of Redemption Corps, or PORC for short. Concierge and various jobs in Area Thirty-One are my responsibility and require that I manage the fallen and place them where they are best suited to serve.

"Do you understand?" she asks.

Not at all, but who cares! "I'm fallen?" I feel a little light-headed, like if I could, I'd faint. Sure, I've sinned, but *fallen*?

Her gaze lands on the golfer, then her smile and her voice flatten. "What happened, Raymundo?"

Raymundo?

"You know more than I do, Ingrid."

"I know you got distracted again."

"Don't talk to me about gettin' distracted." He points the grip of his golf club to his chest. "I'm not the one who messed up JFK's passin'."

Her eyes turn a stormy blue. "That was not my fault."

"And this ain't my fault. I'm just the concierge, is all." He lines up his club and takes a whack at a purple tulip. The flower sails straight down the field, then curves right. "Dang, hooked that one."

Ingrid sighs and turns her attention back to me. Her face softens and she finally answers, "No. You are not fallen."

That's good to know.

"You're special. Do you know how special you are?"

"No."

"You're one in twenty-eight billion, give or take."

I would have said one in a million, but the way she's looking at me makes me believe I am one in twenty-eight billion special. "Do you know why you're here, Miss Brittany?"

I like the way she says my name, like butterfly wings brushing across my skin. "I imagine it's on account of Detroit climbin' me like a wild monkey and jumpin' through the ceiling to steal my customized path to heaven."

"I'm sorry for that. Portal jumping is nearly impossible."

"Nearly?"

"It can only occur if extraordinarily improbable events converge."

"Like what?"

"A jumper is looking for a portal and puts herself in the right place at the right time, and only then if the paths to heaven get congested with hundreds of thousands of people passing in one single tragedy, such as the Vesuvius eruption, AD 79, the Shaanxi earthquake of 1556, and the 1881 Haiphong typhoon." Ingrid shakes her head. "Even though the situation is usually quickly resolved, it is conceivable for a jumper to get lost in the crowd."

The golfer continues to swing at tulips. "Dammit. Sure wish I had my driver."

Ingrid scowls over her shoulder as she says, "Edith Randolph Chatsworth-Jones should have been returned by now."

"Who?"

She looks at me and tries to smile away her scowl. "Detroit."

Edith? Edith is just about as bad as Marfa, but at least Marfa isn't my real name. If I'd known, I would have laughed my ass off. "When's she comin' back?"

"Fore!"

"Raymundo, please! You try the patience of a saint. You're here to help explain what happens next. Not destroy my flowers."

"Nothin' much to explain. Marfa has two choices: live or die."

"It isn't quite that easy," Ingrid explains, taking my hands in hers. "You are being given the chance to live a full life on earth. Isn't that wonderful?"

Suddenly I don't feel so special. "What's the catch?"

"You must assume the life of Edith Randolph Chatsworth-Jones."

The fire that turned her into a kerosene torch must have burned out a porch light or two. "We don't look anything alike," I point out.

"Once you agree to the transmigration covenant, your spirit will assume her body."

Transmigration sounds terrifying. "Do you mean a switcheroo like in *The Change-Up* or *Freaky Friday*?" Only with someone who stomped on my face and left me to live in a vegetative state.

"Yes, that's one way of putting it."

That woman is the devil's handmaiden, and I want no part of her. "What's my other choice?"

"You wait for Edith's portal to open and pass through."

"When will that happen?"

"That depends on unknown variables. Because of the very rare circumstance, it could be next week, or next month, or next year."

Some choices. "Can't God just fix my body so I can live as me?"

"It's too late," Ingrid tells me. "The injuries from your accident were so severe, your body couldn't sustain life." Her smile gets all cheerful like she's about to announce that I won the Texas Lotto. "It's a testament to your strong will that you survived as long as you did."

"Testament to stubbornness and bad temper, more like," Raymundo scoffs.

"Will I have to put up with the pervy wing nut while I wait for a portal?"

"I'm afraid so."

"Are you sure God can't just fix my body?"

She shakes her head. "Your next of kin have been notified."

"That was fast. I just died a few minutes ago."

She shakes her head again. "The spirit realm does not mark time the same as it is on earth. I'm afraid your body is in the morgue."

"I'm in the morgue?" I point to my chest and whisper, "I'm in the morgue?"

"You're bagged and tagged, Marfa," the golfer thoughtfully provides. "Can't come back once you're bagged and tagged."

"Shut up, Raymundo!" Ingrid's eyes turn from calm turquoise to stormy blue, then back again. "Don't listen to him."

"And Momma and Daddy know I'm in the morgue?" I ask myself more than anyone else.

"I'm sorry," she says, sounding like she means it. "Just think about this extremely rare opportunity for a second chance at life. You're really quite lucky."

I don't feel lucky or wonderful or special. I feel my heart cry out for my momma and daddy. "She's a stalker and a bully." And I *feel* mad as all heck.

"I warned you about her, but you didn't listen."

"Shut up, Raymundo," I say. "She didn't care about the consequences of what she did. She thought I was stupid, called me a fat hillbilly, and took my place in heaven!"

"I wouldn't count on a place in heaven if I was you," the golfer scoffs.

I ignore him because I was saved when I was ten, and Ingrid said I'm not fallen.

Ingrid ignores him, too. "She took your portal. Not your place. She did make it past the turnstiles, but she's not as clever as she thinks."

"Heaven has turnstiles?" I never read that in the Bible.

"In order to avoid overcrowding at the gates, souls are directed to turnstiles and processing is slowed. She drew attention to herself when she stole a ticket."

I never read about tickets either. "Where is she?"

"At the moment, she is cooling her heels and awaiting perfect judgment. She will be detained there until her fate is determined."

"Jail?"

"More like the DMV."

I shudder. While it's good to know that she didn't get away with kicking my face and sneaking into heaven, being stuck at the DMV sounds like cruel and unusual punishment. "I don't know anythin' about this Edith Randolph-whatever."

"Chatsworth-Jones."

"What do I say if people ask me questions?"

"You claim amnesia."

"Really?" I think back on an episode of *Dr. Phil*, when a woman on his show said she had amnesia. At the time, I thought she was just pretending because her husband was ugly. If my husband looked like a basted turkey, I'd pretend I didn't know him, too. "That's a real thing?"

She nods. "All those who've accepted a new life have professed amnesia." She must see the confusion in my face and so she explains. "Throughout history, spirits have been offered a second chance at life for a variety of reasons, including, but not limited to, portal jumping."

"So people who have total amnesia are like me?"

"*Some* of them, yes."

"I thought they were just fakin' it."

"A person can't fake it for a lifetime."

I reckon that's true.

"It's worked out for the others. They've gone on to have wonderful lives. Well, except for Tutankhamen, but that was before my time."

"This happened to King Tut?"

"Are you goin' to make a choice?" The golfer taps the back of his wrist like he's wearing a watch. "I've got things to do, you know."

Yeah, I know, and her name is Señora Ana Marie Garcia Lopez. I shake my head to clear that image from my brain. "I thought dyin' was easier than this. This is difficult."

"Then let me make it real simple for you, Marfa." He points his club at me. "You can stick around the Limbo Lounge with me or go live as a skinny rich woman."

"Some choice! A wing nut or a crazy stalker!"

"You wouldn't have her same problems," Ingrid assures me. "You'll still be Brittany on the inside, with all your memories and feelings."

Hmm. If I'm still Brittany inside, I can convince Momma that it's really me. If I'm rich, we can get a better house and a new van. If I'm skinny, I can get a hot boyfriend.

"Ticktock, Marfa."

"*Shut up*, Raymundo!" I'll be back home in no time at all, eating Frito pie and drinking Dr Pepper on the front porch of a brand-new house. Heck, maybe I'll have enough money to buy a ranch. Momma's always dreamed about being a bona fide cowgirl, and she won't have to stand on her sore feet all day or complain about her bunions. Heck, she could get bunion surgery. I could buy Daddy a new truck *and* pull trailer so he can hunt and camp in style and comfort. My mind spins from one possibility to the next.

Ingrid grabs my hands and my attention. "It's time to make a decision."

I'm terrified and emotional, and if I could cry, I would right about now. "What should I do?"

"I can't tell you that, but the window of opportunity is closing."

"Can't I stay with you?"

"I'm afraid not, but if you choose to live as Edith Randolph Chatsworth-Jones, I'll stay with you afterward."

"Like a guardian angel?"

"I wish. I am just the director of Southwest Thirty-One, but I can help you for a time."

"How long?"

"Until you don't need me or break the conditions of your transmigration covenant."

I put one hand to my forehead. How long before Momma recognizes me if I look like Edith? I suppose Edith has family somewhere, but I'm not going to concern myself with that. "Promise I won't be mean and crazy like her?"

"I promise."

Should I live as a rich bitch or wait around in limbo for her to die? For maybe a year! I wish there was a sign or signal to show me what to do. Instead, I get, "You need to get hooty," from the golfer.

"I'm hooty," I snap, and look into Ingrid's face for guidance, but her eyes are blank. "I need more time."

"You're quickly running out of it."

I feel sick, but it's not physical. More like my soul is in turmoil. "I haven't been in your office very long."

"In God's time, no, but a day has now passed on earth."

A whole day! "Okay . . . I . . ." Momma and Daddy are probably planning my funeral. Soon they'll be stockpiling casseroles and funeral cake for afterward. "Okay . . . I . . ."

"She needs help from one of those *Dummies* books."

"I'll do anythin' not to have to hear from this wing nut ever again."

"You have to say the words."

"Suck it, Raymundo!"

"Those aren't the words, Miss Brittany."

I sigh and say, "I choose rich bitch," like I really have a choice.

Ingrid smiles and quickly goes through a list of instructions she reads out of a manual. I have to vow to abide by "the policies and procedures of transmigration." I raise my right hand and swear I'll follow the switcheroo rules even though I don't intend to obey some of them, like not telling people who I am and resuming my old life. I'm not supposed to talk about leaving my body and moving around the hospital either. Evidently, what happens in the Limbo Lounge, stays in the Limbo Lounge.

"What's done can never be undone. Do you understand this covenant you are about to enter?"

"Yes." Covenant? That sounds more serious than "policies and procedures."

"Ready?"

I nod unsteadily.

"Perfect," she says, and the ground beneath my feet fades away. I fall like Alice in Wonderland toward Detroit's hospital room. I have a horrifying thought that I won't fit into her skinny body. I hear my mother's voice saying, "I can't stand the thought of you leavin' me, Brittany Lynn. You're all I got"; then I land smack-dab on Edith Randolph Chatsworth-Jones and I don't hear anything at all.

Someone pinches the back of my hand. "Stop it," I try to say, but I don't think my lips move.

"Wake up." The woman's voice is perky and annoying and I want her to go away.

My hand is pinched once more. "Stop it," I think I say again, but that doesn't sound like me. I'm tired and just want to sink back into the place of sunshine and tulips.

"Squeeze my finger."

I don't want to, but I do so this person will go away.

"Good. Open your eyes."

No. I'm too tired. I just want to sleep, but I'm pinched again. Now I'm aggravated and blink several times. Everything is blurry and too bright. I squint until the fuzzy edges slowly come into focus and Lois Griffin is looking down at me. I love *Family Guy* and all, but I'm going to kill Lois if she pinches me again.

"You're awake," Lois says.

I'm disoriented and don't know where I am. I don't know why I'm here, or how Lois got out of the television. She holds up a silver pen, and I blink several more times. No, that's not right. Lois can't get out of the television.

"Follow the pen." She moves it back and forth, and I do as she asks so she'll get the freakin' pen out of my face.

"Can you tell me your name?"

Something isn't right. My brain is stuck and won't work. Why is Lois wearing glasses?

"Do you know where you are?"

I shake my head.

"You're at the University Medical Center of El Paso."

That can't be right . . . but maybe it is. I don't know.

"You were brought here two days ago."

I'm confused. Lois doesn't sound like Lois anymore. I try to raise a hand to shield my eyes from the glare, but I can't move my arms and legs more than a few inches.

Lois looks at the end of the bed and says to a woman in green, "Contact her parents and let them know she's awake."

Yeah. Once Momma and Daddy come they'll make Lois leave me alone.

A man with dark hair walks into the room and asks, "Are you finally awake?" as if I'm not staring right at him. He's wearing a white dress shirt and a tie with dogs playing poker on it. "Do you know where you are?"

That's the same thing Lois asked. I'm still confused but this time I nod.

He pulls a penlight from his breast pocket and shines it in my eyes. "I'm Doctor Greg Perez."

I try to lift my hand to push his little light from my face, and this time I look over and notice the padded restraints.

"We can take those off if you stay calm."

I'm so calm, I'm about to doze off. "Why . . ." I want to ask why I'm tied down, but my throat is dry and I can't get the words out. Did I do something crazy? Commit a crime? Pass out from one too many Texas Hurricanes again?

Dr. Perez shoves the penlight back into his pocket and unbuckles my right wrist. I watch Lois unbuckle my ankles and move to the left side of the bed. "If you swing at me, I'll put the restraints right back on," she says. What is going on? I'm a lover, not a fighter.

"Can you tell me your name?"

"Brittany." My eyes are so heavy that I can't keep them open. "Brittany Lynn Snider." Sleep pulls me under and I sink into a place filled with the brightest tulips imaginable. This place looks familiar. I've been here before, but I don't recall when. There's a woman with me; she has platinum-blonde hair and tells me I'm special and wonderful and I'm confused. I know her, but my memory of this place and of the woman is foggy. It's there but I just can't grasp it.

She refers to me as a rich bitch, which just goes to show how much she knows. The closest I've ever come to being rich is when I won twelve bucks on a Powerball ticket. As for the other, I can get real aggravated and fly off the handle, but I don't think I'm a bitch. I try to be kind to everyone. Well, everyone but Dingleberry. The last time I saw Dingleberry I flipped her off. It was a few weeks ago, when Lida and I walked into the Drunken Buzzard for some nachos and Miller Lite and she yelled "Tubby Toast" at me from across the bar. She was with her husband, Wally Bob, and they were acting like a happily married couple. I had to laugh because everyone knows Wally Bob's a hard dog to keep under the porch, no matter how many times Dingleberry takes a stick to him.

Bless her pea-pickin' heart.

The woman in the tulip garden waves her hand in front of my face to get my attention. "You're doped up on something."

"I am?"

"But no matter the circumstances, you cannot tell people that your name is Brittany Lynn Snider."

"What?"

"You're Edith Randolph Chatsworth-Jones now."

"Who?"

"You have amnesia, remember?"

In the foggier part of my brain, I know this.

"Edith took your portal and you took her place on earth."

That sounds familiar too. "Yes." I look down at tulips beneath thin bare feet. I don't recognize them, but I think I remember the woman talking to me. "Miz Ingrid?"

"Yes."

Fog starts to lift from another memory, too. A memory of the Limbo Lounge and manicured feet with muted pink polish. "Whose feet are those?" I ask, even though I think I might not want to know.

"They're yours now."

They don't look a bit like my size-ten double-wides. I push my hands out in front of me and turn them this way and that. These hands are too thin and the fingers too long. The bony arms aren't mine either, but I recognize them. I really don't want to hear the next answer either but I have to ask, "Am I really her?"

"Yes. You've transmigrated."

I remember her face now. Beautiful and cruel. "Do I look like her?"

"Yes, and you must live Edith's life. Not the one you left behind. You don't want to end up like Joan of Arc."

I look up. "What?"

"People call you Edie now."

There has to be something of me left. A mole or freckle or a glint in my eyes. There just has to be one thing. "I like Brittany better."

"That wasn't part of your covenant with God. I clearly explained the positives and negatives of your 'total amnesia' arrangement. The policies and procedures were put in place centuries ago for the benefit of participants."

"I don't want to be called EEE-DEEE," I say, dragging the name out for effect. The drugs aren't helping my enunciation either.

"There are worse things in life than being called Edie." She shakes her head at me. "If you insist on being called Brittany, people won't believe you have amnesia. They'll think you're insane. You don't want that."

The whole "covenant with God" thing is kind of scary, but I'd rather people think I'm insane than call me Edie for the rest of my life.

She cocks her head to one side and looks at me like she read my mind. "There is nothing I can do if you break the rules. You'll be on your own."

"Okay," I say, because I don't want to argue. I return my gaze to Edie's feet. "I'm not anythin' like her on the inside." Her toes are kind of bony and the nail polish is boring. I like bright colors and . . . I look up. "Right?"

"Right. You are you on the inside." She looks past me and I follow her gaze. "Remember, what's done can't be undone."

I don't see anything and turn back to face her.

"You have amnesia." Ingrid's turquoise eyes look deep into mine like she's trying to hypnotize me. "Your name is Edie," she says as the door behind me opens and I drift backward. "Don't blow it."

This time I don't land in Edie's body. I simply wake and open my eyes. The medication must be wearing off, because I'm thinking more clearly. A single light shines down on my head, but the rest of the room is dark. Lois Griffin is nowhere around. I recognize the doctor standing next to my bed.

"You're awake," he says, and reaches for a pen in the breast pocket of his white coat. "Do you know where you are?" Of course, he shines his stupid light in my eyes.

"Hospital," I whisper. In my head I hear my own voice, but when I open my mouth, I hear her. I clear my throat and try again. "Hospital."

"Right."

"Which hospital, sir?" The sound of Edie's voice makes me recoil inside. Hearing it is like a whole 'nother out-of-body experience—and I should know. My scalp tightens, my hair follicles tingle, and I try not to freak out.

"You're at the University Medical Center of El Paso."

Yes. I remember now. I remember church and Momma's van and HotGuyNate. I don't know if we ever met up, but here I am in El Paso.

He asks me if I'm hungry, and now that he mentions it, I'm starving. I don't know if someone with amnesia remembers things like food or how to eat, but at the risk of "blowing it," I nod.

"I'll let the nurse know you're awake and she'll have something sent up for you."

I nod once more, because if I hear Edie's voice, I might scream or pass out, or the shrinking-scalp thing might shrivel my brain. Or is it Edie's brain? Either way, I don't want a brain like a prune.

I watch him leave the room and then I take several deep breaths. Just lying here, I don't have to look to know this is not my body. It feels different. My real body is bigger and my boobs fall into my armpits. This body is long and stick-thin and feels as if it can be snapped in half.

Ingrid promised me that I don't have Edie's personality or mental issues. I'm not crazy. I'm me on the inside, and since I'm the one thinking with this brain, I choose to believe it's all mine.

I keep taking deep, even breaths and raise my eyes to the ceiling. I remember the lightning and explosion of sparks and glitter. I wonder if Valentina is still just down the hall and if Clint and the golfer are still fighting over Ana Marie Garcia Lopez in the Limbo Lounge.

Every unbelievable thing, from standing outside my body in the emergency room to getting sucked up through the ceiling, is not part of some wild dream. All of it—Valentina and the other Brittany, Jemma Jennie with the gold fringe and Pearl, Skater Tommy, and crazy Edith—is real.

My body is bagged and tagged in the morgue. Momma and Daddy are planning a funeral and I'd break down and cry if I thought I could stop once I start. The real me is in the real body of a real hateful woman. It's true and not at all believable.

I hear a shock of quiet laughter and realize it's me. It comes from her throat but it's my laugh. It's my ha-ha-ha chuckle and not her hoity-toity cackle. I don't know how long I stare up at the ceiling, thinking about it all, before a nurse comes into my room. She puts a tray on the over-bed table and pushes it in front of me. "Are you hungry?" she asks as she raises the head of my bed. "The doctor ordered broth and crackers." She takes plastic wrap off a glass of ice water, a cup of tea, and two small bowls. "Jell-O, too. Lime by the looks of it."

I've never been a picky eater. I'll eat most anything, except-ing Jell-O. Especially green. I hate the way it jiggles and smells and slides down my throat. Mamaw Rose used to church hers up with shredded carrots and green peas and she'd snarf it up like it was ambrosia. Just the sight of it makes me nauseated. I don't know if Edie likes Jell-O, but it's not on Brittany Lynn's menu.

The nurse wraps a blood pressure cuff around my left arm and squeezes the bulb. "If your system tolerates the liquid diet, you can order from the menu in the morning."

How long until morning? I wonder, and wait until she re-moves the cuff to lift my left hand so I can pull the tray within reach. I recognize Edie's long thin fingers and pink-painted nails from Ingrid's tulip garden, but the bandage covering her wrist stops me. "What happened?" I say out loud, although I think I can figure it out.

"You don't remember?"

I shake my head.

"You lost four pints of blood before housekeeping found you. Another few minutes and you would have died in that bathtub."

Did Edie try to kill herself?

"The Klonopin-vodka cocktail didn't help."

I guess that answers my question. I have no clue what Klonopin is, and my alcohol of choice is tequila, poured into a blender filled with ice and margarita mix.

"The ER doctors didn't think you were going to make it this time."

This time? I put Edie's forearms side by side and stare at the bandages with morbid fascination. "That had to hurt," I whisper to myself. I hadn't felt any pain until now. Now I feel a bone-deep ache radiating outward from Edie's wrists. I hadn't given much thought to why Edie was strapped to a bed or why she was in a coma. Now I feel a twinge of compassion for her, like I do when someone cuts off a snake's head. I can feel bad for the snake, but that doesn't mean I forget it's a snake or forgive it for biting me.

"The hotel sent the toiletries they found in your room— minus sharp instruments, of course." The nurse moves to a slim closet and pulls what looks like a brown vanity case from a piece of matching carry-on luggage. Even from across the room, I recognize the LV monogram, and I doubt it's a knockoff from China. "You can use the water and basin to brush your teeth." She waves her hand toward the blue pitcher and kidney-shaped bowl on the end of the table. She puts the case on the bed next to me. "Do you need anything?"

I shake my head.

"Press your call button if you can think of anything," she says on her way out of the room.

I don't know if a person with amnesia is supposed to know how to pour water, but I'm as thirsty as a draft horse. I reach for the glass but my fingers are numb and can't grasp it tight enough. I can wiggle and flex all ten fingers, but I'm left-handed and can only make a fist with my right. I am somewhat ambidextrous, as most lefties tend to be. I can easily drink some ice water and tea with the right, but I can't manage to get a spoonful of broth to my mouth without it dribbling on the way. I give up and use a straw. By the time I finish, I'm exhausted. Not the kind of exhausted that makes me fall asleep straightaway. More like the kind when I was in high school and had to play volleyball in gym class. The difference between now and then is that I'm not gasping for air and clutching my chest. My face isn't deep red and Dingleberry isn't calling me Tubby Toast.

I grab the vanity case next to my hip and push the food tray to one side. I've never come close to touching real Louis Vuitton before. My wrists hurt and the gold-colored lock dangling from the zipper slips from my fingers. I'm about to pitch a hissy when I finally get it open.

The inside is lined with beige leather and filled with skin-care products that I've never heard of before. The writing on the little blue pots and bottles is in a foreign language, perhaps Swedish. There's a silver tube of Dior mascara (brown), Chanel lipstick (passion red), and Burt's Bees lip balm. At the bottom, a hairbrush and hand mirror.

That's it. No primer, foundation, cover-up stick, contouring bronzer, eye-shadow palette, blush, brow wax, hair curlers, or can of super-hold? I guess you don't need a full face of makeup if you're planning to kill yourself. Or if you're born with Edie's complexion. Not that it matters either way. I'm not supposed to know what to do with a tube of lipstick.

I pull out the mirror and the first thing I notice is clear tape and a nasty-looking IV stuck in Edie's jugular. A tube with a white cap rests on her shoulder.

The day I saw her in this very room, I didn't notice her bandaged wrists or the IV in her neck. I just saw her buckled restraints and wondered why a woman in a coma had to be strapped to a bed. Now I know she was more of a risk to herself than to anyone else.

Beneath the tape, her skin is yellow and bruised. It looks horrible and I know I should feel worse for her than I do. I should forgive and forget because it's the Christian thing to do, but it might take me a minute.

I raise a hand and touch her throat. That hand and those fingers in the mirror do not belong to me. I feel cool fingertips against warm skin as if they are mine. My head gets light, and I raise the mirror inch by inch until her icy blue eyes stare back at me. The last time I saw her, she looked cuckoo, but it's me behind those ice-cold eyes this time. It's me looking cuckoo this time, too.

Ingrid promised I wouldn't be crazy like Edie, but I'm getting all worried about it anyway. I tell myself that anyone would feel crazy if someone else's hand touched their skin and it felt like their own.

Anyone would feel bizarre if their heart raced beneath a bony chest they don't recognize. Anyone would freak out if they looked at themselves but saw someone else staring back at them. A shiver runs up my spine and every hair follicle on my head tingles again.

I pull the mirror back far enough to see Edie's full face. She's as beautiful as she was the first time I saw her. I push her thumb across her chin and lower lip, and again I feel a sensation so foreign yet so familiar.

"Hello. Testin' one, two, three. I'm in here somewhere." I try to laugh but it turns into a sob, and I take a deep breath and let it out slowly. "I live in Marfa with my momma. I love fish tacos as all git-out." But I don't sound like me. "I love red cowboy boots, country music turned up real loud, and singin' my heart out."

The words are mine but are spoken from the lips of a stranger. I tell myself that everything will be okay and not to get emotional, but my emotions are like a tsunami crashing into me. My eyes ache and fill with actual tears. "I'm me," I reassure myself. To prove it, I sing my latest lyrics. "I have a big heart and bigger dream . . . Big dreams that don't fit in a small town . . . I'm outta here." Edie's voice cracks, and evidently, she can't carry a tune in a tin bucket. I know I gave up on my dream of being the next

Reba or RaeLynn—of standing on a big stage and belting out my music. I gave up singing in public, but like the beat of my heart and the breath in my lungs, it's always come natural. I knew I'd lose some of me in this arrangement—okay, most of me—but I never thought I'd lose the talent God gave me at birth.

It's not like I had a lot of time to think it through or sort it all out in my head. I guess I just figured I'd see something of myself in her. I guess I just assumed I'd have my singing, like always. I guess I didn't want to believe I'd be so . . . gone.

"I'm Brittany Lynn," I say into the mirror. Then my vision blurs and I can't see anything at all.

9/6

I wake up with a headache from my crying jag. I'm still emotional, but things do get better when I get food. Real food—or real hospital food, rather. I have bacon and scrambled eggs and toast. And coffee. It's not a horchata latte with cinnamon milk, or a macchiato, but it's caffeine and that's good enough for me.

Last night I was overwhelmed, but I'm in a better frame of mind this morning. My thinking is clearer, and I resolve to make a plan. I need to take baby steps. No more Edie overload. I need to get used to her voice before I try to sing my songs. I need to get used to the sight of her hands reaching for a spoon or a toothbrush before I reach for a mirror and see her mean eyes looking back at me.

It's going to take time to feel comfortable living the life of a stranger. Other than her bullying me and me hating her guts, I don't know much about Edith Randolph Chatsworth-Jones. I know she wore a blue slip when she was found in a bathtub, and that she ended up in the Limbo Lounge at the same time as me. I know she was selfish and entitled and had the same meanness as Dingleberry. I know she tried to talk me into selling her my path, and I know she thought she could blind me with dollar signs, and that I'd fall for it because I'm just a dumb cosmetologist. I know she was relentless in order to get what she wanted. I know that there must have been something so horrible in her life that she picked up a razor blade and cut herself. I know she was serious about it and waited until she was alone.

Dr. Perez checks in on me right after breakfast. He says my vitals look surprisingly good and he snaps on gloves to cut the bandages from Edie's forearms. I gasp at the black sutures stitching together angry red slashes and delicate skin. Her left wrist suffered more damage than the right, with several ugly gouges like she was digging at her pulse.

"That's a horrible sight," I say just above a whisper. That might be Edie's voice, but those are my words. So are "How could anyone do that to themselves?" The pain alone would have stopped most people after the first cut.

Dr. Perez looks back at me. "I heard you were having some memory lapses." I remember that I have amnesia and don't know what I'm supposed to say. So I just give him a blank stare like he's speaking Borneo. Not that I know if that's a real language or where to find Borneo on a map.

The nurse I mistook for Lois Griffin enters the room and the doctor turns his attention to her. "There's still some weeping, but it's not as inflamed."

"Her color's better." She opens a tray of gauze and scissors. "And she ate her breakfast."

He pours sterile water over some gauze pads, then cleans the stitches. Those might be Edie's wrists, but I can feel the swipes of wet gauze, the sting of antiseptic; I suck in a breath. "Has she taken her medication?"

Medication? Edie's on medication? I guess that makes sense.

"Right here." She pats her pocket and pulls out four bubble packs. She pops out two capsules, one beige tablet, and a little blue pill. She puts them on my tray, then pours a cup of water.

I don't want to take Edie's medication—unless it's something for pain. I'm a real baby, and I wouldn't complain about some pain pills or a shot of something good or a morphine drip. "Which one of these is for pain?" Or am I not supposed to know about pain medication? I guess it's too late now.

"Those are your psychotropics."

The doctor puts some sort of ointment on the sutures and he and the nurse look at me like they expect me to pop those pills in my mouth. I pick them up and reach for the cup of water with my right hand. That seems to be enough for them and they return their attention to my wrist and continue to talk as if I'm not right here.

"She can take something for pain as needed."

I pretend to swallow each pill one at a time. I drink the entire cup of water, then gingerly shove the pills under me. When these two leave, I'll wrap them up in a tissue and throw them away. The last thing I need right now is psychotropics messing with *my* mind.

"Are her parents here?"

"Tomorrow afternoon."

My parents are coming? No, wait. Edie's parents are coming? She said they wouldn't ever cut their vacation short for her, and it seems she was right. They were called yesterday and aren't in a rush to see Edie.

"They're staying at a vineyard and flying in from Napa Valley."

"Staying at vineyards is my idea of the good life."

Vineyards? That sounds fancy, like they swish wine in their

mouth and spit it out. I'd never waste wine, and I don't want to meet hoity-toity wine swishers. I'm not ready.

Dr. Perez lets the nurse bandage my wrists while he turns his attention to Edie's belly. "Has she been up and about yet?"

"Not yet."

Maybe I'll be ready to meet them next month or maybe next year or *maybe never*.

His hands and fingers are cold and he pokes and prods and digs around like he's rearranging Edie's guts. "Does that hurt?"

"Yes, sir. Hurts as all git-out." Maybe I can pretend to be in a coma again. At least until Edie's parents go away.

He gives me a strange look but keeps talking like I'm not here. "She feels impacted. Get her walking around and her bowels moving." He straightens and turns to the nurse. "Order her a stool softener."

Wait. What?

The nurse nods as she wraps tape around the gauze. "I'll take out her catheter so she can use the bathroom."

Edie has a catheter? In her—or my—private area?

"She hasn't evacuated since she arrived."

Evacuated? Does he mean poo? I think he means poo.

He snaps off his gloves and tosses them in the garbage. "She might need a Fleet."

He's not talking about the Seventh Fleet. He means the kind of Fleet that Mamaw Rose had in her bathroom. I'd holler *hell no!* but I'm supposed to have amnesia.

"The nurse will take out your IV and catheter." He turns and finally talks to me directly. "We should have you in a new room shortly." He pulls out his stupid penlight and shines it in my eyes for the millionth time. "Do you know where you are?"

"Hospital."

"In what city?"

I don't know if I'm supposed to remember anyone mentioning it, so I shrug.

"Do you know what you were doing at the Plaza?"

The Plaza? That's the fanciest hotel in El Paso. I only know because I heard it on the news a year or two ago. I don't have enough money to walk in the door, let alone book a room. "No, sir."

He shuts off the penlight and shoves it in his pocket. "Tell me your name."

I just point to the label on my plastic water pitcher because I don't know if I'm supposed to say Edie or play dumb.

"Don't you know?"

The only thing I know is that I don't want to make Ingrid mad and get yanked up to the tulip garden again. I don't want to make mistakes like King Tut or Joan of Arc, so I shake my head and give him a big, blank look. Then, quicker than a sneeze, a psychiatric doctor pays me a visit and asks all sorts of questions about the event or events that triggered my last self-harm episode. I'm assuming he means Edie's suicide attempt.

"Are you depressed?"

I'm more confused than depressed, so I shrug again.

He types something into his electronic notebook and continues. "Did you self-harm out of anger or sadness or punishment for self-perceived wrongs?"

"What?"

He looks down and reads from his screen. "Did you self-harm to make yourself feel normal, distract yourself from your feelings, or to make others aware of your feelings?"

"I don't remember."

He types for a few moments, then looks up at me. "On the

self-harm scale from one to ten, ten being the highest, where are you?"

Negative zero to the hell no, but I'm probably not even supposed to know what he means.

He looks into my eyes like he can read my brain. "Do you feel like harming yourself today?"

"No, sir."

He's quiet for a few long seconds. His brows pull together as if he doesn't know what to think about me. I understand. I don't know what to think about me either. "I'll consult with your private physician and get back with you."

When he leaves I lay my head back. Keeping quiet and playing stupid is harder than it seems. Exhausting, too. I close my eyes to try to take a nap, but the nurse comes in and gives me a couple of pain pills and the dreaded stool softener. She takes out the IV and catheter and I drink a lot of water in the hope of avoiding the nuclear option.

She helps me with hospital slippers so we can walk like the doctor ordered. My knees almost buckle when I stand.

The nurse grabs my elbow and says, "You haven't been on your feet for a while," but I don't think it's that as much as these aren't my long legs. We walk slowly across the room and I take deep, even breaths so I don't get light-headed. Edie's free arm falls straight down her side, her thighs don't rub together, and her breasts don't stick out. I feel light and narrow and bow-legged. I don't know how to move in this body.

"You're doing good," she says, and steps out into the hall.

I stop just outside my room's entrance as all thoughts of Edie exit my head. The hall is exactly the same as the last time I walked it, when I was me and the golfer was a wing nut.

"Do you feel dizzy?"

I look up and down the familiar brown carpet, half expecting to see him or Valentina or Cliff.

"Do you need to go back?"

"No, ma'am." I'm getting that out-of-body feeling again, but I'm not turning back now. There is something I need to see, and we continue a little ways until I stop at a room on the right.

"How are you feeling?"

"Okay." I stare into the room where I was hooked to machines and where Momma bargained with God for my life. Where both Momma and Daddy cried over me and where I saw them last. The bed is empty. There is nothing left of me, and I am once again reminded that I am good and truly gone. Tears that I hadn't been able to shed that night sting my eyes. "Were my parents here when I died?" I wonder out loud as my heart squeezes in my chest.

"No, but we called them when you stabilized."

I look at the nurse and wipe at my eyes with the sleeve of my gown. With everything that has happened, and with the time difference between the earth and spirit planes, I don't know if I was alone when I passed. "What?"

"We let them know you were here, and they were contacted when you woke from your coma."

I blink several times. "Oh." *Those* parents. I turn back and glance into each room as we pass. There are new people in both Pearl and the other Brittany's rooms. Valentina is gone, but sadly Tommy is still here. I don't want to "blow it," but I have to know that Valentina is okay and didn't take a turn for the worse. "Why is this room empty?" I ask.

"There's been no one to fill it since the last patient was discharged."

"Discharged to where?"

"A rehabilitation hospital in San Antonio."

Good. "I hope that person will be okay."

"She's facing years of rehab, but she has youth on her side and may regain the use of her arms and legs."

May? I think of Valentina, of her ponytails and braces and her dream of being a Dallas Cowboys cheerleader. I wish her odds were better than *may*.

By the time I make it to my room, I'm too exhausted to think about my parents or Valentina or Tommy. I don't know if I'm supposed to remember how to use the bathroom, but I'll risk it. I'm not going to wet my pants, but the experience is disturbing on so many other levels that I'd rather not think about. Fortunately, I'm quick to fall asleep, but unfortunately, I'm still having freaky dreams. This time I am at my own funeral and when I try to talk to anyone, they scream and run away. Worse, I'm wearing a moldy velvet suit, green and without a hint of sparkle.

A nurse wakes me up at noon to take my vitals again and I recognize her. She's the nurse who walked through me, got zapped, and made the golfer's day.

A guy from food service brings me a hamburger, fries, salad, spice cake, and a Dr Pepper. It's what I'd ordered from the kitchen, but I can't even finish half before I feel full enough to bust.

After lunch, I am moved to a bigger room on a different floor. The wallpaper has a random pattern, and there's a window that looks out at the endless Texas sky and congested parking lot. The nurse wraps cellophane around the bandages and asks if I remember how to shower. Using the bathroom by myself is one thing, but washing my hair is something I probably shouldn't remember. I shake my head, and she grabs Edie's vanity case from the bedside table and says, "I'll show you."

I'd really rather she didn't, but I suck it up and follow her into the bathroom. She helps me with the snaps on the hospital gown and moves to the shower. The gown slips to the floor and Edie's nude body fills a mirror above the sink. That's the new me, but my face burns like I've been caught looking at something I shouldn't. Like I'm standing outside some skinny woman's bathroom window peeking in. I turn away and step into the shower. There's nothing I love more than a long, warm shower, but there are three of us in here today and I can't wait to get it over with.

I focus on my pretend amnesia while the nurse shows me how to wash myself. She teaches me how to shampoo and condition my hair, then gives me two thin towels. She dries me off and helps me into a clean gown. If I'd survived my accident, this would be my life. Someone else washing my body and dressing me. Likely that someone would be my momma. As much as I'm sad that I died, as sorry as I am that I left her all alone, I'm glad she doesn't have to change my diapers and clean my privates.

The nurse shows me how to brush my teeth and pats my shoulder because I'm a fast learner. She leaves to get my underwear and returns with something black and tiny that fits in each of her palms. I don't have to pretend amnesia when I ask, "What's that?"

She holds it up. "A bra." It's black and sheer with little velvet hearts, and I know that in my entire life I've never fit into something that small. Or the matching thong she holds up either.

"Anything else?"

"Yes."

Good. I'd rather have comfy undies that don't ride up on me.

"Three pairs of black pants and blue sweaters, black pumps, three more thongs with matching bras, and a nightie."

"Is the underwear all the same kind?"

"Identical."

The nurse helps me into the lingerie, and I assume the nightie isn't appropriate when she hands me a clean hospital gown. I can tell right off that me and the thong are not going to get along, and I resist pulling at it.

There's no 1,600-watt Conair stuck to the wall like at the Super 8, and the nurse towel-dries my hair and shows me how to brush out the tangles. She cuts the cellophane from my forearms, then leaves me alone to finish with my right hand.

I don't recognize myself on the outside. I don't recognize my reflection in the mirror or the sound of my voice, but I'm still me. I have a new life, but I don't have to forget where I come from. I still have the same thoughts and dreams, just different circumstances. If I want to open my own salon, I'll have to go back to school to get my certificates, which is a pain in the butt, but will be a lot easier this time around. I can go to an Aveda school in Austin or San Antonio. They're classier than where I graduated from, and I can drive the six hours to see Momma or she can drive down to see me.

I set the brush on a side table and wonder what Edie did for a living. Something snobby, no doubt, not that it really matters now. She's about to be one hell of a cosmetologist, and the irony is sweet.

My idea of heaven has changed throughout the years, but I've never envisioned it as a cross between St. Ambrose Parish and the Department of Motor Vehicles, only with harder benches.

As a child, I used to think it was filled with my two favorite things in the world: puppies and sprinkle doughnuts. I thought angels hopped from star to star and wrote my name across the sky. The first time I visited Italy, I was sure heaven must look like St. Peter's Basilica. Once I thought I found it on a beach in Bora Bora, but that turned out to be too much rum and sun and a Brit named Trevor.

I've pictured heaven as sailing at sunset in Key West, attending fashion week in Milan, or lounging on clouds as soft as the seats in Father's Phantom, while cherubs massage my muscles with their chubby hands. God knows I love a good massage.

This looks like a cloud plateau. There are no pearly gates, no trumpets, no angels singing hallelujah. Nothing but blue sky and white mist. Black windows and blinking numbers, and the never-ending stream of people.

"Now serving number five-zero-two-four at window number seven."

I don't know how long I've been listening to numbers, watching people move past me to a ticket window, scrutinizing the systems and analytics.

"Now serving five-zero-two-five at window number eighty-seven."

I watch an older woman in a pink fluffy robe move forward, and I've come to the logical conclusion that the zeros on my ticket are an error due to a system glitch or processing mistake.

One of the flashing lights draws my attention to the bank of windows. "Serving number five-zero-two-six at window number ninety-six."

My number will never get called because I don't have one. I've already looked around for an information booth or window, but there isn't so much as a mail slot for complaints. No matter how far I wander, I always find myself back where I started.

I've pushed my way to blinking windows and showed my ticket and I shouted for help. I asked for the date and how long I've been here. The window just flashed a number that wasn't mine and didn't answer my questions. People come and go but I'm stuck here with no apparent way out.

A woman plops herself on the hard bench beside me and crosses legs that appear to have been swallowed by faux-python boots with five-inch heels. The rest of her horrendous ensemble includes a black pleather skirt, a sheer white top, and a cheap red bra. There are occasions when tawdry undies are appropriate and fun, but there is never an excuse for cheap lingerie. She looks more 8 Mile than Pretty Woman, and it looks like she's tried to chew the black polish off her stubby nails.

She does have one thing going for her, though: a real ticket with a real number, and 5,029 is coming up quick.

She doesn't know it yet, but she's holding my ticket. "When did you get here?" I hope she voluntarily hands it over and saves us both the indignity of a physical altercation. She won't be as easy as Brittany, but I've taken Krav Maga and can drop her with a jab to her solar plexus if need be.

"Now serving five-zero-two-seven at window number sixteen."

"A while." Her cheeks are smudged with mascara-stained tears, and she holds up her ticket. "Only one more to go, then I'm next in line for heaven."

A whore in heaven? She looks like she's been dragged through hell backward. Her circumstances are certainly pitiable, but no more distressing than mine. I sit on the board of several charitable organizations, I'm a shareholder in my family's multinational conglomeration, and I'm a distinguished art buyer. I deserve a real number more than a prostitute does. "I wish you were staying longer. I'm sure we'd be great friends."

She looks me up and down. "I doubt it, Paris Hilton."

I gasp. Paris Hilton! I'm younger and prettier, and I don't have to make myself sound ridiculous for attention. I smile like I don't want to choke her. "Good one," I say with a laugh and stick out my hand. "I'm Edie."

When she shakes my hand, I can feel the ticket. "Chablis Chardonnay."

Of course that's her name. "Is that French?" I know when I hand her number through the window, they'll be expecting a hooker, not me, but I'm more important than a woman who gives twenty-dollar blow jobs on Michigan and Livernois.

"Sure."

"Le chic." She tries to pull her hand free but I clasp it tight in both of mine. "Everyone else around here is so boring."

"I'm not your scissor sister."

What? What? With a streetwalker? Oh, good Lord. "Charming." I almost let go of her hand in disgust, but I keep my eye on the prize.

"What's your problem?"

"I want your ticket." I yank her wrist toward me.

"No!" She pulls back.

"Now serving five-zero-two-eight at window one-three-three."

"I'll pay you a million dollars for it." I'm running out of time and we go back and forth in a tug-of-war with her hand.

"There's no money in heaven. Let go of me!"

"What's your hurry? You're going to hell." Chablis Chardonnay is stronger than she looks, but playtime is over. "Stay here where it's nice and cool."

"Dumb-ass bitch!"

"Cretin."

I yank hard but she breaks free. The ticket flies from her hand, and before it lands on her python-covered thighs, I snatch it out of the air.

"Who's the dumb-ass now?" I toss my ticket in her face and run like a pissed-off hooker is chasing me, because she is. In those heels, she's no more a match for me than Doreen and Dan. I can hear her cussing me out as I bob and weave and finally stop when I no longer hear her foul mouth. I position myself behind a group of tall Swedes for better cover. I stand on tiptoe but can hardly see over their shoulders. Not that it matters. A green light flashes toward the first few windows and I run toward it with the ticket clenched in my tight fist. "I'm coming, God!"

"Serving number zero-zero-zero, zero-zero-zero, zero-zero-zero at window number five."

What? I stop near window five as Chablis Chardonnay hands over my ticket. I'm confused. The number in my hand should have been called next. Did God make a mistake? Did I fight for a new ticket only to have my old number called? Is that ragged hooker taking my place in heaven? What the hell is happening?

10

I don't know how many doctors one person needs, but during breakfast the next morning of toast and coffee, an orthopedic specialist pays me a visit. He unwraps my bandages, has me try to touch my fingers and thumb on both hands, then wraps me up again. He says my right hand will heal, but my left will likely need surgery to repair the nerve damage. Both need therapy and rehab, and no one will say how long that will take.

The orthopedic specialist is barely out the door when Dr. Perez and the shrink I met earlier stop by. Both doctors question me and ask about where I was born and the names of Edie's parents. I tell them I don't know, which happens to be true. Dr. Perez asks my age.

"I don't know." But I think Edie is the same as me. "How old am I?"

"Thirty."

"What?" My jaw drops and I sit straight up in bed. "Thirty!"

"How old do you think you are?"

Twenty-five! "I don't know."

The shrink leans forward and presses me. "You had a strong reaction to being told you're thirty. Why?"

Because not only did Edie steal my spot in heaven, she robbed me of five years of my life. I sit back and pull up the sheet. "It just sounds old."

The doctors take a momentary pause to chuckle before launching into more questions.

"Do you recall your last visit to Livingston?"

"Where's that?"

"It's a psychiatric hospital."

"Edie was in a psychiatric hospital?" I correct myself and say, "Me?" I guess I shouldn't be surprised. Edie was crazy and tried to kill herself.

"Where did you attend college?"

Chip Daniel's College of Hair. "I don't know—where?"

"Wellesley."

I've never heard of it so it's easy to give them a blank stare.

"What's your current address?"

Probably Detroit, not that it matters. When I leave the hospital, I'm heading to Marfa. I can't tell Momma I'm Brittany— at least not right off, but I'll figure it all out once I'm home.

The doctors just look at each other and whisper; then the shrink asks, "What are your parents' names?"

"I don't know, sir."

"Your brother's name?"

"I have a brother?" I always wanted a brother.

"Where did you spend your gap year?"

"What's a gap year?"

The shrink gets an alert on his tablet and frowns. "Did you hide your medication in your bedsheets?"

Oh yeah. I forgot to get rid of those.

Both doctors look at me like I'm a felon.

"I don't want to take pills."

"They stabilize your moods and help with your depression, impulsivity, and suicidal ideations."

Wow. All those meds and Edie was still crazy. "No."

"We can't force you, but stopping your medications led you here."

They can't force me? Good to know. "I don't remember what led me here. But I can tell you that I don't need that stuff."

Dr. Perez and the shrink busily type something in their notebooks as a middle-aged couple walks into the room. We eye each other suspiciously as they move to the end of the bed. They look wealthy and snooty, and offhand, I'd say Edie's folks have arrived.

"Your parents are here to see you." Dr. Perez states the obvious and smiles like he expects us to fall on each other's neck.

"What is this nonsense with your memory?" Edie's mother asks, blowing Dr. Perez's dream of a happy reunion. She is blonde like Edie and has frosty eyes. She has the same hoity-toity voice, too, and I wouldn't be all that surprised if she calls me a cretin.

Both parents are tall and thin and wear matching navy-blue blazers with gold patches on the breast pockets. They're so stiff and formal that I can't imagine Edie ever calling them Momma or Daddy.

"Well?" her mother says, and I shake my head because she's as scary as her daughter. I don't know if she's crazy, too, but I don't want to say the wrong thing and find out.

"The doctors say you're having memory problems." Edie's father has gray hair, slicked back with pomade and a wide-tooth comb. Out of the two, he appears nicer.

I give him my best blank stare and smile because I want him on my team.

"Have you lost your voice along with your memory?"

Without looking at Edie's mother, I answer her. "No, ma'am."

"Please." Edie's father puts a hand on his wife's arm but his dark brown eyes are directed at me. "What are you doing in El Paso, Edith?"

That's a good question. "I don't know, sir." Out of the two I'd rather answer Edie's daddy.

"You talked to Amanda an hour before you left home."

"Who?"

"Your TZE sister."

"I have a sister?"

Claire shakes her head, annoyed. "You've been friends since you pledged Tau Zeta Epsilon in college."

I've never pledged anything, and my best friend since second grade is Lida.

"She's playing games again, Marvin."

"Don't get worked up."

Clearly these two do not know the definition of "worked up." In my house, "worked up" means someone's about to pitch a hissy fit and knives are an option. Edie's mother is cold and controlled and hasn't even raised her voice. Personally, I'd welcome a hissy fit with homicidal undertones any day over this woman's icy calm.

"You lied and told Amanda that you were going to Hawthorne," she says, and I can practically see frost hovering over her words.

Marvin pats her shoulder and I think that maybe he's going to tell her to go easy on me, but he says, "The stress isn't good for your health, darling."

Her stress! What about *my* stress? These people are getting me agitated. I need something for my nerves. I need Valium or Xanax or propofol. I know they've got some around here somewhere.

"What should we tell Blake?" Marvin wants to know.

Blake Shelton? *Tell him he's as hot as a helping of HELL YEAH!* Their eyes drill into me and even if I wasn't faking amnesia, I know better than to be a smart-ass. "I don't know a Blake."

Darling looks like she wants to choke me. "This is disgraceful," she says, and I swallow hard.

"How could you have humiliated that fine man and his family?"

They're a tag team. A tag team with mean faces like Edie's. I am outnumbered and helpless. My thong is riding up, and I want to tell them to go to hell.

"How could you humiliate your family?"

"The last time was bad enough." Darling brushes the front of her blazer like it has lint on it, *as if* a piece of lint would dare come within ten feet of her. I know I wouldn't. "We can't show our faces at the yacht club."

The last time Edie tried to kill herself? Or did she humiliate "that fine man and his family" more than once? Not that that should be a concern at the moment. Edie tried to carve out her veins, I'm wrestling with a complete meltdown and a wayward thong, and they're worried about showing their faces at a stupid yacht club!

"What are your plans, Edith?"

Getting as far away from you as possible.

"Well?"

At the moment, not getting riled up and letting my jumpy nerves get the best of me.

The psychiatrist intervenes. "What do you remember before your accident?"

The dashboard Jesus. "Nothin'."

"Nothing at all?"

"No, sir."

"Look at her arms, Marvin." Darling points toward me. "Look at what she's done now."

"Don't let that upset you."

Darling is going to get a lesson in upset if she keeps pointing her bony finger at me.

"What's the first thing you can remember?" Dr. Perez wants to know.

That's easy. "Lois pinchin' the back of my hand."

"Lois . . . ?"

Oops. I can't say Lois looks like Lois Griffin because I have amnesia. "I don't know."

Marvin and Darling turn to each other and talk in hushed tones, and while Edie's wrists might be a mess, there's nothing wrong with her ears. I hear words like *sacrifice* and *selfish*, *attention* and *ungrateful*. They glance at the doctors and huddle closer. "We'll discuss it when we get her home."

News flash. Not going anywhere with Marvin and Darling. No way. Not now. Not ever. I've got my own plans, thank you.

"I spoke with your doctor. . . ." The shrink pauses to scroll through his notes.

"Barb Ware," Perez reminds him.

"That's right. Doctor Barb Ware."

"Bobwyre? Y'all are pullin' my leg."

"Barb Ware," the shrink says again.

"That's what I said. Bobwyre."

"Not barbed wire like a fence. Doctor Barbara W-*a*-re. W-a-r-e."

Dr. Perez spells it out for me like he's reading from one of the golfer's *Dummies* books.

I can take a joke. I can laugh at myself, too, but I'm not in a laughing mood. I'm overloaded and overwhelmed, and my last nerve is worn as thin as a whisper. I want to yell at everyone to get out, but I hear Momma's voice in my head telling me not to be a hothead and fly off the handle, so I swallow past the words burning my throat. I need a cool head and tongue, and thanks to the good Lord and baby Jesus, I control myself and say, "Well, bless your heart, Doctor Perez."

Darling points her finger at me again. "Why is my daughter speaking with that horrible Southern accent?"

I put on my best church smile and say like God's watching, "Bless your heart too, darlin'." Momma would be proud.

"You sound like a hillbilly."

Hillbilly? What is with these people?

"Edith, I won't have you embarrassing the family with that ignorant accent," Marv joins in.

That's it. "I'm not Edith!" I sit straight up and the hot words I've been holding back erupt in a rageful torrent. "Edith's a mean psycho and I hate her. My name is Brittany Lynn Snider. I'm twenty-five years old and I live in Marfa with my momma, Carla Jean Snider. I love cold beer and fish tacos, and you better trust and believe that I'm wearin' my space panties to Boogie's Tex-Mex three-for-one taco night." They look like they're witnessing an alien abduction, but bubba, hold my beer, I'm not finished yet. "I believe in God and baby Jesus and that Texas is heaven on earth. If y'all think I'm going anywhere but home to my own momma today, all y'all are crazy as sprayed roaches."

Wow, that felt good.

Ingrid was right. There are worse things than being called Edie. One of them is sitting next to a girl named Carol who eats her own hair. I'm told that it's called trichophagia and it's really gross to watch. Even worse when she coughs up a hair ball.

"What do you think, Edie?" Another is being locked up in a psychiatric hospital somewhere in Michigan.

I look at therapist Rhonda and squeeze the stress ball in my left hand. I hear a collective groan from the others in the group and say, "I think I don't belong here."

"Not again."

"She says that every morning."

"Twelve times since she's been in group. Of course, we only meet three times a week. Monday, Wednesday, and Friday. We definitely don't meet on weekends."

"Make her stop saying that."

"God, you people are boring."

There are six of us in this cognitive therapy group. There's bipolar Ellen, impulse-disordered Anna, obsessive-compulsive

Liz, trichophagia Carol, psycho Katrina, and me. I'm the only sane one around here, but they're all looking at *me* like *I'm* crazy. Ingrid warned me. She told me not to blow it. I wish I'd listened.

"We're supposed to be talking about how Katrina's a bitch."

"You're the bitch, Helen."

"It's Ellen, and quit smiling at me! Make her stop staring at me!"

Morning sunlight falls on Katrina's demented smile. Her hazel eyes are a freakish blue and green and aren't quite focused, but that could be the medication they've put her on. The good Lord knows I've been dosed up on some heavy shit since I arrived three months ago. I guess that's what happens when you lash out at people who already think you're a lunatic. They believe you're going to try to kill yourself again all because you yell, "Edith's a mean psycho and I hate her." They say you're having a psychotic break and blame it on you hiding your psychotropic medication. Before you know it, you're shipped off to a goddamn mental institution and forced to take a cocktail of medications that turns you into a drooling mess. Then they keep adding days to your treatment because you're a drooling mess who can't remember a goddamn thing about yourself.

Oh, and another thing that's happened to me since that day in El Paso when I was packed up and shipped out against my will: I've been swearing like a certified sinner.

I blame Edie.

"I'm not staring at you, Helen."

"My name is Ellen!"

"Ladies, use the problem-solving strategies we've talked about," the therapist says loud enough to get everyone's attention. "What should Ellen and Katrina have done differently?"

Liz raises her hand. "Ellen shouldn't have called Katrina a bitch. Katrina shouldn't have called Ellen Helen. Edie shouldn't say she doesn't belong here all the time. Anna should stop stealing everyone's pencils and glue and Carol should stop eating her hair."

The therapist nods. "How should they resolve their feelings?"

Anna jumps to her feet. "Role-play!"

"No," I beg. "Not role-play."

Katrina stands and does a few stretches like she's preparing for a street fight. "I'll play Helen," she says, and I try not to smile.

Carol pulls out a strand of her hair. "This won't end well."

"Don't eat that!" Liz tells her. Carol gives Liz the side-eye and puts it in her pocket.

"You can't play me." Ellen turns to therapist Rhonda. "She can't play me. It's against the rules."

"Katrina never plays by the rules."

"Not once in forty-two days. She definitely doesn't play by the rules."

Ellen waves in my general direction. "Edie can play me."

"Yeah. Edie never has to role-play. It's her turn."

"Definitely her turn."

"That's not goin' to happen, y'all." I squeeze my stress ball a few more times, then shove it in the pocket of an Ithaca College hoodie. Apparently, Edie had a box of clothing from the last time she was here at good old Livingston Mental Health—nicer sounding than *mental hospital* or *nuthouse*. It was filled with mostly sweatshirts and tracksuits, flat velvet shoes, and normal underwear. Her parents sent them along, and nothing says "we care" like a smashed-up box sent by UPS. Then again, I did call them roaches.

"We all have to show respect for each other in group," therapist Rhonda reminds us. She takes a pencil from behind her ear and writes something in the notebook on her lap. "Katrina, you know your role is to watch other members use the problem-solving strategies we've learned in group to express your feelings in a more constructive way."

Katrina shrugs and sits back down. Carol and Anna volunteer to role-play the other two women, and there's nothing quite like crazy people trying to act like they're not crazy by repeating monotonous "strategies."

"I should use appropriate language when expressing myself," Carol says in her deadpan voice. "And not call a person a bitch."

Anna nods in agreement. "I need to consider other people's feelings. I definitely need to play by the rules."

I look at Katrina and her lunatic smile. Out of all the women here, I like her the best. To say we're friends would be a stretch, but yesterday she came into my room and wanted to use my tinted lip moisturizer and mascara. She colored a little out of line, poked herself in the eye, and I was afraid she'd go psycho on me. She just made a joke and laughed and told me that Livingston is the best mental hospital she's been in. I don't ask how she knows. Best not to pry open that can of crazy worms, but sometimes I get the feeling she isn't as demented as she appears. Although I don't know why she'd fake being a psycho when the goal is to get out of here. At least that's *my* goal. Since I've been here, I've watched patients come and go, and I definitely want to *go* ASAP.

I don't really remember the first sixty days. I was locked up in ward C, where I had to use the toilet in my tiny room and wear a heavy suicide smock. I slept a lot and lived a nightmare when I was awake. I was scared and confused and cried all the time. Edie's lawyer, Garver something, came to visit. He talked about the courts and my patient's rights, and I couldn't understand what any of it meant. I got the feeling he worked more for them than for me.

I was getting sicker and more lethargic, and the doctors noticed that the medication that worked for Edie in the past didn't work for me. They were baffled and scanned my brain for damage due to blood loss after Edie's suicide attempt.

Lucky for me, they were so shocked by the imaging, they scanned it a bunch more times. They didn't find damage (praise God and baby Jesus), but saw instead a drastic change from Edie's last neuroimaging. Goodbye to her dark blue and pale yellow brain, hello to my brilliant gold and orange. I was re-evaluated and retested and diagnosed with profound retrograde amnesia and complete autobiographical memory loss. The doctors determined my amnesia is likely caused by one or more of the following:

1. Blood loss and coma
2. Psychological trauma
3. Emotional shock
4. Hysteria
5. Dissociative break
6. They don't really know.

When I first got here, the staff asked a lot of questions about why I think I'm Brittany Lynn Snider and why I hate Edie, but I learned my lesson. Even when I was a drooling mess, I insisted that I didn't remember, and eventually they stopped asking.

The good news is that faking amnesia is getting easier. The

bad news is that the staff believes my amnesia is temporary and that the key to unlocking my memory is through "triggers." What I know and they don't is that no amount of word association, sound pairing, and photos is ever going to make that happen.

"I never said Ellen's a bitch." Katrina stands and points to her nemesis. "*I said* Helen's a bitch."

Predictably, problem-solving skills descend to hell and we're dismissed until Monday. Thank God I have the weekend before I have to rejoin the ladies who actually need cognitive therapy.

I've been in ward B for a month now, and I've been tapered off the strong psychotropic drugs. Now I take a low-dose antidepressant, which I figure I probably do need due to my depressing situation.

Everything that had been in Edie's vanity case in El Paso was returned to me in a plastic red pouch with my name written in black Sharpie. The hospital has a policy against arriving with Louis Vuitton, which is best, given the kleptos around here.

Since landing in ward B, I have more freedom, and by more freedom I mean I was awarded a seat on the minibus to Meijer for good behavior. I bought scented lotion and good shampoo and conditioner, cosmetics, a black Carhartt knit cap, and a mini calendar. I mark off every day right before bed, and that might not seem like a big deal, but it's progress toward the end of the tunnel. I don't see light yet, but at least there's a tunnel.

I can leave my room and wander around, and I can attend church services in the lobby on Sundays. The preacher who comes isn't as fiery as Johnny J., which is for the best, I suppose. No one wants fired-up crazy people running around.

I eat my meals in the cafeteria, although that's a privilege

I can sometimes do without. Like when Twitchy Lisa (not my name for her) accuses everyone of having an affair with her husband, Roy, which is really laughable. Roy is bald and spotty and not in a good way. Lisa has nothing to worry about, but she seems to target me more than others. The doctors say it's because she sees me as the biggest threat. I don't care about the reasons; I'm over trying to *reason* with her.

After group, I return to my small room and pull out a black-and-white composition notebook. Spiral notebooks are against the rules—the wire might be used as a lethal weapon.

I glance over the lyrics I wrote before the lights were turned out last night. My left hand is still numb, and if I don't have my little rubber ball to squeeze, I touch my fingertips to my thumb like I learned from the orthopedic rehab therapist. Squeezing and finger touches have become so routine, I just do them without thinking about it.

My right hand is a lot better and I'm getting better at using it. I cross out words and add others to the piece I've titled "Groan-a-Lisa." "I don't want your husband," I sing in Edie's pitchy voice. "He's all yours. I'd rather stab my eyes out than look at his sores." So maybe those aren't my best lines, but the chorus is pure gold.

Hey, Groan-a-Lisa, I don't need your crazy around me. I've got bigger problems than the ones you fight. I got problems that keep me awake at night.

Listen up, Groan-a-Lisa, don't bring your crazy around me. I don't care about your emotions, your struggles, or what you fear. All I care about, Lisa, is how I get the hell out of here.

Okay, maybe not Grammy-worthy lyrics, but this is my life and they mean something to me.

Meals at Livingston are always served with plastic utensils

(the lethal-weapon thing) and always at the same time. The dining room doors open at precisely 7 a.m., noon, and 6 p.m., in order to avoid confusion, agitation, and conspiracy theories. The food isn't great, but I've had worse. The Chat-N-Chew Chili Wagon comes to mind.

Today's lunch is some very bland rigatoni and a mixed-greens salad. I trade in my pasta for an extra salad. I figure Edie must have been vegan, because I crave fresh veggies like I used to crave snack cakes. I remember my first real meal after I was moved to ward B. I was feeling more like myself and ate roast beef and potatoes, dinner rolls and real butter. I ate until I was tight as a tick. Afterward, I got sick as a dog. I discovered Edie's digestion can't take a healthy appetite. I learned to eat more like Edie and less like Brittany to avoid some serious agony. Three-for-one taco nights and space panties are a thing of the past.

There are a few other things I've discovered about Edie, too. Like, even if I was allowed to have a razor, there's no need. She's obviously had laser hair removal on just about every part of her body—yes, even down there. Ouch! Her toenails grow at an alarming rate, and she had eyelash extensions when I first got here. The regrowth on her head is a medium brown, not blonde, and the stylist in me cringes when I see those roots. I usually pull her hair into a high ponytail under my cap.

I've been told that she goes by Edie Chatsworth-Jones and that her mother's name isn't Darling; it's Clarice like in *Silence of the Lambs*. Different Clarice, same feeling of horror.

And I've been told that she was committed to Livingston the first time a year and a half ago for downing a fistful of Klonopin and a bottle of vodka in a guesthouse on her parents' property. Marv and Claire had been understandably horrified, but shortly after leaving Livingston that time, she'd convinced them (and a few doctors, too) that she hadn't really wanted to die. It was a cry for help and attention, she argued, but no one is suggesting that this time around. Not after she added thousands of miles and a razor to the equation.

After lunch I have an appointment with one of a handful of doctors who treated Edie a year and a half ago. This time it's with Dr. Lindbloom, a psychotherapist who likes to drop the word *Mensa* into conversations like the golfer used to drop "double-eagled on the eighth." Since I have amnesia, he goes into detail about what that means practically every time I see him.

He's a short, nerdy-looking guy with brown corduroy pants and a wiry ponytail that would benefit from a sharp pair of scissors. If I liked him and could give him a professional consultation, I'd recommend that he massage his scalp with jojoba or argan oil, but I don't like him. He doesn't seem to like me either, but I don't want to cause trouble for myself. I have two more months before I'm *adios, amigos*. Dr. Barbara (aka Bobwyre) tells me that my discharge paperwork is moving along, and barring any unforeseen problems, my release date is October fourth. I like Dr. Barbara. She's been Edie's shrink for a long time. I think I can trust her, but "unforeseen problems" worries me, and I don't want to say or do anything that could add more days to my sentence.

"I'm reading Rhonda's notes and it looks like you are reluctant to participate in group therapy," Dr. Lindbloom says.

I'm lying on a leather couch that feels and smells like a saddle. "I participate plenty, but I don't like role-play." My eyes are closed and I reach into my pocket and pull out my squeezy ball. "I'm shy."

"You weren't shy when you were here before."

I don't know if it's me or if Edie got on his bad side when she was here before, but unlike the other doctors, I've only seen him once a week since I got let out of ward C. Folks generally like me, and I reckon the world is filled with people who don't like Edie. "Well, I don't recall bein' here before."

I hear him shuffle some papers before he asks, "What comes to mind when I say 'Hawthorne'?"

A tree. "Nothin'."

"Hmm." He makes that sound a lot, sometimes dragging it out because he thinks I'm "malingering," which is a fancy word for faking. He's right, but he is not the medical director or chief physiatrist, Dr. Ryan, and he can't do much about it but stick to the treatment plan. That doesn't sit well with him, and it seems to me as if he thinks he can trip me up and catch me faking just to prove he's right.

"Hmm . . . What do you think when you hear 'Magnus'?"

I think it sounds like Magnum and that makes me think of condoms, but I doubt that's what he means. Although I'd love to see his face if I said it, but I can't. I have amnesia. I probably shouldn't know about safe sex. "I don't know what that means."

He turns on the sound of blaring horns in heavy traffic. "What word do you associate with this sound?"

"Big city."

"What big city?"

"New York."

He turns off the recording. "Hmmm . . . Why did you say New York?"

"Because you asked."

"Can you imagine yourself in New York?"

"Yes."

"Where do you imagine yourself?"

"High-rise apartment."

"Your high-rise apartment?" he asks, sly as a debutante.

"No."

"Whose apartment is it?"

"Ramona's."

"Hmmmmmm . . . Is Ramona a family member or perhaps a friend?"

"Neither. She's on *Real Housewives of New York City*. It was on last night. She and Sonja are a hoot and a half." I turn my head and look over at him. "It was a rerun."

His hand is on his forehead like he's in pain and he's clicking the top of his pen. "On your group worksheet you wrote that Anna is a 'kleper.' What does that mean?"

"That I can't spell 'kleptomaniac.'" Out of everything, I think that my miraculous ability to read and write gives Dr. Mensa the biggest mental seizures. The other doctors chalked it up to the mysteries of amnesia, like my handwriting being totally different, but he can't let it go at that. I didn't mean for it to be a big deal; I simply didn't want to pretend ignorance and start kindergarten a second time.

After another half an hour, I think the doctor and I have had enough of each other.

"Same time next week," he says as I move toward the door. "Do you need a card or will you remember?"

"If I forget, all y'all know where to find me." I shove my ball in my pocket and look over my shoulder at him. "I don't think I'm goin' to get my memory back." Maybe he's as tired of these sessions as I am and we can just stop.

"Don't worry about it." He stands and moves toward me. "We'll keep working at it until you do."

That's what I'm afraid of. "Doctor Barbara says I can get out October fourth. That's only two more months."

"You'll be reevaluated the last week of September."

"And since I don't pose a threat to myself or others, y'all can't keep me in here."

"Don't let your expectations overshadow your treatment." He shoves my chart under his arm. "Remember what happened last time."

"No."

"Your temper got the best of you."

Yeah, losing my temper hasn't worked out for me lately. Sounds like it didn't work for Edie either, so I smile and say, "See ya next week, Doc," and hope maybe something intervenes between now and then.

Maybe if I talk to Dr. Barbara, she'll say I don't have to go to his office anymore. She has a nice face and seems to care about me. She gives me hope and at the moment, that's all I have.

I keep my head down as I make my way to my room. I have a lot to think about and don't want to get stopped by anyone. Unfortunately, I feel Twitchy Lisa's eyes on me a second before she's by my side. "Don't say it," I tell her.

"Where's Roy?"

"I don't know." Of course that answer doesn't satisfy her, and she dogs me to my room.

"I saw you with him."

"Leave me alone, Lisa."

"Where are you hiding my husband?"

I reach the safety of my room and slam the door in her face. I'm living in an altered universe. Like *Freaky Friday* without the fun stuff. Four months ago I was working next to my momma at the Do or Dye, and now I have a schizophrenic woman chasing me down the hall. Ingrid said she'd help me out like a guardian angel, but I haven't seen her since El Paso. I don't know if her time to help me is up or if she's mad because I blew it. I remember her saying something about not seeing me if I don't play by the rules.

I lean against the door and touch my numb fingertips to my thumb. *One, two, three, four,* I count in my head. Living in this altered universe is hard and still crazy, but some things have gotten better. I can look in the mirror and take a shower without having a breakdown. Living in a tall, skinny body almost feels normal now. I'm used to feeling my knees knock together and my arms swing at my sides. When I eat or write or reach for something, I don't see her hands now. I don't get mentally tripped up over where she stops and I begin . . . unless I look at Edie's wrists. The ugly scars remind me that some things will always be a mystery.

When I push away from the door my gaze falls on an empty spot next to my plastic vanity case. My pink grapefruit body lotion filled the empty space before lunch. I don't have to wonder what happened to it. That's twice this week. I yank open the door.

"What have you done with Roy?" Great, Lisa is still waiting to interrogate me.

I don't even bother to answer as she follows me down the hall to Anna's room, where I storm in and pull my lotion from her klepto grip. "Touch it again and I'll break your fingers," I say, and walk out. Of course, Twitchy is waiting and starts in on me again.

"Where's Roy?"

"He's hidin' in Anna's room." I know Lisa's mental illness is not her fault and that she can't help it. I know I should feel bad about lying to her and threatening Anna's sticky fingers, but I don't. Momma would say I should be more Christian, but Momma isn't locked up 24/7 with crazy folks.

Which brings me to one more thing: I'm not as nice as I used to be.

I can't blame all of that on Edie.

12

A few days after Katrina poked her eye with my mascara, women start knocking on my door for makeovers. I never signed up to be Livingston's resident cosmetologist, but I'm not mad about it. It helps break the tedium of doctor appointments and group, game night and music night, and I need to use my right hand to practice the professional makeup courses I took online last year. It passes the hours between X's on my calendar.

"More black eye shadow." This is the sixth time in two weeks now that Katrina has sat in my chair. She never earns a seat on the minibus, but she gives money to the others to buy black makeup and red lipstick.

"It's not eye shadow. It's eyeliner, and you know I can't give you more since you acted like a zombie and scared Helen at movie night."

"It's Ellen."

"I know."

She laughs as I back-comb her black hair. "You're not as boring as you look."

"And you're not as demented as you act." I've learned that the key to getting along with Katrina is to never show fear.

At first, the women were just walking into my room for makeovers and updos, but it got so busy that I had to make an appointment book and set my hours.

The staff didn't know what to think about my skills. Edie doesn't have a history with cosmetology but can suddenly style hair and apply cosmetics like a pro. When asked about it, I just shrug and give them my usual answer: "I don't know." Shortly after, a doctor found a case study from Denmark in which a plumber with a ninth-grade education fell asleep in a train station after hitting his head and woke seeing the world as triangles and waves. He started writing equations everywhere and talking about quantum physics. He amazed top mathematicians and physicists and solved some sort of complex system that everyone had been working on.

Now, I don't know the first thing about all that brainiac stuff, but if an uneducated plumber can wake up solving the mysteries of the universe, a Michigan socialite can wake up knowing how to style hair.

The staff at Livingston eventually agreed that self-esteem boosts could be a part of everyone's therapy. There are limits and rules and I'm more than okay with that. Every woman has to bring her own cosmetics and hairbrushes for sanitary reasons. I can't cut hair for obvious potentially lethal consequences, but I can give them a Brittany Lynn Snider fashionable style. Some arrive with the jumbo self-gripping rollers and the teasing combs (without picks) that I recommended. I can't exactly keep up on the latest tricks and trends without a computer, but it's good to practice the skills I do have for when I go home. With half of my left hand still numb and my grip still weak, braiding is difficult, but I'm adapting and getting better. It helps that I give them all the Do or Dye signature finish: enough extreme-hold to survive a cat-five hurricane.

After three weeks, it became necessary to make a list of rules and tape them to my door:

1. Absolutely NO walk-ins—that means everyone!
2. Be on TIME.
3. Take your meds BEFORE appointment!
4. That means YOU!

The next time we meet in group, Ellen tells everyone she sees a hidden meaning in the rules and thinks "No Time Before You" is the name of my "salon."

Of course, Katrina objects. "It's a list of rules, Helen." I've given Katrina three French braids like she wanted. They aren't quite as tight as I'd like because of the mobility in my left hand, and she's stuck about ten bird feathers in them.

"It's Ellen."

These two women are relentless and I don't get between them.

"Edie gets to name her beauty shop."

I look across at Carol and her comb-over bouffant and apple-green eye shadow. The hair is great and hides her biggest bald spot. The eye shadow . . . Well, she likes it.

No Time Before You Salon sticks, and I guess it's fitting, given my amnesia situation. The salon gives me back a piece of myself and helps me pass the time from one month to the other. It reminds me of who I am and where I come from. Not that I need to be reminded that I'm not in Texas. It might be September now, but it's cold as heck in Michigan.

Not all the women who book appointments are happy,

though. Renee from room 10b thought her eyebrows were too dark and Michelle from 23b didn't like the side ponytail she asked for. I point out that they got what they paid for. They argue, and I get so aggravated that I do something I've dreamed of since the day I started cutting and styling hair in beauty school. I draw a red arrow on a piece of paper and tape it above my trash can. I call it "the complaint department."

Katrina thinks my complaint department is hysterical. While I wouldn't go that far, I'm so pleased with all the X's filling my calendar, I lose my mind for real and agree to an appointment with Twitchy Lisa for a makeover. She says it's her fifteenth wedding anniversary, and Roy's coming to have dinner with her in her room. I wouldn't know what to say or do if Edie's family came for dinner or anything else. Not that I have to worry—no one has even called and I'm fine with that.

I back-comb and spray Lisa's hair halfway to heaven, and she never once accuses me of hiding her husband somewhere. Her mind does wander around in her head, but it's the first time I actually have a coherent conversation with her.

I stick to her neutral color palette and she leaves happy and looking almost normal, but a few hours later, she walks into my room and tries to hand me a three-page letter of complaint written on legal paper. I'm sitting on my bed, working on some music, and point to my trash can and tell her, "File it in there," under "no good deed ever goes unpunished."

I write a few more lyrics to "Groan-a-Lisa" and put an extra-thick X through September 27. I have three days of evaluations ahead of me and I can't get distracted by a schizophrenic woman. If all goes well, I'll get released on time. I'm already anxious and excited and, yes, a little bit worried.

I sail through the first evaluations, but I know my last appointment with Dr. Lindbloom won't be as easy. I don't have to lie on the couch, and he stares at me until I start to feel uncomfortable and count my fingertips. "I don't know what I did the last time I was here at Livingston," I say to fill the awkward silence. "But you obviously didn't like me."

"On the contrary, Edie." He uncrosses his legs and shuts my file. "You're brilliant and we had some extraordinary conversations."

He doesn't hate Edie? I'm confused. "Like what?"

"Art, philosophy, the brilliance of Debussy, the symbolism of Angkor Wat."

"Angkor what?"

"Wat."

"That's what I asked you." I shake my head. "I know a little bit about art, but the other three are a mystery."

"Talk about art, then."

"I know what I like." He just stares at me again, waiting. "Well, in Marfa, Texas, there was an artist named Donald Judd." There isn't a soul that was born and raised in Marfa who can't recite everything there is to know about Donald Judd. His art museum, studios, and foundation are about the only things that keeps tourists coming to the small town. "He was a Minimalist and created oversize art that represents the existence of space, scale, and time with already existin' things. He installed fifteen huge concrete blocks in the desert and created smaller stacks of blocks made out of wood, aluminum, and plexiglass. Some of his boxes are in the Guggenheim."

"When were you at the Guggenheim?"

"I don't know if I was ever there."

He sits forward in his chair. "Hmm . . . How do you know so much about Donald Judd's work?"

Okay, I walked right into that trap. I can't lie and say I read it, because there aren't Donald Judd art books around here. It isn't likely that I saw a biography on TV, so I fall back to my usual answer. "Beats the heck out of me. I guess it's the same as knowin' how to braid hair and stylin' updos." I shrug. "Like that one fella from Denmark who was a plumber before he hit his head and now he's smarter than Einstein. Doctor Barbara told me about a woman who woke up from a coma speakin' three different languages that she never spoke before."

"I'm aware of what she says." He sits back looking dejected and defeated. Even his ponytail looks sadder than usual. "You said you appreciate Donald Judd's art forms. Continue with that."

"I said I know what I like." And I like painted skulls and horns more than installation art.

"And you like this artist." It occurs to me that he's been trying so hard to trip me because he wants the old Edie back. It isn't Edie he dislikes, but *me*.

"I wouldn't go that far. There's a magazine about the Southwest in Doctor Ryan's waitin' room," I say, which is true, but I thumb through *People* instead. "I *appreciate* a paintin' called *Dawn at the Alamo* I saw in there." He raises a hand to his forehead like he always does, like it's the sound of my voice coming from brilliant Edie's mouth that's been paining him all along. So naturally I add, "Painted cow skulls are pure genius, and if I get my hands on some tie-dye longhorns, I'll be happier than a tornado in a trailer park." I smile, and he can't get me out of his office fast enough.

I don't have too long a wait before I learn that I am being discharged on time. Even Dr. Mensa recommended my release. The day before I leave, my therapy group gives me a little party in the game room. There's a cake with bright flowers and red punch, and I get talked into back-combing hair. I bust out my can of super-hold for the last time and try not to think about tomorrow. I'm excited to leave, but leaving doesn't mean I'm free to do as I please. It feels like I'm leaving one involuntary confinement for another, and I'm not sure living with Edie's family isn't going to be worse. I don't have money or credit cards or even a cell phone. I was trapped here for five months, and I'll be trapped with Marv and Claire for . . . I don't really know.

I don't know Marv and Claire's rules, and all I've been told by the nurses is that someone named Donovan is coming to drive me home to Hawthorne. I don't know who Donovan is. I don't know one thing about Hawthorne and no one's asked if I want to be driven there.

"I wish you didn't have to leave," Katrina tells me that night as she helps me pack.

She reminds me of Valentina, only older and nutty. "You've been a good friend," I say, and given the circumstances, I guess that's true. "You've made livin' here better, and I would have been bored without you."

"I need to say something but I don't want you to think I'm crazy."

Too late. "Okay."

She shifts her weight from one foot to the other. "Sometimes when I look at you, I see something's different."

That stops me, and the shirt I'm folding falls to the bed. "What do you see?"

"I see that your spiritual energy is at odds with your physical being," she says, and her hazel eyes turn a deeper shade of green.

I wonder if this is a test, if Ingrid's testing me before I leave the mental hospital, and I carefully say, "That's real interestin'." Is Katrina only acting deranged as part of Ingrid's plan?

"You have a mysterious aura. I've never seen anything like it."

"I didn't know you're psychic." She shrugs a shoulder and I breathe a sigh of relief. There's no plan. She really is deranged. "Give me a holler when you get out," I tell her, but I doubt that will ever happen.

"What's your phone number?"

"I don't know." Which is the truth. "I don't know where I live, either."

"I'll figure it out. Everyone's information is on the internet if you know how to find it."

I've done my share of stalking, but I've never been able to find *everyone's* information. "We can have coffee and catch up." Where there are people around and she can't stab me.

She nods and hugs me tight, stunning me with her sudden emotion. Now I feel lower than a snake for thinking she could stab me. That probably wouldn't happen. At least not in broad daylight.

I never was the popular girl. Not in my hometown, or at school, or when I sang at competitions. I was always just there. Even on Daddy's side of the family, I was "Pudge's girl," like they didn't remember the name of his only child.

I've never known what it's like to be the center of attention until I walk toward the front doors at Livingston the next morning. A lot of the women have gathered to say goodbye to me, Brittany, the No Time Before You cosmetologist, and I feel as if I should have bedazzled my blue tracksuit and stuck a tiara on top of my Carhartt hat. If I didn't have my red vanity case in one hand and a plastic personal belongings bag in the other, I'd wave back. It feels like I've been voted the most popular girl at Livingston Mental Health, and that makes me smile with mixed emotion as the doors sweep open to let me out.

A crisp morning breeze brushes my face and carries with it the smell of what I now associate with autumn. There is a world of difference between Marfa and Michigan, and I breathe this new kind of fresh air deep into my lungs. I wish it was my first breath of freedom, but it's not.

A silver car with suicide doors is parked at the curb and a man is loading my cardboard box of clothing into the trunk. He's wearing a sharp navy suit, white dress shirt, and blue tie, and I gather he must be Donovan. I stop by the back bumper because I don't know what to do. Should I introduce myself or not?

"May I stow those for you?" He points to my plastic bag and red case.

"Yes. Thank you, sir." The trunk is spotless and looks like it just came from the showroom. "What kind of car is this?"

He shuts the trunk and says, "It's the Phantom."

I've never heard of a Phantom, but it sure is fancy. "You must be Donovan." I don't know what he's been told, but it feels awkward not to introduce myself, so I stick out my hand. "I'm Edie."

He nods and gives my hand a quick shake. "Good to see you again, Young Edie."

That stops me. "Is there an Old Edie?"

"Your grandmother," he answers in an even tone, so I can't tell if he believes the amnesia story or not.

"Is she still alive?"

"Alive and well." He moves to the back door and opens it for me. "Your mother arranged an appointment for you at Chantal."

"What's Chantal?"

"A ladies' spa. Your mother knows you'd want a massage with Ginger first thing when you arrive in town. It's been a while since you pampered yourself."

I don't know if this is her way of pampering me or putting off my homecoming. The closest I've ever been to a spa was when Lida and I made appointments at Tina's Tranquility off Highway 90 in Alpine. Tina's idea of tranquility turned out to be a grueling massage and a flute CD playing in the background. I was sore for days and never went back. I suspect Tina and Ginger have different ideas when it comes to spa treatments. "Do I go to Chantal very often?"

"Regularly."

That's what makes me nervous. What do they know about Edie? What have they heard, and what questions will they ask that I can't answer?

"They're ready for you."

I'm not sure I'm ready for Chantal. I climb into the car and sink into soft white leather. I am engulfed in luxury and don't think anything will ever top this. Then Donovan gets in and asks, "Can I turn on the seat massage for you, Young Edie?"

Massage? Two massages in one day? "Yes, sir."

As we pull away from Livingston, classical music surrounds me from all sides and warm massage rollers start at my shoulders and slowly move down my back, working out months of stress from my kinked-up muscles.

I've died a couple of times, but this is the closest I've ever been to heaven.

13

Before getting shipped off to Livingston, I knew very little about Michigan. I knew it was the state on the Great Lake that looked like an oven mitt. I knew that Kid Rock and Eminem were from Michigan and that Detroit was about as far from Marfa as you can get and still be in the US. Everything else I know about the state came from movies, the History Channel, or human-interest stories that give the impression of burned-out buildings and rampant poverty.

I still don't know a lot about Michigan, but today I can add to my limited information. The scenery is filled with so much color, my eyes don't know where to land.

I look past the wet road and broken highway lines flashing past my window to green rolling hills crammed with trees turning colors with the season. The leaves are yellow and orange and red and combinations in between. I've never seen anything like it outside of movies and books. It's like driving through a beautiful photograph and as different as can be from the Chihuahuan Desert.

With each mile, my nerves unravel like a frayed rope and I'm holding on tighter and tighter. Since the day I wrecked

Momma's van, other people have directed my life. In all that time, I've only been given one choice: live or die. The only say I've had in my life has been whether I wanted baked or mashed potatoes.

One Sunday I was Brittany Lynn Snider and by Wednesday I was Edie Randolph Chatsworth-Jones. One Sunday I controlled my life, and that Friday I was shipped off to a mental hospital. Everyone but me has determined where I go, what I do from hour to hour, and when I go to bed.

No one asked me if I want to live with Marv and Claire. Maybe I could have said "hell no" if I had been asked, but the thing I've learned since I died is that no one has to ask if there's only one option.

My stomach starts to ache as I think about Marv and Claire and what they might say and what I shouldn't say when we see each other again. I start talking to Donovan and asking questions so I don't have to think about it.

He turns off the music and politely responds as before, but now his answers are brief, like he doesn't need to explain things that I already know. As if I know that Michigan is known for fishing, Ford Motors, the Red Wings—and that oak trees have orange leaves in the fall.

I assume Hawthorne is some kind of mansion, because people don't name their houses or double-wide trailers. "Do I live in Detroit with my parents?" I know that's where we're headed, but I hope Edie lives in a different house or apartment so I won't have to stay with the parents for very long.

"Your parents live at Hawthorne in Grosse Pointe Shores, where you and your brother were born and raised."

Grosse what? "Where's that?"

"Northern shore of Grosse Pointe."

If Edie lives in Grosse Pointe, why was her name Detroit? "Where do *I* live?"

"The Westin Book Cadillac in downtown Detroit."

"That sounds like a hotel."

"You live in a residence above the hotel, Young Edie," he explains, more briefly now, like he thinks my amnesia is a pile of BS and I'm annoying him.

"I'm sorry about askin' so many questions," I say, and catch his gaze as he looks at me through the rearview mirror. "But I don't remember."

"I was told that you might have some memory loss."

Some? "You don't have to believe it." We look into each other's eyes and I say to him, "Just please know that I do." I roll down the passenger window and let in the autumn air. I don't blame Donovan for not believing me. No one is going to believe me. Heck, I wouldn't believe me either.

Donovan says something about Detroit and I roll up the window. "Pardon me, sir?"

"We're an hour outside of Detroit," he tells me.

"Thank you."

I don't have a way to tell time, but I think we travel about forty-five more minutes before the hills flatten and the occasional house gives way to rural spread. Rural spread gives way to compact cities and congested traffic, and then we cross a bridge and drive between towering buildings that block out the sky. I'm fascinated and terrified all at the same time and feel like I've been drop-kicked to a new planet.

"We're almost at Chantal," Donovan tells me.

The streets and sidewalks are crowded with all kinds of vehicles and people. I crane my neck and gaze up and feel the size of an ant. The closest I've ever come to a big city is when Momma and I drove to Katy for the Little Voices singing competition. Katy's thirty miles from Houston but we were too afraid to drive into the heart of the city.

Amid the sound of car horns and revving engines, the Phantom pulls to a stop in front of a limestone building, marked by age but renovated with big modern windows. To one side is a single gold canopy with black letters that spell out a very understated "Chantal." Donovan opens my door, and I slide out and into air that now smells of exhaust with a hint of pub food.

I stand and take a 360 of my surroundings. I must look as lost as I feel because Donovan asks, "Are you all right, Young Edie?"

My heart pounds and I swallow hard. "Everythin's bigger than all hell and half of Texas." The door to Chantal opens and a woman in black steps out.

"The front desk will call for me when you're ready to leave."

I look at Donovan and want to grab on to him as tight as my fraying rope. "Aren't you comin' in?"

"It's a *ladies'* spa." I'm not sure, but I think he's embarrassed.

"Okay." I let out a breath and turn toward the spa. I've been through a lot in the past five months, I can do this. I put one foot in front of another and tell myself I'm a twenty-five . . . no, I'm a thirty-year-old adult, and there's nothing to be afraid of.

"Hello, Edie." The woman at the door has red hair, and if I was at the Do or Dye I'd guess she's a 5c, but different brands have different names and formulations for their color lines. Whatever brand, it's vibrant and the sort of quality I'd want at Shear Elegance. "Welcome back."

The inside of Chantal is mostly white with touches of gold and black. It's oddly quiet and I don't see other guests as I am shown to a room with a spa chair and massage table. The towels are folded to look like swans, and I'm handed a thick robe. Pink champagne sits next to a plate of tiny hors d'oeuvres and I nibble and read the latest *Vogue* before Ginger enters the room. Her hair is pulled back into a ponytail that looks like a black whip, and she proceeds to beat the hell out of my muscles just like Tina. No matter how many times I say "ouch" or "Gawd almighty," she takes it as a sign to double down. By the time she leaves, I'm sore as all git-out and wonder if Clarice is still holding a grudge about being called a crazy roach. I wonder what else she might have in store, but the next three hours are bliss. I'm pampered like I'm queen of the world. I take note of everything because who knows what my future holds or what dreams I can make come true.

I forget about the scars on my forearms until the manicurist massages my hands and wrists. This isn't Livingston, where suicide scars aren't out of the norm and where there's always someone with bigger issues than yours. This is the real world, but if the manicurist is surprised by my forearms, she doesn't show it. The only thing that does raise a brow is my choice of red finger- and toenail polish. Evidently, Edie always wears the same pale pink.

The only real shock of the day comes after my roots match the rest of my blonde hair. I tell the stylist to trim an inch, curl it with a three-quarter barrel, and back-comb the crown. I read *Elle* and *Harper's Bazaar* when what I really want is a *People* or *US Weekly* to find out what's happening in the world—who's getting married, having a baby, or the latest cheating scandal. Sometimes it's reassuring to see that perfect people have regular problems just like everyone else.

Everyone except me. No one has my problems, at least not that I know of. I flip a page in *Elle* and see Miley Cyrus in a fishnet minidress and a thong. I can't believe the girl who in-spired me to be Brittany Wittany went from Hannah Montana to swinging naked on a wrecking ball and twerking in latex, seemingly overnight.

Then it hits me. I gasp and my mouth falls open. You too, Miley?

The stylist looks at me through the station's mirror as she curls and pins my hair. "Are you okay?"

"Yes." I nod. For a split second I thought I'd discovered someone like me, but Miley's never lost her memory, just her clothes.

Other than asking if I'm okay, the stylist isn't chatty. In fact, no one really talks at Chantal. They just do their thing, pour champagne, and serve hors d'oeuvres. I wonder if it's the spa's policy or if no one wants to talk to Edie because she's been evil to them. Either way, I'm just relieved that I don't have to give them my amnesia smile or answer questions. I just have to kick back, get pampered, and drink champagne, which brings me to something I noticed. Edie is a lightweight. I wouldn't call myself a big boozer, but I keep up with the best of them—namely on Momma's side. I can hold my own, but Edie's half lit after a few glasses of champagne.

By the time I emerge from the gold doors and back into the exhaust fumes, I'm looking like a Dallas Cowboys cheerleader. My hair is shiny and bouncy and back-combed halfway to heaven like God intended. My brows have been tweezed, my face steamed with lavender, scraped with an epi-blade, and perked up with a yummy facial concocted just for Edie. My skin is as soft as a baby and I smell like a mandarin and cranberry cocktail. I feel more like myself and that feels mighty fine.

Donovan pauses as he opens the door for me. He blinks

several times but he doesn't comment. My makeover has struck him dumb. We drive for twenty minutes through the orange and grays of the setting sun before the car slows and turns onto a narrow road. Gates with an *H* in the middle swing open, and I assume the *H* stands for Hawthorne. I should be sick with anxiety. My stomach should feel heavy with dread, but champagne bubbles make my insides feel tingly, and everything looks rosy from my champagne goggles. I'm too tipsy to feel fear, but I need to remember that liquid courage can turn into stupid juice real quick, and I've gotten myself into trouble a time or two. Triple-shot Thursdays come to mind, and the last thing I want to do is shoot my mouth off at Marv and Claire and wake up at Livingston again.

The road is lined with trees changing color for the season and lit with lamps atop tarnished posts. The road turns into a circular drive that has a fountain in the middle with a bunch of fish heads spitting water into a big clamshell. If I had a penny, I'd toss it in there for luck, but I don't have any money at all.

Donovan stops the Phantom in front of what looks like a museum made of white stone. Or maybe one of those old grand hotels on a lakeshore where fancy people go to golf or yacht or whatever it is that fancy people do. The car stops at wide steps and dramatic wood-and-stained-glass doors. "This is someone's house? It's huge."

"Hawthorne is forty thousand square feet and had forty-two rooms when it was completed in eighteen-ninety-three. It has been modernized three times, bringing the total number of rooms to thirty-three, not counting the pool, bowling alley, and wine cellar."

And just like that, my stomach gets tight and I'm not feeling so rosy.

"Your parents are waiting for you inside," Donovan tells me, and I follow him up the steps to the front doors.

The inside of Hawthorne looks like a museum, too. It's unreal, like there should be velvet ropes to keep tourists from wandering off carpet runners and touching anything. But there are no ropes or runners. No tour guide. Just me and Donovan for now.

My gaze travels up walls made of dark wood and covered with huge paintings and tapestries hanging from gold cord. I tilt my head all the way back to look at the enormous domed ceiling made with the same stained glass as the front doors. Large urns of fresh flowers sit atop even larger pedestal tables. The room on my left is bright yellow and white and there's a marble fireplace with naked ladies carved in it.

The house smells of old wood and lemon oil, roses and lilies. Everything about it is rich and grand, but not exactly what I'd call warm and inviting. "Are people actually livin' in this place?" I ask myself more than anyone else. Those naked ladies look cold enough to sneeze and I notice their breasts are very perky.

"Until the first of the year," Donovan tells me. "Then we close this house and open Chatsworth in Palm Beach."

I can never remember the difference between Palm Beach and Palm Springs.

"It's warmer and more relaxed at Chatsworth."

Chatsworth could be made of ice and still be warmer than this place. As for relaxed . . . a distant *tap-tap* of heels on tile floors pulls me up straight like I'm on strings. The sound quiets as if muffled by carpet before it returns just a bit louder. With each tap, the strings pull tighter, and no amount of alcohol can dull the nerves running up my spine. Then I see Edie's mother across the foyer walking toward me, wearing a floral-print dress that seems to flow about her with every step she takes. I might have been on pain meds and raw emotion the last time I saw her, but I instantly recognize the upward tilt of her head and frozen eyes. She is beautiful and has skin like it's been kissed with dew.

Her gaze takes in my hair and I can't tell if she approves of my shiny curls. "Welcome home, Edie."

Not that it matters. I like them enough for the both of us. She kisses both my cheeks and leaves a trace of Chanel as she pulls away. "Thank you, ma'am. I appreciate the invitation." Her lips compress with the first hint of emotion. To her, I sound like a hillbilly. I don't want to make her mad, but I was raised to say ma'am and sir, please and thank you, and how's your momma and them. And like Momma always says, good manners are a good habit.

"Your father is in Chicago but will be home in time for dinner. I know that he is looking forward to seeing you. We both are."

I doubt that, since neither bothered to *see* me when I was an hour and a half away at Livingston. I just smile and say, "That's nice."

"Dinner will be served at seven thirty in the conservatory. It's more intimate for our small group. Your grandmother is here, so please be on time. Cocktails are in the blue drawing room at seven, but your appearance is not mandatory."

I could probably use a cocktail or two—or ten—before this night is over. An awkward silence stretches between us like she's waiting for a response. "Thank you," I say, and purposely don't call her ma'am. "I don't know where the conservatory is, but I'll be there at seven thirty." The only conservatory I know about is in El Paso, but I doubt she's talking about a big building where folks play music and dance ballet.

"Good. Novia will help you get settled in your room."

I turn to tell Donovan goodbye, but he has already left. I didn't even hear him go, and when I turn back around, a woman I've never seen before in gray and white moves toward me. Her black hair is pulled back and her dress is an honest-to-God maid's uniform.

"Welcome home, Young Edie," she says, reminding me that Old Edie is around here someplace.

"Thank you, ma'am."

I follow Novia up the wide stairs that split at a landing. We continue up the right side, and like everyone I've met today, she doesn't say anything. I wonder if it's Edie, her family, or the whole state of Michigan, but folks sure aren't talkative around here. Aren't Midwesterners supposed to be nice?

We walk down one hall and then another before Novia throws open a set of double doors. Everything is blue and white and silver and it's like stepping into the movie *Frozen*. The windows across the room start at about waist height and continue all the way up to silver valances hanging just below the ceiling. I move to the windows and look out at the yard. Dusk is creeping across the manicured lawn, and lights turn on and illuminate pathways and flood a really tall flagpole with four flags flapping in the wind. Across the yard, reflections of light bob up and down on a lake and outline the shore.

"What lake is that?" I ask Novia.

"Saint Clair, of course."

Of course. Where else would Clarice Chatsworth-Jones live? I point down the shoreline to a lighthouse or something. "What is that?"

Novia comes to stand next to me and follows my gaze. "Grosse Pointe Yacht Club."

I remember Marv and Claire saying something about not showing their faces at their club. "Do Mar—" I catch myself and say, "Do my parents belong to that club?"

"Yes."

I turn around and see that Novia has opened a couple of doors, so I walk across the room and stick my head in each. The first is a fancy bathroom and the second is the biggest closet I've ever seen. It's stark white, and the clothes are neatly hung, not at all like my crammed closet at Momma's house. There are different partitions according to if they're pants or dresses or whatever, color coordinated (mostly black), and some are in garment bags and clear plastic like from the dry cleaner. There's a big round ottoman in the center and a wall filled with boxes of shoes and handbags in dustcovers, made by some designers I've heard of and some I haven't. At the end of the closet are drawers and cabinets and there's a built-in safe, too. I move to the wall of shoes and stop in front of the Christian Louboutin section. Like a homing beacon, my eyes go straight to the word *crystals*. I pull out the box and find a red felt bag inside. Sensing that I am about to discover sparkle nirvana, I move to the ottoman and take a seat. I reach into the felt bag and pull out a pair of pumps that about stop my heart. They are clear and covered in crystals that dazzle blue and silver beneath the light. The soles are red just like in the pictures I've seen in *Vogue* magazine, but there isn't so much as a scuff on the red bottoms. My flat shoes are off quicker than a prom dress and the stilettos are on my feet. I turn my ankle this way and that, and I swear to the good Lord and baby Jesus, they look like Cinderella's glass slippers, only with a five-inch heel. I walk about the big closet, unused to teetering on stilettos. I like how they sparkle like diamonds and *click-clack* on the hardwood floor. I fall but catch myself on the ottoman on the way down. Just as fast I'm back up, feeling glamorous in Edie's—no, *my*—fabulous shoes. Edie was vain and selfish, but it would be wrong to let all these fabulous shoes go to waste because I hate her. After all, Jesus said, "Let nothing be wasted," and that goes double for sparkly Christian Louboutin pumps.

"Your intercom is on your nightstand. Let me know if you need anything."

I turn toward Novia standing in the doorway. I got so carried away, I forgot about her. "The time." I sit rather than fall in front of her. "I'd like to know the time."

She looks at her wrist. "It's six thirteen. You have a clock next to your bed and another in the bathroom."

She glances at my face, then quickly looks away. I can't tell if she's shy or if she doesn't want to risk eye contact. "Thank you," I say, and Novia just nods and leaves the room without a word.

Again, is it me or are people just tight-lipped around here?

14

I find out at dinner that it's not Michigan that's the problem. It's not Edie's family either. They all kissed the air above both my cheeks and said how glad they were I was home. Claire asked a few questions about my overall healthy appearance and couldn't take her eyes off my hair. I'd touched up the curls and height and sprayed it down as best I could with Edie's light-hold. Marv stared at my thick lashes and winged eyeliner as he inquired politely about my amnesia. Big brother Burton said, "Oh please, Father"; then they all went back to their conversations with each other.

It's Edie. No one wants to talk to her if they don't have to.

"What's this I hear about your memory?"

No one but Old Edie.

Silence falls on the round dinner table surrounded by plants and fruit trees. I look across the blue-and-white china, crystal glasses, and silverware I've never seen and don't know how to use. There's a flower centerpiece with a lit candle in the middle that flickers in the reflection of the conservatory glass walls. The whole evening's been awkward and weird.

"What have you heard?" I ask, because I don't want to say the wrong thing. I've already committed the faux pas of wearing jeans, a chunky blue sweater, and boots with a low heel. My ankles are a bit sore from stumbling around in heels, and I dressed for warmth when everyone else looks like they put on their Sunday best.

"That you can't recall a thing about yourself." I don't know Old Edie's age, but she looks like an albino prune with a white shampoo and set. Her boyfriend, Harold, sits beside her. He's kind of collapsed inside his suit jacket like he's a Slinky. No one talks to him either, and I can't tell if he's fallen asleep or died.

I touch my fingertips one-two-three-four, one-two-three-four, and smile and nod like I have amnesia.

"That's what your parents told everyone," she continues, and I wonder who "everyone" is. Old Edie points a fish knife, which I've realized is different than a dinner or butter knife, at Edie's brother. "Isn't that right, Burton?"

"That's what we've been told." If Edie is a duplicate of her mother, Burton is a younger version of Marv.

Old Edie isn't done and points to the woman sitting to my right, Burton's wife, Meredith. "How about you?"

"I haven't heard anything." Meredith has natural auburn hair, brown eyes, and a dusting of freckles she's covered with powder. She's the kind of woman that the more you look at her, the prettier she gets. I'd guess she's a few years older than Edie, but she looks tired. I've been told she and Burton have a six-month-old baby boy named George and a four-year-old daughter, Rowan, which could explain it.

"Of course you haven't. You wouldn't speak up even if you did hear something." Old Edie scowls at me. "I heard you were in a hospital to get your memory back."

Harold lets out a snore that revives him, and he looks around to see if anyone noticed. "Capital idea." I guess he's not dead. "I'll have a cognac."

Old Edie ignores him and stares at me until I say something. "Which hospital, ma'am?"

"Which hospital, Marvin?"

"It's not important, Mother."

I smile, and everyone goes back to their conversation that Old Edie interrupted. I dig back into my bass covered in almond slices and cream sauce and topped with carrot ribbon. It's almost as good as fish tacos but a lot fancier; I've never seen such a fuss made over a meal in my life.

There's a different plate and set of utensils for everything. I wasn't born in a barn, but I don't recognize half of them. After a few obvious false starts, I watch Meredith out of the corner of my eye so I know what to use for which course, and I notice they rest their knives and forks at certain places on their plates. I reposition my utensils to match theirs, and I feel like the girl in band who's one beat behind everyone else in school. For some reason, they don't eat dinner rolls like regular people. They tear off a bite-size piece and spread it with a dab of butter before they eat it. It seems a waste of time, and my left hand makes it even more difficult. I give up and slather the inside of my roll with butter all at once. They all seem to notice, but no one says anything. Probably because I have amnesia.

"Excellent meal, Clarice," Marvin says, and I turn my head to one side to look at him. I'd guess him to be in his sixties, and if it wasn't for his hair, he might not be bad-looking for a guy his age. "You always know what to serve." He lifts his wineglass as if to toast her.

"It's Edie's favorite." She looks at me and smiles like she's making an effort to welcome me home.

"It's delicious," I say, and since she's made Edie's favorite meal, I'll make an effort, too. "How did you get the almond slices in such perfect rows?"

Her smile falls a bit and everyone looks at me as if I've been hit with a stupid stick.

"I didn't," she says. "Chef Larry cooked for us tonight. We'll have him for another month before Chef Paulette takes over."

"I thought Mar—Father said . . ." Am I the crazy one around here?

"I plan the meals at Hawthorne," Claire explains, like planning and cooking have equal importance.

"Fine job." Harold rouses himself and joins the others in a toast.

I raise my glass, too, like it's normal to toast a meal plan. I take a few small sips of white wine instead of chugging it like I usually would. I didn't quite catch the name of it, but it must be fancy because everyone swirled it in their glass and smelled it. Someone said it was harvested on specific days under a full moon, and they all raved about hints of this and that, and spicy notes, and something on the nose. For all the hoopla, it's okay, I guess, but I'd rather have a Shiner Bock or a Lone Star Das Bier Y'all.

After the fish is cleared from the table, we're served lemon sponge cake with brandy glaze and wash it down with little cups of espresso. This time Claire did have something more to do with dessert than just planning. She selected the lemons from the trees a few feet away.

"What did you do to your hair?" Old Edie asks me.

I look up from my boozy cake, feeling tipsy just off the brandy fumes. "Do you like it?"

"It's lovely," Meredith tells me.

"Thank you." As with the rest of the family, her smile is kind of tentative, but I think she's sincere. "Your hair is beautiful. Lots of women pay a lot of money to have hair like yours," I tell her. "Have you ever rinsed your hair in cranberry juice? Of course, it's sticky as all git-out, but it's a natural boost for gingers and smells wonderful."

She goes stiff, like my expert color analysis has turned her to stone.

The same can't be said for Old Edie. "Your hair reminds me of my old cocker spaniel, Elvis," she tells me, then leans forward and yells down the table, "Marvin, do you remember Elvis?"

"Of course, Mother. Father had him delivered when I was home for Christmas my junior year at Yale. Beautiful dog."

"Yes." She smiles as if reliving a fond memory and picks up a dessert fork. "Such a lovely scamp." She turns to me and her scowl reappears. "Silky, but I would not want to wear him on my head."

"No, ma'am." I don't know if it's the wine, or cake, or the vision of Old Edie with a cocker spaniel on her head, but I start to giggle.

"Did someone tell a joke?" Harold wants to know.

"Ask Young Edie."

"Huh? What did you say, dear?"

Old Edie cups her hand around her mouth and yells at her boyfriend, "Young Edie's hair looks like Elvis."

I shake my head and put my napkin on the table. "You're a hoot and a half." I scoot my chair back and stand. "If any of y'all would kindly point me in the direction of the ladies' room, I'd appreciate it."

They all stare at me, then point to the doorway. "Down the hall, through the music room, first door between the Chinese urns," Burton says, and I think that's the most he's spoken to me since I met him.

"Thank you." I follow Burton's instructions and find the two urns. When I reach for the door handle, a child's voice stops me. I catch a glimpse of a girl dressed in frilly pink and holding something white and furry. Her voice is joined by the deep laughter of a dark-haired man by her side. They disappear into the conservatory as quickly as they'd appeared.

I guess we've got company. The good news is that no one wants to talk to Edie, so I can just say, "Hello, it's nice to meet y'all and good night." Then I can take another soak in Edie's tub, maybe turn on the jets this time. Before I leave the bathroom, I wash my hands and fluff my hair at the crown. I'm liking this new blonde bombshell look. It takes the kind of time I never had for myself when I was working at the Do or Dye.

By the time I make it back to the conservatory, the table has been cleared and the family is sitting at the far end of the room on big stuffed couches. A little red-haired girl in a pink dress and white stockings is sitting at Meredith's feet and a small white dog is in her lap.

Claire looks up at me. "Rowan's come for a visit and look who she's brought."

I glance around for the man with the deep laugh, but he's nowhere to be found. "Who?"

"Magnus, of course."

I remember Dr. Lindbloom asking about Magnus, and I wonder if that's the name of the dark-haired man. If so, it's unfortunate.

"Mommy's home," the little girl says, but she doesn't sound too happy.

"Your dress is very pretty," I tell her so maybe she won't

be sad about her mommy being home, although that doesn't make sense. Meredith told me that she lives down the street. The little dog's ears perk up and it lifts its head. "I love pink." The dog jumps out of her lap and runs at me like I'm made of bacon. It yips and quivers and dances around on its hind feet in front of me. My daddy has always had a dog or two. The kind that fetches stuff, rides in the back of a truck, and would kill a rattler if it came down to saving Daddy. This is not that kind of dog. This is the fussiest poodle I've ever seen. It's white and its fur is shaved into pom-poms on its head, feet, and the end of its whippy tail. There's a blue bow between its ears and a pale blue collar around its neck. "I have a dog?"

"For three years now."

"Is this a boy?" I'd never make a male dog look like such a sissy. Rowan comes to stand beside me, and I get down on one knee as she pats the top of its head. "Magnus is a good boy."

So Magnus is the dog's name. Its beady black eyes look into mine and the stupid thing growls at me. "It's all right," I say in a smooth friendly voice and reach for his collar. The damn thing snaps at my hand and I pull back just in time.

"I know you think I'm too rough with Magnus, but I took really good care of him while you were away."

"Well, thank you. He looks like you took good care of him."

She nods as the stupid mutt snarls at me like he has a super animal sense and can detect I'm not Edie. "Don't get mad at me because your fur's cut like a girl," I say, and the sound of my voice makes him snap his teeth at the air in front of his nose as if he wants a chunk of me. Apparently, he has a problem with the new Edie. He's not alone, and needs to get in line right behind Dr. Lindbloom. "He likes you better," I tell Rowan, and lean back.

She nods and her brown eyes look into mine. "We love each other, Aunt Edie."

"Rowan," Meredith calls to her daughter. "Come here. You know that's Aunt Edie's dog. He doesn't belong to you."

Rowan hangs her head and walks back to her mother. The little dog gives one last snarl and follows.

He doesn't belong to me either. I rise to my feet and look around. None of this belongs to me. It's foreign and uncomfortable and I miss Momma and Daddy. I miss Marfa, and the Do or Dye, and knowing where I belong. My heart is so homesick, my chest aches. The beautiful glass room is suddenly stuffy and the scent of citrus is heavy in my lungs. I excuse myself with the pretext of taking Magnus outside before bed, but no amount of coaxing can persuade him to stop barking at me, let alone follow.

I step outside without him and shut the conservatory door behind me. The chilling lake breeze tousles my curls and invades the loose weave of my sweater. I pull in my shoulders and cross my arms over my chest. The house casts wide swaths of light and shadow across a stone terrace and concrete banister. The railing runs the length of the house and is lit up every ten feet or so with lampposts that continue down the stairs and into the garden. I walk to the railing, and the sound of my boot heels joins the rhythmic clang of metal hitting the flagpole. Beyond the garden, moonlight cuts a path across the lake's surface. It's like *The Great Gatsby* out here minus Leo. Breathtaking and beautiful, and I can't wait to leave.

These people don't want me here any more than I want to be here. I'm uncomfortable and they're uncomfortable, and I don't know what they expect or how long I have to stick around. Marv and Claire and I are meeting with Dr. Barb in the morning. I guess we all need to discuss an aftercare plan and my life going forward. I don't know about them, but all my life needs is money, a cell phone, and a one-way airline ticket.

The breeze brushes my hair across my face and carries the scent of lake water and damp garden and a cigar. A flash of orange catches my eye and I turn and look into a corner of the terrace hidden in inky shadows. The orange flash fades to a red glow. I gasp as a dark outline pushes away from the railing, and a man walks through a trail of weak light, shifting across him with the breeze. I glance at the door and then back at him. I don't think I could make it to the house if he decides to grab me, but I can scream really loud.

He's dressed in a black sweater and black jeans. Patches of light slide across his dark hair and the side of his face, and I think this is probably the man who brought Rowan and Magnus. Either that or he's waiting around to rob the place or kill us all in our sleep. "Howdy."

He stops within the variegated shadows, and I can't get a clear look at him. "Howdy, Sunshine."

Sunshine? "I don't think we've met." I don't offer my hand for obvious reasons. "I'm Edie."

"I didn't recognize you with all that puffy hair."

He doesn't give his name and probably assumes I know it. "I added dimension and volume."

"You look like you've been in a beauty pageant. Down south where big hair seems to be a competitive sport." He raises his cigar to his mouth and his cheeks get sucked in as the end glows red.

Well, that's true enough. "Thank you." I've styled pageant hair and I know.

He tips his face up and blows a thick cloud of smoke that lingers in the light above his head. "It wasn't a compliment."

I feel my brows lower. "Are we friends or family?"

"Neither."

I guess I can add him to the list of people who don't like Edie. He can get in line behind Magnus. He steps further into the light and I get a better look at his face and shoulders. Now he makes me nervous for a whole different reason. He's hot as hell and all of Tinder. He's big. The kind that comes from lifting weights and rescuing women from burning buildings. I wind a curl around my finger out of habit. "Are we sworn enemies?"

"More like we have a mutual aversion."

Aversion? "You mean I don't like you?" I ask, because I can't imagine having an aversion to a man who looks like Mr. February in the Houston Firefighters Calendar.

"I don't lose sleep over it. You don't like anyone."

That's probably true of Edie, but not me. "I take it you don't like me."

"No, but you don't lose sleep over it, either."

There's an obvious history between him and Edie that didn't end well. It's like that saying about heaven having no rage like love turned to hate. "Were we lovers?" I ask, because getting hot and steamy with this guy would be one memory worth recalling.

He chokes on cigar smoke. "Jesus."

Jesus doesn't have anything to do with it. "Were we?"

"No." He coughs and clears his throat. "This is the most we've spoken to each other in over ten years."

You don't have to talk during sex. Sometimes a man can open his mouth and ruin the fantasy you got going in your head, but I get what he means. He's not friend or family but he brought Rowan and Magnus. "I get the feelin' that no one around here wants to speak to me, either." I think of Marv and Claire and our short conversation before dinner. "Just my parents," I say, because maybe they're trying.

"Your parents are stuck talking to you."

That's not nice, but it might be true.

"You have your girlfriends. At least that's what you call them."

The closest I've had to friends since I left Marfa are the women in my cognitive therapy group, and I don't think that counts. Well, except for Katrina, but I don't know that I trust her with sharp instruments. "Since you seem to know so much, what would you call them?"

He chuckles and takes a pull of his cigar. A smoke cloud streams off his lips, but he doesn't answer.

I shiver from the cold and rub my hands up and down my arms. He's handsome and I wouldn't mind hearing what else he knows about Edie. I could ask the family, but they all look at me like I just got let out of the loony bin, which I did. "Everybody around here is walkin' on eggshells—except Old Edie. She said my hair looks like her old cocker spaniel."

"Elvis?" His chuckle turns to laughter.

I smile because it was funny. "I guess that's what passes for 'welcome home' in this family."

"I'm sure your mutt is glad you're back."

"Magnus? I tried to pet the dang dog and he almost bit my hand." I shake my head. "He snapped and snarled at me for no reason."

"Maybe because you named him Magnus."

"Maybe because he's as ugly as a stump full of spiders and just as cuddly."

"That's a fair description of all your dogs."

All? "How long have we known each other?"

He looks at me like Donovan did. Like he doesn't want to keep answering questions that he thinks I know the answers to.

"How long?" I push him.

He turns his attention to the lake and his voice is as deep as the shadows stretching to the shore. "I can't think of a time when I didn't know you," he says.

A shiver runs up my spine but I'm certain it's from the cold this time. "It's probably a good thing we don't like each other."

"Why's that?" he asks, and raises his cigar.

"Talkin' to you is a chore." I sigh. "Like puttin' socks on a rooster."

A lazy stream of smoke fills the air in front of his face. "I'm trying to be nice."

I shake my head and look at the toes of my boots. "I'd hate to meet you on a night when you're not tryin'."

The conservatory door swings open and Meredith steps outside. "There you are," she says. "How long have you been out here?"

I didn't know anyone was keeping track.

"Not long." He moves closer to put out his cigar in an urn filled with some kind of plant. I was wrong about him being Mr. February. He's the whole dang calendar. "Edie's been keeping me company."

"And it's been a hoot and a half."

Meredith turns her head as if she sees me for the first time. "Oh!" Her gaze shifts between us. "Edie, I see you've met my brother, Oliver."

"*Now serving zero-zero-zero, zero-zero-one, two-seven at window fifty-three.*"

The number I wrestled from Chablis Chardonnay's grubby hands has been skipped two thousand seven hundred and fifty-three times now. My original ticket filled with zeroes was called a while ago. I'm not sure how long I've been sitting around since then because there's no way of knowing, but I do KNOW I should be in heaven instead of a whore! I'm Edie Randolph Chatsworth-Jones of Grosse Point Shores. Yes, THE Chatsworth-Joneses, and I can trace my ancestry back to the Mayflower. There's only one reasonable explanation for why I'm still here.

I tried to pull one over on God and he's not happy with me. I get it. It's like sneaking into the Yondotega Club dressed as a man. (I was terrified my father would find out.)

I lean my head back against the hard bench and sigh. God wants me to sit here and think about what I've done. He wants me to feel remorse, but I can't fake something that I do not feel. He'll know, because if there is one thing I've learned since I planted my feet on the garish sparkly path, it's that there's no outsmarting God.

"Now serving five-zero-two-eight at window one."

"What?" I sit up straight and look at my ticket even though I know the number by heart. I glance up at the blinking window in the distance and take off running like a prison escapee. I weave in and out of the crowd, duck and dodge and yell, "I'm here," as I slide the ticket through the window and toward a hologram of . . . Judge Judy?

"Edith Randolph Chatsworth-Jones," she begins. "You are here because your spirit has left your earthly body. Do you understand that you are dead?"

"Yes." It can't be Judge Judy, but it sure looks like her. "Where am I? How long have I been here?"

She looks over the top of her glasses at me. "God does not mark time in days and minutes."

"It feels like an eternity!"

She rolls her eyes and shakes her head. "Death comes to all human beings and is not the end of your spiritual existence. God has a plan for all his children and has created a place for all in his kingdom. Loved ones who have passed await a joyous . . ." She continues on and on like this is a long-winded recording. ". . . but your destiny lies elsewhere—"

"Elsewhere? What are you—"

"I'm speaking!" She bangs her gavel like we're on The People's Court. *"Elsewhere in the Progression of Redemption Corps."*

"The progression of what?"

"This is your final judgment." Judy bangs her gavel again. "Pay up, Edith Randolph Chatsworth-Jones."

Final judgment? That sounds ominous as hell. The hologram begins to fade and I call out, "You can't mean hell. Judy, come back. I'm a good person!" Before I have time to further argue my case, I am pulled through a sudden crack in the mist. I'm terrified of being trapped in dark places or locked inside my own dark thoughts. The crack seals itself and I'm in a place filled with color. This can't be hell, unless hell looks like Holland in April.

A platinum-blonde woman stands in a field of vibrant tulips. She is dressed in white and her eyes are clear turquoise. She glows from the inside out, but she doesn't have wings.

"Am I in heaven?"

"No. You are in my office."

"Office?" Rows of different-colored tulips stretch as far as the eye can see. This is crazy.

"I'm Ingrid, director of Southwest Thirty-One."

I don't have a clue what that means, but she's obviously in charge, so I give her a pleasant smile. "It's a pleasure, Ingrid. I'm Edie Chatsworth-Jones."

She shakes her head. "Not any longer. There can be only one Edie Chatsworth-Jones, and she's alive and well and living in Michigan."

This is getting crazier. "I'm Edie and I'm right here in your office. Apparently in the Netherlands."

She waves a hand and rows of flowers are replaced by a Times Square–size video screen. "What do you suppose happened to Brittany Lynn Snider after you took her portal?"

I'm too smart to fall into that trap and keep my mouth shut. On the screen, Hawthorne comes into focus. I recognize the garden lighting, and the lamps and urns along the terrace. The conservatory is lit up, which means my parents are dining at home. My heart squeezes and my eyes burn like I'm tearing up without producing actual tears. I never meant to disappoint or hurt my mother and father. I wish things could have been different.

The conservatory door opens and a woman steps out in a Givenchy sweater like the one I wore in Aspen last year. Her hair *is big and bouncy like a rodeo queen's, and as she moves into the light on the banister, she looks oddly familiar. Her face is . . . I gasp and point to the screen. "That's me!"*

"Well, you're partly right. That's Brittany Lynn Snider. When you stole her path to heaven, her spirit was transmigrated into the physical being of Edie Chatsworth-Jones."

"What is this? A bad science-fiction movie?" I clutch my chest in horror. "What did she do to my hair?"

"Her hair."

"And her makeup. She's wearing—" I gasp. "Is that Oliver Hunt? What's he doing—she's talking to him. We hate each other. Make her stop!"

"She can live her life any way she chooses within the boundaries of her contract."

Contract? "That isn't her life. It's my life and she can't waltz into it and wear my clothes and shoes. She can't drive my Bentley and live in my penthouse or have my dog. She's an impostor!"

"You aren't listening, and we have work to do."

"What work?"

"Raymundo!"

The concierge for the hospital in El Paso appears with his golf club over one shoulder. His hideous mustache moves with his mouth when he says, "Let's go, Marfa."

Marfa? "I'm not Marfa."

"Since Marfa is now you, you're now Marfa."

I point to the screen again, but this time I have tacky blue fingernails and pudgy hands. I look down at a "Don't Mess with a Texas Girl" T-shirt, big boobs, and bigger thighs squeezed into tight jeans. I pat myself down just to make sure what I'm seeing is real. "Am I fat? I haven't had a potato or a crumb of bread for ten years. I work out five days a week. I can't be fat."

Ingrid shakes her head. "Don't mess this up, Raymundo," she says, before I'm pulled through a sudden crack in the tulips and land in a plain hall.

"Welcome back," the golfer says.

I look around and see Noah parting the Red Sea in the fish tank. Heaven Can Wait is on the television and people are chatting it up or playing cards. I know this place. For all the trouble I've gone through, I'm back where I started.

The golfer bangs the head of his club on the floor and says, "Can I have all y'all's attention?"

So, I know where I am—but why am I here?

"This is Marfa, the new apprentice concierge at UMC El Paso."

"Noooooo!"

15

For my first morning away from the strict schedule that has controlled the past five months of my life, I would have liked to have slept in. Surfaced when I wanted and had coffee in bed, but no one asked me what I wanted. I get up early and barely have enough time to do my hair before I'm driven to Dr. Barb's with Marv and Claire. Donovan picks us up in a white Cadillac Escalade with four cushy seats in back. Two face front; the other two face the rear. There's a television and minibar, and guess who gets stuck across from Marv and Claire, wondering if it's too early to crack a bottle of something?

"We thought it best that people don't know everything about your absence," Marv tells me, and I hear the cover story for the first time.

"When asked, we've said you were vacationing on the Amalfi Coast. The weather turned nasty, as it does, and you fell and hit your head."

"That's how you lost your memory," Claire adds. "You have been at a memory care rehabilitation hospital, but all efforts failed, and you are back home."

"Which 'memory care rehabilitation hospital'?"

"No one will ask, but if they are so ill-mannered, say it's your personal business and leave it at that," she answers.

"Or that you don't remember."

"Are y'all jokin'?"

They both look at me with twin expressions of confusion.

"No."

"Why would we joke about this situation?"

Maybe because it's convoluted. I want to tell them that you have to keep this amnesia stuff simple (or ASS for short) so it won't trip you up. I learned that in Dr. Lindbloom's office, but apparently I've spent the past five months at a memory care rehabilitation hospital, so what the heck do I know?

I understand the reasoning behind the cover story. I'd rather people not find out Edie tried to kill herself and got shipped off to a mental institution. That's embarrassing for both of us. I look out the window and grab my squeezy ball out of a black Chanel bag I stole from Edie's closet. To avoid a second clothing faux pas, I've dressed in black pants and a plain black sweater, as if there was a real choice. A majority of Edie's clothes are either light blue or black, like she had a dress code or a fear of color. Thank God her shoes aren't as boring. I picked out bright pink pumps with silver spikes lining the toes and four-inch heels. You can take a girl out of Texas, but you can't take away a Texas girl's shine.

I've never been a woman partial to heels, given that I inherited Daddy's wide feet, but Edie's feet are thin and slide right in snug as a bug. I have a newfound appreciation for stilettos, which make my legs look a mile long and my butt look amazing.

Once in Doc Barb's office, I turn my ankle this way and that so the patent leather picks up the glimmer of the lights. The pointy toes and spikes on these Alexander McQueens make me feel like a lethal weapon.

"What do you think, Edie?"

I look at the doc sitting at her desk, then at Marv and Claire across the room. Since Livingston, I've picked up a bad habit of tuning people out. "Come again?" Which makes me realize how much I miss sitting around gabbing like I used to.

"We were discussing the plan going forward and your staying in Michigan until spring."

"And visits to Palm Beach, of course," Claire says, like a warden adding time onto my prison sentence.

"Y'all can't force me to stay or go anywhere, right?" I like Doc Barb, but I've been living under other people's rules for far too long.

"Yes, but there are so many things you simply don't know anymore," Barb reminds me. "For example, who's your dentist?"

I look in the Chanel bag like the answer's in there and pull out my squeezy ball.

"Or your GP or ob-gyn? You don't know who to call if you need medical help."

"I'd call nine-one-one."

"Nine-one-one isn't going to come if you need your teeth cleaned or your annual mammogram."

True, but I don't plan on sticking around.

"Who's your banker and what are the passwords to your accounts?" Marv asks me. "We read your paperwork from Livingston. Your handwriting and signature are different."

I hadn't thought about that. When I wrote in logs or did my step work, I was learning to write with my right hand and didn't stop to think that my signature might be different from Edie's.

"You need to change your signature on your properties and financial portfolios and . . ." Claire pauses to lift a hand from her lap. "Everything."

I have properties and financial portfolios? I've never had more than a five-thousand limit on my Visa.

Claire drops her hand. "Talk to Garver. He'll know what's best."

Oh yes. Garver Smith. Squeeze-squeeze-squeeze. The guy who's supposed to be my attorney and took Marv and Claire's side to have me committed.

"Garver's good but he has his limits. I'll make a call to Burgin-Wesler," Marv adds. "Wes is familiar with Edie's financials."

Claire turns her attention to Marv. "And Edie's charities and LLC and—"

I put a hand to my forehead and stop listening. I just want to go home. To Texas. I just need a one-way ticket and a carry-on filled with undies and a toothbrush. And maybe some of Edie's shoes . . . and that gold sequin dress I saw this morning as I was pulling on my black pants.

"Edie?"

And that amazing Dior purse, and the pink crocodile Birkin, and the Chloé bag that Lida and I had seen in *Elle* and drooled over.

"Edie?"

Heck, I'll just pack up Edie's Louis Vuitton luggage and make my getaway.

"Edie?"

I blink and snap out of my fantasy. "Yes, ma'am?"

"Before your release from Livingston, we talked about you staying in Michigan under my care," Doc Barb reminds me. "With monthly visits and check-ins every Friday."

Yeah, but I didn't mean it. "For how long?"

"Let's see how you do for the first few months. If you're feeling good and making progress, we'll scale back the check-ins."

"Doctor Ware has approved your travel to Palm Beach, and you can do your weekly check-ins from Chatsworth." Claire gives me a warm smile, and this time her smile doesn't freeze when she looks at my hair. "Isn't that wonderful?"

No. "But I can travel to other places and check in from there, too."

The doctor shakes her head. "Your brain imagery doesn't show illness, but we can't know if your profound memory loss won't trigger your episodic depression," she says, but I know the answer. Zero, since I have neither memory loss nor depression. "You just left full-time care and can't rush your recovery. You need to take it slow. If you continue to improve, I think we can revisit this conversation in four to six months."

"That seems best," Marv agrees.

"Four to six more months? Best for who? I'm tired of people runnin' my life and pushin' me around." When Edie came up with her path-stealing scheme at UMC El Paso, she promised me more money than I could spend in two lifetimes. I don't need that much. Just enough to open Shear Elegance, and maybe a little extra so Momma and me can live our lives in comfort. I figure Edie owes me at least that much.

"How much time do you imagine before you're strong enough to take care of yourself?" the doc asks, and I'm starting to feel betrayed. She's never said anything about another four to six months.

"Just enough so I can sign a credit card without gettin' my behind tossed in jail."

"What do you need?"

A plane ticket. "I don't know, but I've been locked up and might want to travel."

"Where will you go?"

Home. As soon as possible. "I don't know. Someplace where folks aren't afraid of me."

"We aren't afraid of you, Edie." Claire looks from me to the doctor. "We're afraid *for* you."

I know they are trying, but I get the feeling that I make them as jumpy as they make me. "Y'all look at me like you're afraid I'm a hired killer and eye contact will put you on my hit list."

Claire shakes her head. "It's been a tough five months for everyone and we're just being cautious."

I don't want people cautious around me. I don't want people to walk on eggshells like I always had to with Dingleberry. Marv and Claire are not my favorite people, but that's no way to live. "If Livingston didn't turn me into a killer, nothin' will," I joke in an effort to lighten the mood. I miss joking and embellishing, and I have a burning urge to bring up the time Daddy killed a wild boar with his pocketknife. I can't because I have amnesia, but I wouldn't be a true Texan if I let a little thing like total memory loss stand in my way of *bool-sheet*. "Thank the good Lord and baby Jesus I never used that shank I made out of toothpicks and bobby pins. Twitchy was at the top of my 'People to Kill' list, I'm not gonna lie," I say, but I'm the only one smiling. They look horrified, and I turn to Barb. "Oh Lord, don't tell me I killed somebody and don't remember."

"No." She shakes her head and I sigh with relief. "We're just not used to your kidding."

"I never kidded before?" Thinking about Edie, I guess that's not a big surprise.

Marv and Claire shake their heads.

"*Never* told jokes?"

Marv finally breaks the silence. "Never."

That's not a surprise either. "We should all give it a try some-time. You know, 'Knock knock,' 'Who's there?'" Thinking back on the conversation on the drive over, I suspect neither of them has a sense of humor."

"Knock-knock jokes are for children," he says matter-of-factly, and he doesn't know it yet, but he just earned himself a mess of knock-knock jokes.

"Marvin." Claire puts her hand on her husband's knee. "No one wants to upset you, Edie."

Marv is being rude, but I'm in control of my emotions. "How can I get upset? I don't remember anyone or anything before May. I woke up not knowin' who or where I was." I pause to look directly at Edie's parents. "Y'all remember that day." They both give a slight nod and try hard not to look away. I appreciate the effort, but I feel a rant working its way to the surface. "I've been told about my life from birth to thirty, but I don't remember it. I'm told I went to some fancy schools and had a fiancé; I couldn't tell you what I learned or the name of the guy I was supposed to marry. I'm told I know a lot about fancy art and music, but all I can say is that I like painted skulls and country and western. Doctor Lindbloom said I was brilliant. I figure he must know since Mensa is his favorite subject."

Doc Barb laughs. "Lindbloom loves to talk about himself."

Finally, someone lightens up. "The pair of you could say I'm a thief and a triple-dipped psycho, but that's not me." That's the other Edie.

"It's difficult to look at our daughter and know that you're not the same person we've known for thirty years. You don't remember us or your brother. You don't remember how much you loved trimming the Christmas tree when you were little or how excited you were when you named your first sailing dinghy *Swift Winds*."

For the first time, I see a little crack in Claire's icy image. The corner of her mouth wavers, and even though she doesn't cry, she feels more human to me. Like she's more than an unfeeling block of ice. I haven't given much thought, if any, to how they must feel about the new and improved Edie. Hell, I don't know either. "I'm sorry about that."

"It's difficult to realize that you really did try to kill yourself. You really do hate your life. You really do want to die."

Marv puts his arm around Claire's stiff shoulders. "Darling, things will work out."

"Edie?" Doc Barb looks at me. "What are you feeling?"

"Sorry. That must be horrible." I shake my head. "I don't want to die, and I'd never kill myself. It's a calcified fact that I *hate* pain, and the sight of my own blood gives me the heebie-jeebies. Lord knows I had to give enough of it at Livingston."

"Edie, I think your parents need more from you than saying you hate pain and the sight of blood."

I know what the doc wants. "Aren't you my doctor? Shouldn't you be an advocate for me?"

"I am. I want what's best for you. Your amnesia is rare and we know more about the far side of the moon than we do profound retrograde amnesia. You are vulnerable, and the more you learn about yourself within safe boundaries, the better your long-term success will be."

This is one of those amnesia catch-22's.

"Your father and I . . ." Claire pauses long enough to look from me to Doc Barb, then back again. ". . . think a slow reintroduction to society is appropriate. Nothing big; we'll take you to a

few intimate cocktail parties and small events until you're con-
fident on your own and comfortable talking with old friends."

"That sounds mighty nice," I say, but the last thing I want to
do is go to some pea-pickin' cocktail party and pretend I have
amnesia. "But I don't have old friends, and y'all are uncomfortable sittin' around a dinner table talkin' to me. I think the
longest conversation I've had so far was with Old Edie when
she said my hair looks like her dead dog." I lift a hand and let it
fall into my lap. "Oh, and with that guy Oliver on your terrace
last night."

Claire's eyes round like she's in shock. "You spoke to Oliver?"

"Oliver Hunt?" Marv sounds just as incredulous as his wife.

"He didn't say his last name, but if he's Meredith's brother,
that's him."

"And the two of you spoke?" Marv asks.

"Yes, but he said we don't like each other."

"Well . . ." Again the parents are speechless.

Doc Barb closes my thick file on her desk as she stands.
Thank God the hour is over and I can . . . I can . . . I have no
idea, but on the drive to Hawthorne the parents seem to believe
I agreed to the four-to-six-months plan.

"I have a referral for an orthopedic surgeon," Claire tells me
on the way home. "His name is Doctor Graham and he special-
izes in hand and wrist reconstruction and comes highly recommended. Lee Brooks-Abrams went to him after the unfortunate
Ugotta Regatta mishap."

I look down at my hands and the sweater covering my wrists.
I've been afraid to admit that my left ring and pinky fingers are
starting to curl inward, despite physical rehab. I don't think it's
all that noticeable yet, but I'm afraid it's going to get worse. The
parents must have been in contact with the OT I worked with at

Livingston. I wonder what else they know about what happened to me all those months I thought they forgot about Edie.

"His work is miraculous. She has full use of her hand, and you can't even see her scar unless you're looking for it."

The scars are an embarrassment for them. I don't judge them because they are for me, too, and I can't see a day when I don't wear long sleeves to cover them up.

Marv glances up from his cell phone. "Outstanding. Graduated in the top three percent from Harvard Medical School."

"I'll call the doctor's office, if you'd like."

"Thank you," I say, and just like that, my plans to escape Michigan are put on hold for a while yet. The parents are being pushy, but I'm not going to look a gift horse in the mouth. I'd love to have better use of my left hand, and I have to stick around a bit longer anyway. I'd like to hold a pencil and a pair of shears when I go home.

I realize I need a more realistic plan than "get out of Livingston and go home." I can't go anywhere without money or identification.

I'm revising the plan:

1. Get money.
2. Get ID.
3. Get surgery.
4. Get home by Christmas.

16

Thank the good Lord and baby Jesus I'm getting a new cell phone, and it's at Marv's suggestion, of all people. After our meeting with Dr. Barb, he shows me to an office that is so enormous, there's room for the Resolute desk (okay, not the one in the White House, but it looks just as big and impressive), a conference table with three computers hooked to some sort of electronic hub in the middle, and a leather couch and group of chairs in front of the mahogany fireplace. The whole room has huge bookcases with sliding ladders. It smells like old books and money. If all that isn't overwhelming enough, the chandeliers above my head are big enough to crush an elephant if they crashed to the floor.

I expect Marv to take his place behind the big desk, but we sit at the conference table instead, and he shows me how to boot up a computer and log on to the internet using a touch pad. "The world runs on technology, and it's important for you to learn how to use the internet," he says as he moves the cursor up toward a row of three different web browsers and overshoots them all. "These new keyboards are useless." He slides the arrow too far down, circles back, and finally clicks the Explorer app. "I might be a bit rusty."

Him showing me stuff I learned in grade school is painful for a lot of reasons, but I play stupid and say, "Oh," and "Wow," and "Gosh, look at that." Then he pushes the keyboard in front of me, and now I have to play really stupid, like I don't know my way around a computer or the internet. Like I don't know how to pirate Netflix and HBO and binge-watch *Stranger Things* and *Jane the Virgin* while Momma ODs on '80s music videos on YouTube.

I say things like, "Is that how I use this?" and "That's amazin'."

"I know that your mother touched on the subject of your memory loss earlier," Marv says. "We've also discussed it many times in private."

I just bet they have. We look at each other, my hands still on the keyboard.

"We had hoped the issue would resolve itself at Livingston, and our Edie would be back to us by now." He presses his lips together, but I see no other signs of emotion. "We accept that your condition is severe and most likely permanent. You may be prone to emotional outbursts and display inappropriate coping mechanisms. You may need to relearn social boundaries and norms."

Yeah, yeah, I was told the same things, but I'm not worried about it because I don't have amnesia. I'm in control of my outbursts these days, but I have a feeling Marv and Claire are going to think I'm inappropriate anyway.

"Your mother will help teach you social norms. There's no one better than Clarice, you don't have to worry yourself about that."

Unless it's choosing the right pickle fork, I don't need help.

My momma raised me right. I don't burp or pick my nose in public, and I always have on clean drawers when I leave the house.

"We know that the daughter we raised is gone."

Now I feel bad for Marv. He's not all weepy, but he must be sad. Some folks have a hard time expressing emotion. I, on the other hand, have the opposite problem. "I'm sorry you lost Edie."

He gives a curt nod and a lock of gray hair escapes his pomade. I don't know why he slicks his hair back like a gangster, but if I were to advise him, I'd tell him to fire his barber and consult with a professional stylist. I could give him some free suggestions on how to update his look with a pompadour fade, but I doubt he'd appreciate my intervention.

"We've come to terms with the new reality." He clears his throat. "As difficult as the new reality may be."

I'm going to choose not to get offended, because he's probably hurting on the inside. "I think we'll come to terms just fine," I say, although I'm more than a little skeptical. "Once we get to know each other, we'll be happy as clams at high tide."

"You did love clamming as a child." He rakes his hair into place and slides the keyboard back in front of him. "You and Oliver always fought over who had the biggest basket."

That must have been before our "mutual aversion."

Marv turns his attention to the computer screen and says, "My great-grandfather, Boone Hawthorne, moved to Detroit after the Civil War and started selling cigars on Griswold and Lafayette. From there he purchased land and built a distillery and made whiskey to go with those cigars. Hawthorne Cigars and Spirits opened in 1870."

I can see Marv with a stogie and a whiskey on the rocks. "Is the store still there?"

"No. The tobacco barns are still in operation just outside of Saginaw, although due more to prestige than profit. The distillery was demolished during Prohibition, but by then Boone had diversified into pharmaceuticals and cast-iron manufacturing." He logs off the internet and navigates to an icon of a black tree on a blue background. He only misses once before he clicks on it and tells me, "This is the Hawthorne Corporation, a multinational conglomerate that has its roots on Griswold and Lafayette." He taps the trackpad and adds, "You need a new phone."

"What?" I want to clap my hands and shout, "Hallelujah! Thank the good Lord and baby Jesus," but I have to hide my excitement behind my amnesia mask.

"A cell phone. Our telecom department handles this sort of thing."

Something as simple as a cell phone is ordered through the corporate business account. Marv connects to the telecom department, enters a password, and pulls up a page of options. When I say options, I mean that I can choose the latest Samsung in bronze, black, or white. My excitement plummets even further when I realize this is a company phone. Anyone in the IT department can look at phone calls and texts. All my selfies and personal information will be uploaded to the company cloud.

I choose the white Samsung, but I don't care anymore. "Did I have one of these company phones before?" I'm hurting on the inside like Marv. I slump in my chair and keep my emotional outburst to myself.

"Three. You left them in your apartment last May. They were outdated, with information useless to you now, and were destroyed. This new phone will better fit your present needs."

I bet Marv and I have very different ideas when it comes to my "present needs." "Like?"

"Banking. Access to credit cards without providing a signature. Your code to the penthouse. 'Magnus' is the only password you need to open your password chain."

"I have a penthouse?" I remember Donovan mentioning something about Edie living above a hotel, but he never said the word *penthouse*. "In Detroit?"

"Yes. At the Book Cadillac on Washington Boulevard. The residence entrance is on Shelby."

I sit up a little straighter and ask just to be sure, "Do I own it?" I don't let myself get excited quite yet. "Or do you own it?" Like my phone.

"It's yours," he answers, and looks like he wants to smile but can't quite manage it. "I was skeptical, when you told me the price of that unit would double in three years, but you were right."

Me? Brittany Lynn Snider from Marfa, Texas, has a penthouse in Detroit. I shake my head in amazement. "Well, butter my butt and call me toast."

He makes a sound like he's in pain as he taps one more link, then signs off. "You should have your phone tomorrow. Mimi will help you with the rest."

"Who's Mimi?"

"Your personal assistant, although your mother has enlisted her help while you've been away."

"I have a personal assistant?"

"Clarice needed a new assistant after Mrs. Goldstein retired this past June and put yours to work. Mimi is with Clarice and Meredith in your mother's office upstairs. I believe they are waiting for you."

"Why?" We stand and I watch him move behind his big desk.

"One of your events, God only knows which." He sits down in a big leather chair, looking like a president.

"Thank you for the phone," I say, even though it's not all what I'd hoped for. Because I don't need to relearn social norms, I add, "I appreciate it."

"You're welcome, Edie." He leans his head back, suddenly looking like he's a *worn-out* president. I think of my daddy and how he pops a beer first thing when he gets home from work. His latest dog waits with at least two tennis balls in its mouth and shakes with excitement until he takes it out back. People hear his laugh from Marfa to Alpine. Daddy isn't a perfect man, but he knows how to have fun. I suddenly feel bad for Marv because I don't think he laughs much or cracks a real smile, but he ruins it by saying, "Please be aware of your mother's feelings and think before expressing yourself. Buttering your behind is inappropriate."

And just when we were starting to get along, too. "Hey, Marv."

He gives me his attention without moving his head. "Yes."

I doubt he'd play along with a "childish" knock-knock joke. "Why couldn't the bicycle stand up by itself?" But I have a mess of stupid kid jokes. "It was two-tired." He just stares at me like he doesn't get it. "It's a joke."

"Is that what you call it?" His expression doesn't change.

"Yep. I'll have another to tell you tomorrow."

"I look forward to it."

Novia appears like she was summoned and shows me to Claire's office. It's more feminine than Marv's, with a much smaller Resolute desk. I find Claire and Meredith sitting around a pedestal table with four floral chairs, sipping tea with a woman in black pants and a red blouse. I thank Novia, again proving my social norms are just fine.

"Edie." The woman I'm guessing is Mimi stands up from her chair and walks toward me. Her dark hair is pulled back in a ponytail and her lipstick matches her blouse. "Welcome back," she says, and opens her arms. Now, I'm from Texas and we're a friendly bunch, but we don't go around hugging strangers. That sort of contact is limited to close friends and family. Johnny J. preaches it's the same as dancing. Hugging, dancing, and tight clothes can lead to sinful thoughts. Not to mention a wicked grin, washboard abs, and a happy trail sliding beneath a button fly.

I return Mimi's hug because that's how folks are around here. She kisses the air above my cheek. "Thank God you're home. We have so much to catch up on," she whispers next to my ear. I'm sure she knows of my memory loss, but I don't know what to make of that. "Meredith is being her usual pain."

I don't know Meredith, but I can't imagine her being a pain to anyone. I don't want to make a premature judgment. I'm not sure about Mimi yet, and I'm adding her to the running tab of people who think Edie's lying about amnesia. Or the ELAA list:

1. Dr. Lindbloom
2. Donovan
3. Burton
4. Old Edie
5. Magnus: he *knows* I'm lying
6. Oliver

And the jury is still out on:

7. Mimi
8. Marv
9. Claire
10. Meredith
11. Harold: not sure he knows who *he* is half the time.

"We're just going over the guest list before we send out invitations to the Hawthorne New Year's gala," Claire tells me. "The theme this year is 'Golden Years,' and guests are to arrive in gold and black or combinations of the two."

"Last year's theme was 'Baby It's Cold Outside' and guests arrived in fur. Or . . . a . . . faux fur, rather," Meredith adds. She lifts a hand from the table, covered in a white-and-pink-striped cloth, and motions toward three gold teapots with roses painted on them. "Would you prefer chamomile, chai, or Earl Grey tea?"

There's only one kind of tea, and that's Texas sweet tea, and it's poured into a Mason jar filled with ice because everyone knows it tastes better that way. "Chamomile," I say, to fit in with these poor misguided Northerners.

"Milk, sugar, or lemon?" she asks as she reaches for one of the pots and begins pouring.

Milk? What the heck? "Sugar, please." I take the empty seat next to Meredith. My place is already set with a pink cloth napkin and a little gold spoon. Meredith hands me a cup and saucer and a little sugar bowl with the same rose pattern.

"Thank you." I look at the steam rising from the tea and decide to give it a moment. "I doubt I'll be much help with the party, but I'll try."

Mimi pulls out a folder and hands it to me. "This is the list so far."

I set it next to me and am much more interested in watching Claire drink her tea. She sits ramrod straight and brings the cup to her lips. No slurping. No raised pinky. No dribbles on her yellow blouse. It's so prim and proper. Watching her is like watching Queen Elizabeth drinking tea on *The Crown*.

I rub my left thumb across my fingertips and put the napkin on my lap. I've gotten a lot better at using my right hand, and I

grab the little gold spoon and shovel sugar into my cup. If I con-
centrate, I should get through this like a regular aristocrat. I stir
until the sugar is dissolved, then tap my spoon against the cup's
rim until I'm sure it's not going to drip on Claire's tablecloth.

The only time I've ever had hot tea was when I had strep
throat and Momma put honey and lemon in it. It did help my
throat, but it tasted like honey and lemon and old weeds. I place
my spoon on the saucer like everyone else and carefully raise the
cup. When it's halfway to my lips, I notice that all three women
are looking at me. "Y'all good?"

"That's your great-grandmother's wedding porcelain."

This must be one of Claire's teaching moments. "It's real
pretty." I sit straight and take a sip without spilling a drop. The
tea doesn't taste like weeds, but it's bland as all git-out. I set it
on the saucer, quite proud of myself.

"How's Magnus today?" Meredith asks as she raises her cup.

"I think Magnus and I have come to an understandin'. He
stays on his side of the house, and I stay on mine." Which isn't
a hardship, given I doubt I could find his side of the house even
if I went looking for him.

"What's wrong with Magnus?" Mimi asks. "He loves you."

"He loves Rowan more, and I think he would be happier
livin' with her."

"No. Rowan knows that she can't have a pet until she proves
she is responsible enough to care for an animal. All she has to do
is pick up after herself and remember how to tie her own shoes."

Heck, I'll pick up after the kid and tie her shoes if it gets
her one step closer to Magnus ownership, although I'm fairly
certain that Meredith and Burton have housekeepers. If not,
they should take one of Marv and Claire's. Lord knows there's
a passel around here.

"But if you don't mind, she'd like to walk him once a week for you."

"Sure. Anytime she wants is fine with me. Do you need Donovan to pick her up?" I ask to seal the deal.

"We live just down the street."

Even better.

The attention turns from Magnus to the gala thing, and I pick up my gold spoon and scoop some more sugar. Last night when I returned to my bedroom after dinner, the clothes I'd left in a pile on the closet floor had vanished and my shoes were put away. The wet towel I'd left hanging on the rack to dry had been replaced and my bed turned down.

"Edie?"

It was creepy. I stir one more time and tap the spoon on the rim.

"Edie?"

I look up. "Yes, ma'am."

"Please put the spoon down." Claire places her hands on the tablecloth in front of her. "That's Baroque."

"Oh. Sorry." I take a real good look, but I don't see anything. "Broke where?"

Claire closes her eyes. Meredith is suddenly fascinated with the papers in her folder and Mimi starts to laugh. "That's funny," she says.

"What's funny?" I don't understand their reactions.

"Your joke."

"That wasn't a joke." These people are so confusing, with their rules and boundaries and stupid humor. "What's worse than rainin' cats and dogs?" I ask, stretching way back in my memory for dumb jokes. "Hailin' taxis." I take the napkin from my lap. "*That's* a joke." Maybe not a very good one, but a heck of a lot better than a broke cup that isn't broke. I stand and push in my chair. "I'm worn thin as Bible paper. If y'all will excuse me, I'm goin' to my room."

Meredith catches up with me as I'm trying to remember which way to go. "Edie," she calls to me.

I turn toward her and wait beneath a painting of flowers and a stream. I step out of my heels because I discover something I didn't know before just now: high heels are comfortable until the second they're not.

"I don't believe Clarice accented the *a* when she said 'Baroque,' and it did sound like she said 'broke.'" Meredith spells the difference and gives me a short history of the seventeenth century. "I'm not saying this was your mistake, but I wanted to save you from embarrassment if it ever comes up again."

She's trying to help me without making me feel dumb. I appreciate that, and I look into her brown eyes and at the freckles sprinkled across her nose. She's cute as a button and I can't imagine her being a pain to anyone.

She puts her hand on my arm. "I know your memory loss must be difficult, and I hope I haven't hurt your feelings."

"You haven't hurt my feelin's." I guess I can take her off the list of people who might think I'm faking.

"Think of 'Baroque' as a homophone. Like 'die' and 'dye,'" she says.

I use homophones in my lyrics all the time. "'I was *ridin' high* on your love, but you were *writin' hi* to another girl.'"

She smiles and drops her hand. "I *bawled* when I saw Georgie's *bald* head for the first time."

I smile, too. I've never had a sister, and Meredith seems like a good enough person. "I'd love to meet Georgie. I don't know for sure, but I think I like babies."

Her smile kind of wavers.

"Didn't I like babies before?"

"There are some women who aren't naturally maternal."

I suspect there's a lot more to it. "Did we like each other?"

She is far more diplomatic than her brother when she says, "I'll bring Georgie over when Rowan walks Magnus."

17

I don't know why anyone would think Meredith is a pain. Maybe she has two faces, but I don't think so. She appears to be one of those rare people who are genuinely kind. I can gather from what Meredith *didn't* say that Edie didn't like her, but that's no surprise. Last night Oliver said Edie didn't like anyone. I'm sure that's an exaggeration. There must be at least one person she liked.

I find my bedroom and shut the door behind me. The curtains are open now and the bed is made. I'd left a cup of coffee on the nightstand and it's gone. Am I supposed to leave a tip? A thank-you note? I don't think I'm ever going to get used to this.

I toss my shoes on the floor and sit on the edge of the bed. What am I supposed to do now? I met with Doc Barb and the parents this morning. Marv showed me how to use a computer and ordered a phone. I had tea with Claire, Meredith, and Mimi. And I don't know what to do with myself now. I'm so used to living on a schedule. Even my free time was filled with No Time Before You Salon. As crazy as it sounds, I miss it. Even more crazy, I miss Katrina, too. Maybe because she liked me, and I never got on her bad side. We were friends. Not like with Lida, but like being friends with a cat. Cute, smarter than it seems, and attacks for no reason.

If I'm bored now, what's there to do with myself for the next month or two? I think about my conversation with Marv and wonder when I can move into Edie's penthouse—no, *my* penthouse—but I doubt it's up to me. Dr. Barb said I need four to six months of progress before I can be on my own. In four to six months, I'll be living in Texas.

My gaze falls on the intercom Novia mentioned last night. It's the size of a tablet, and I pull it onto my lap. This is more than just an intercom. I'm looking at integrated technology, and it doesn't take long to figure out how the system operates. I kick back against the padded headboard, tap the kitchen icon, and order a ham sandwich, potato chips, and a Dr Pepper like I'm at a restaurant. While I wait for lunch, I open and close the shade across the room, then pull up different security cameras in the house and around the property. Nothing much going on besides someone making my sandwich, people in gray uniforms polishing wood, and the landscapers raking leaves outside.

I can connect to the internet and surf the web, and if anyone wonders how a person with amnesia can operate the tablet, I'll say Marv showed me.

My fingers are itching to type *Marfa* and then pull up the Do or Dye web page and see Momma's picture. I want to search for old news articles from the day I had my accident and see if there's any mention of me or why I was in El Paso. More than anything, I'd love to connect to Google Earth and see both Momma's and Daddy's homes, but I can't risk someone seeing my searches and tossing me back in Livingston faster than I can say "Google search."

Lunch arrives and I eat my sandwich as I look up anything I can on Edie Randolph Chatsworth-Jones. I discover she was an art dealer and a benefactress, sat on the boards of several charitable organizations, was a shareholder in Hawthorne Corporation, and traveled often. There are a lot of photos of her at galas and events and on the covers of *Entrepreneur* magazine's "Women to Watch" issue and *Elle*'s issue titled "The New Generation of Power." Maybe Dr. Lindbloom was right about Edie being brilliant.

There's a whole lot of information about the family on Wikipedia. I skim most of it because I'm not interested in acquisitions of multinational conglomerations (and yes, I had to look up the definition of *multinational conglomeration*) and looking at a family tree of people I don't know is boring.

There's only so much I can read about these dull strangers, and I toss the tablet on the bed. There's only one *non*boring thing to do around here, and I head to Edie's enormous closet and pull my sweater over my head and shuck my pants at the same time. I'm wearing silky black panties and a matching bra that I found in drawers neatly filled with lingerie. Thankfully, Edie owns more than thongs.

I step over the black pants on the floor and move straight to the rod filled with big garment bags. Each bag is labeled and I grab VERSACE 2019 MET GALA first. It's stuffed with embroidered red velvet and a corset-like bodice sewn with intricately cut jewels. It looks like some kind of jeweled headpiece is crammed in there, too. I'm curious to see the whole outfit, but there's no way I can get all that material stuffed back in the bag if I do. I grab a thinner bag and pull out a light blue satin dress that I immediately pull over my head. The fabric is folded and twisted on the shoulders and has a corset built into the lining. I lose the black bra and zip the dress up the back the best I can. It hits just below my knees and I find a pair of light blue pumps that tie around my ankles. I look at myself in the mirrors, fluff my hair, and pull it to one side. "Beautiful," I whisper. I forgot that Edie was so beautiful. That I'm beautiful. Then I catch a glimpse of my arms and hide my ugly wrists in the fabric. I can never wear this dress in public without long gloves. Or at least until I have the surgery Claire talked about earlier.

Some of the garments are so horrible, I just zip the bag back up and move on. Whenever Lida and I used to thumb through high-fashion magazines at Porter's or happened to see runway shows from New York or Paris on the television, we'd ask each other, "Who buys that stupid crap?" Now I know.

I try on the gold sequin gown I'd discovered this morning and twist my hair into a classic bun at the nape of my neck. The dress has a train and is heavier than it looks, but I walk about the bedroom waving like I'm a queen. A make-believe queen living in someone else's castle.

Trying on all these fancy clothes is fun and all, but I feel like I've snuck into someone else's closet. After five months, I am me—neither fully Brittany nor fully Edie. I'm used to looking in the mirror and seeing me, but I don't think I'll ever get used to Edie's money or the luxury that comes from it. Hawthorne is wrapped in heritage and is a way of life. It represents a deep vein of wealth that drips money and makes me feel like an impostor wearing someone else's clothes.

I look in the mirror and run my hand across my stomach, disturbing the sequins. This is my life now, and if God didn't want me to live as an heiress, I wouldn't be here. The Bible says to obey God in all things, and I'm a good Christian woman at the end of the day. He wants me to wear this golden gown and all the other clothes in this closet. Momma always says that to go against God is a sin.

By the time the integrated tablet beeps, I'm wearing a silky white blouse with a big bow beneath my chin and a pair of black velvet shorts. I move to the bed in thigh-high boots and see Claire's face filling the screen. She must see me too and says, "I wanted to remind you that dinner is in the dining room at seven tonight."

I glance at the clock. Uh-oh. "I'll be there. Thanks." I have ten minutes to change out of the shorts and boots, dig for the black pants I wore earlier, and shove my feet into soft leather flats. With one minute to spare, I turn a corner and walk into the dining room at Downton Abbey.

Marv and Claire smile at me from the far end of a table that is so long, I can't guess how many people it seats.

"We thought you'd like to experience the most formal room at Hawthorne." They wait for me and Claire does the air-kiss, so I follow her lead. Marv pulls out her chair for her, and I move to take the seat across the table from her. "Wait for your father to hold your chair."

"Oh." Beneath the sparkling chandeliers and light bouncing off the silver, I feel my cheeks burn. "Sorry."

Marv pats my shoulder and pushes in my chair for me. "You look beautiful."

Wow. A pat and a compliment. "Thank you, sir."

We're served a pear salad, then chicken with what looks and tastes like bruschetta and pasta. Claire places her napkin in her lap and my etiquette and social norms lessons begin.

We make small talk, strained and at times painful, while I try to remember where to set my wineglass.

"Chester Chadwick's eightieth birthday is on the fifteenth. That's a week from this Friday. It's a small cocktail party. Perfect for your first outing."

"I don't know anyone."

"You need to reintroduce yourself." I tune Claire out when she starts naming all the different people who will be there, but my ears perk up when she says, "You have a consultation with Doctor Graham on the twentieth."

I look at my wrists covered in white silk cuffs. "I hope he can help."

"Edith," Marv says, and I look up at him. "Money can't fix everything, but it can damn sure fix most things." I think that's Marv's way of being optimistic, and he raises his wineglass in the air. "Clarice, thank you for another excellent meal."

I raise my glass, too, and dinner is over shortly after. We air-kiss each other's cheeks good night and I return to my bedroom. I've decided to commit to Edie's twice-daily skin-care regimen. If I read the labels on the bottles, even those in a foreign language, I can figure it out. It's just a matter of matching products.

I clean up the mess in the closet before I relax and search the tablet for a television icon. There's a thumbnail of Magnus, and I type his name as the password and a new screen pops up with just a few different apps. I browse Edie's emails, which are mostly business related and, again, boring. The few lunch or dinner dates with friends, she signs *Smooches, Edie.*

There are some photos of art and a few of Edie with a man a few inches taller than her. He has sandy hair and a big smile. They look beautiful together.

One of the icons is the "Find My Phone" app. I click it even though I fully expect a "can't find" message. Marv said Edie's old phones had been destroyed and my new phone won't be here until tomorrow.

To my surprise, a US map fills the screen, then steadily shrinks until it stops on Grosse Pointe Shores. It gives an address, but before I start tearing things apart looking for a phone, I type the address into MapQuest, and a red marker pops up in the middle of Hawthorne. Marv didn't mention a fourth phone, but maybe he didn't know about it. If I were Edie, I'd want a line for personal privacy.

I start looking everywhere: under the bed, in the closet, drawers, anything with pockets. I search purses and inside shoe-boxes, but after several hours, I lie in the middle of the ottoman, staring at the ceiling medallion and surrounded by hundreds of handbags and shoes.

Novia comes to ask if I need anything before the staff leaves for the night. Her eyes get big and she says, "Are you packing for a vacation?"

Then an idea strikes and I sit up. "Do I have luggage?" I re-member glimpsing a Louis Vuitton carry-on in El Paso.

"Yes." She carefully steps through the collateral damage on the floor and presses on a mirrored wall. It clicks and slides open to reveal more designer luggage than one person needs, but I don't need to tear through it all. The familiar-looking carry-on is right in front.

"Thanks. Have a nice night." I wait for Novia to leave be-fore I grab the small suitcase and toss it on the ottoman. Then, like a kid on Halloween, I rip it open and dump it out so I can see what I've got. The vanity case falls out, but it's completely empty. I check the carry-on inside and out, and I'm about to give up when I spot a hidden zipper in the outside pocket. In it I find what looks like a wallet insert. I flip it open and discover Edie's Michigan driver's license, a black American Express card, a J.P. Morgan Reserve Visa made out of some kind of metal, and a Dubai First Royale MasterCard trimmed in gold.

None of that is even half as good as the blue cell phone

and matching charger I pull out next. It's an iPhone. The same iPhone model I had last May, too. Perfect, no learning curve.

I plug it in next to the bed and wait for the phone to charge. It seems to take forever until the Apple logo fills the screen, followed by a selfie of Edie and Magnus. He's licking her cheek instead of snapping at the air. I hold it up long enough for it to recognize my face, and all her apps pop up.

It's eight thirty in Michigan, but it's six thirty in west Texas. The Do or Dye closes at seven. My heart races as I open the phone icon and touch the ten numbers that I've waited over five long months to dial. I can hardly hear the ringing over the pounding in my ears, then . . . "It's a fabulous hair day at Do or Dye. What can I do you for?" It's Lorna, and I never thought I'd be so happy to hear her voice.

"May I speak with Carla Jean?" I take a deep breath and let it out, and I feel like I might die. What am I going to say? I didn't think of that.

"She's not here, sugar. Can someone else help you?"

"No." I didn't think of that either. Momma always works Tuesdays till close. "When will she be back?"

"She's on vacation."

Vacation? I always have to drag Momma kicking and screaming on a vacation. "Where?"

"Of course, that's private information."

Lorna picks now to worry about anyone's privacy? There isn't a secret north of the Rio Grande that she hasn't told.

"I can give her a message for you if you want."

"No, thank you, ma'am." I hang up and dial Momma's cell, which I would have done in the first place if she wasn't notorious for losing it in the depths of her "Love Is in the Hair" tote bag.

"Hello, this is Carla Jean." It's been five long months since I last heard my momma's voice. Tears fill my eyes and clog my throat. I open my mouth to say hello, but nothing comes out.

"Is anyone there?"

"It's me," comes out in a whispery sob. "I miss you."

"Is this a prank call?" She puts her hand over the phone and talks to someone else. Then she says, "I'm goin' to hang up. Please don't call again."

"Wait!" She doesn't disconnect, but I have to think fast of something that will keep her talking. I clear my throat and say, "I'm with the Publishers Clearin' House."

"Lord love a duck!"

"Your entry has been chosen in the final round for our super prize."

"Pudge! Pudge! I'm in the runnin' for a super prize. I don't recall enterin' but I'm in the final round. Praise Jesus!"

Pudge? Daddy? Sure enough, I hear him in the background. "Well, Carla Jean, if you don't remember enterin' it's likely a scam."

"Is this a scam?"

"No."

"Honey, hang up and call the FBI."

"You don't have to enter to win!"

"I have to go now." *Click.* For the first time in my life, Momma actually listened to Daddy.

"Wait, what are you doin' on vacation with Pudge?" I say to the black screen. I don't know whether to laugh or cry or just sit here, staring at the phone, stunned and feeling like a mule kicked the wind out of me. Where's Floozy Face? I hit the message icon, but I can't exactly ask what in the heck is up with her and Daddy. I should write down what I want to say so I don't get so flustered next time. While I give it some thought, I notice that Edie's last text was sent to someone named Wicky. I open it and land on:

Hey, handsome, when is your plane arriving?

I have a feeling this is going to be good, and so I scroll up as far as possible.

April 5, 12:01 p.m.

Edie: Last night was incredible.

Wicky: You were amazing. I can't wait until we're together again. God, I'm hard just thinking about it.

Edie: Next time we see each other at the clubhouse, imagine me naked and wanting you.

Wicky: On your knees?

Edie: After you.

April 7, 9:15 a.m.

Wicky: The first night I saw you, I had to have you. I couldn't help myself.

Edie: At the Chippewa exhibit? Glad we found an empty room.

Wicky: The bark canoes haven't rocked like that for over a hundred years.

Edie: I adore you.

Wicky: I adore you, lover.

April 14, 3:16 p.m.

Edie: Meet me at the Townsend. Executive suite. I don't know the number.

Wicky: On my way. Wear something sexy.

Edie: Even when I'm in a business suit, you know I'm wearing something sexy.

Wicky: God, you make me hard.

April 19, 7:52 p.m.

Edie: I can't possibly marry Blake.

Wicky: What are you going to do? Haven't you sent the invitations?

Edie: Oh God.

April 23, 9:00 a.m.

Edie: It's over. I did it. My parents are beside themselves.

Wicky: Be brave.

Edie: I'm leaving town on the 30th. There are three pieces of Nestora Piartoe pottery up for auction in El Paso. It's a good excuse to get out of town.

Wicky: Marvin and Clarice will come around. They just might need a little time.

April 29, 10:36 a.m.

Edie: Are you up for west Texas? I'm leaving in the morning and not telling anyone. I'm desperate to get away from the whispers and judgments.

Wicky: Name the place and I'll be there. Just thinking of you naked makes me hard.

"Yuck, that's the third time he's said 'hard,'" I say to myself through a pained groan. Edie told him she was desperate to get away, and all he could talk about was getting naked and hard. "Wicky" sounds like a real asshat. Maybe Edie and I have one more thing in common. We wasted time on asshats.

April 30, 11:20 a.m.

Edie: I'm at the Plaza in El Paso. These past eight days have been hell. Mother and Father still aren't speaking to me and Burton is horrified by my decision. When hasn't Burton been horrified?!

Wicky: Your brother was born with a stick up his ass. The only Yalie I've known to reject a tap from Bones. Idiot could be a senator by now.

Edie: He's as boring as his wife. She's nauseating, and he lectures me on how I should live my life.

Wicky: Your brother loves his moral high ground.

Edie: One of us has morals?

April 30, 1:12 p.m.
Wicky: I can't wait to hold you in my arms.
Edie: God, get here fast.

April 30, 5:46 p.m.
Edie: Hey, handsome. I was shown the pottery before the auction. I think my client will be thrilled. When is your plane arriving?

April 30, 6:52 p.m.
Wicky: I'm still in Lansing. Have a big case coming up. I don't know if I can get away tonight.
Edie: I'll come to Lansing.

April 30, 8:35 p.m.
Wicky: No. Don't come.
Edie: Please. I love you.
Wicky: I can't do this any longer.
Edie: Do what?
Wicky: This.
Edie: What are you saying?
Wicky: I love my wife.

18

I give Momma two days before I call her again, but it goes straight to voicemail. She's left a recorded message that no child should ever have to hear: "Pudge and me are gettin' busy, if y'all know what I mean. Try back in a few hours—beeeeep."

I clasp my throat and try not to gag. My folks are too old to get busy. They hate each other. Where's Daddy's wife? This is worse than Momma getting an Espinoza Especiale in the back of Jorge's taco truck.

Between Momma and Daddy "gettin' busy" and Claire's etiquette lessons, my brain is upside down. Over afternoon tea, Claire shows me how to stir and sip without breaking the Baroque. She tells me how to give compliments, even if I have to stretch the truth to spare someone's feelings. Like, "Your baby is beautiful," she says. "Even if the poor thing has the misfortune to resemble a hairless rat."

I prefer the Texas way of complimenting folks to spare feelings. Like gushing over someone's new hairstyle because you can't think of one good thing to say about her ugly baby.

Plainly, Claire and I have two different ideas when it comes to "stretching the truth." There's stretching the truth and there's bullshitting. I'm practiced at both, but saying a rat baby is beautiful is beyond my capabilities. I admire Claire's *bool-sheet* skills. I didn't think she had it in her.

At night I learn the difference between red and white wineglasses and cake and fruit forks, and that polite dinner conversation is different from lively cocktail conversation.

The Friday after my release from the loony bin, Edie's personal trainer, Rod, calls me on the company phone and wants to know when we should start working out again. He uses words like *cardio* and *boomerang* and my muscles get cramps just thinking about it, but if it gets me out of Claire's etiquette boot camp, I'm in. I tell him I don't want to boomerang (even though I don't have a clue what that means) but I'll jog with him, and he shows up at Hawthorne the next day.

I'm in a cream-colored jogging suit and white-and-gray running shoes with extra-cushy soles. Rod makes me stretch and lunge to warm up my muscles before I pull on my Carhartt cap and take off with him. We don't make it far before I get a side stitch and my lungs hurt. I grab the ache just below my ribs and move to some soft grass, where I collapse to my knees. "I'm done for the day."

Rod jogs in place and tells me, "We're just getting started."

"We worked out at the house."

"Stretching doesn't count." He checks the gizmo strapped to his arms and says, "We've only run half a mile."

That's more than I've run since high school PE. I'm breathing a little hard but I'm not wheezing like a pack-a-day smoker. "That's good considerin' I haven't worked out in a while. I need to start out slow."

"We are. I've cut your run from ten miles to three."

Ten miles? Is he on drugs?

"Come on. You've only made it as far as the golf course."

"Great. Let's get a cart. I'll drive us home."

"We have two and a half more miles."

I fall onto my back and spread my arms straight out. "You're high if you think I'm movin'."

"This isn't like you."

I laugh and watch the clouds gather in the sky. "You might have heard; I've been in the hospital."

"I was told you had an accident and have trouble with your memory. There's nothing wrong with your legs though." He stands over me and looks down. "You can do this, Edie. When we're done for the day, you're going to feel great. You'll be glad you worked through the pain. You ran the Boston Marathon in just over three hours." *Three hours?* He continues with his pep talk but I tune him out. Rod's a good-looking man. Blue-eyed with sun-bleached blond hair, abs so tight bullets could bounce off him like Superman. I wonder if he and Edie had their own special workout. If they got naked and sweaty. When he pauses to take a breath, I ask, "Were we more than workout buddies?" I let my gaze travel to his waist and spandex-covered bulge. Well, that's just sad. Maybe he's cold.

"I'm a professional trainer!"

I guess that means no. "Sorry, I was just askin'." I sit up with my legs out in front of me. Getting professionally trained and boomerangs and marathons were the other Edie's thing, not mine. I'm not saying I won't exercise or stay fit, but I'm not running unless Rod chases me with a shotgun. "I not only lost my memory in that accident, I lost half a lung and a couple of ribs," I bullshit, because Rod is too hard-core for the new Edie. "One wrong move and a jagged rib can puncture a lung and pierce my heart." I look at him through sad eyes and sigh. "I'm fragile."

"Oh. Your parents didn't mention that. Do you want me to walk you back home?"

I shake my head, because I don't think he knows how to "walk" without turning it into some sort of endurance training. "No need."

He starts to jog in place again. "Call me when you're better."

"You know I will, for certain." I watch him run off like he can't get away fast enough. I crawl to my knees and stand up. The back of my jogging suit is wet from the late-morning dew, and the cream-colored velour has turned dark brown on my butt and the backs of my thighs. The good news is that Hawthorne is less than a mile away. The bad news is that I can't remember how to get back. I was watching my feet or thinking about how much I hate jogging, and I didn't pay attention because Rod knew the way.

I move across the parking lot of the St. Clair Shores Golf Club to the street. I look left and right, and I remember passing that giant pine tree on the next block. I lean forward for a better look, and some jerk honks his horn from behind me. I jump so hard I almost wet myself. I put a hand on my heart and turn around as the tinted window of a white sports car slides down a few inches.

"Are you lost, Sunshine?"

The other night, I'd wondered if he was handsome in the light of day or if darkness was his friend. Sometimes turning on the light kills the mood. Charlie Buck and his wonk eye comes to mind. "Are you spyin' on me, Oliver?"

The window slides down the rest of the way, and I swear to God my heart stops along with my breath. His deep green eyes look up at me, and if it wasn't for his hard jawline and the cleft in his chin, his dark lashes might make him look girly. "Why is your butt wet?"

Oliver Hunt is definitely a leave-the-lights-on kind of guy. It's been a long time since I've had one of those. I pull off my hat and run my fingers through my hair. "Wanna give a girl a ride home?"

"You'll get the seat wet."

"I'm worth the sacrifice."

"It's Swiss leather."

"Well, in that case . . ." I step on the backs of my running shoes as a car honks and pulls away from the parking lot. Oliver sticks an arm out of the window and sunlight pinwheels off his gold watch as he waves. "Who's that?" I ask, and kick off one shoe and then the other.

"My golf partner."

"It looked like a girl."

"That's because she is a girl."

I reach for the drawstring at my waist. "Is she your girlfriend?"

"No."

"Do you care for her?" I slide my pants down my right hip.

"She finishes under par, that's all I care about. What are you doing?"

I push down the other side and am careful not to take my underwear with it. "Takin' my pants off so I don't mess up your Swiss leather."

"Stop!" He looks side to side like he's afraid someone might see us—but not before he gets a real good look at the top of my lacy bikini panties. "Give me your hat."

"Why?" I hand it over and he puts it on the passenger seat.

"Get in before someone sees you."

I grab my shoes and run around the other side, and I have to take a quick step back so the gull-wing door doesn't hit me in the head. "You almost knocked me out."

"I'm not that lucky."

The car's so low to the ground, I kind of fall into it. The door lowers and I dump my shoes on the floor. "Are you sure about the pants?" I look around for the seat belt. "It's not like either of us is goin' to get excited, given our aversion and all."

"I'm sure." He shifts the car into gear as I click the belt across my chest and lap. "How'd you end up in the club parking lot with wet clothes?"

"I was joggin' and got a stitch in my side so I sat on the grass." He revs the engine and pulls out of the parking lot. The car smells and sounds like money, and I figure Oliver must be as loaded as the Chatsworth-Joneses. "Then I realized I don't know the way back home." I look out the windows and pay attention to landmarks and street signs this time.

He takes a right and we drive down a street with big houses and manicured lawns. "Don't you have a cell phone?" he asks.

"I don't have pockets, but I was with Rod and he knew the way." It looks like everyone around here is loaded, too. Even the smaller houses are grand. "He was my personal trainer and all." Oliver takes a left and I can see the gates to Hawthorne. "He's too dedicated and hard-core for me nowadays." I shrug. "I scared him off with my punctured-lung story."

He looks over at me and pulls into the drive. "I'm not even going to ask." The gates open and we take off toward the house like a bat out of hell. He barely stops the car before the door lifts.

"Wanna come inside?" I wouldn't mind if he helped me out of my wet clothes.

"Not a chance. If Marvin and Clarice see us together, they'll get the wrong idea and think we're dating."

I pick up my shoes, grab my hat, and kind of hoist myself out of the car. I turn to tell him he'd be lucky to date me, but he shuts the door in my face. I don't even have time to say, "Thank you for making sure I got home safe and sound," before he speeds off toward the entrance like he can't get away from me fast enough. "You have issues," I yell after him.

He doesn't seem to be alone in his desire to get rid of me. That night during dinner, the parents don't mention seeing Oliver. Instead, Claire teaches me the "language of cutlery." At first I think she's joking, but she says that where I place my knife and fork has meaning and signals things like when I'm taking a pause, ready for the next course, or finished. I'd noticed the strange way they placed their cutlery the first night we had dinner in the conservatory. I had no idea it was a "language."

I'm a little buzzed from the wine, which makes me think this is even more stupid than it probably is. "Are you pullin' my leg?"

"Of course not. You never want to thoughtlessly insult the hostess with the wrong message." Claire looks across the table at me. "If you break the rules of etiquette, you risk not being invited back."

"What if I thoughtlessly break wind?"

She lifts her chardonnay to her lips, and her gaze gets kind of squinty as she looks at me over the top of her glass. "Don't."

I wonder if she means don't thoughtlessly break wind or don't try her patience. I suspect both.

Perhaps feeling an impending emotional outburst from me or Claire, Marvin joins boot camp. "Generally, people are polite and don't mention such things."

I'm bored and tired of boot camp, and I *am* purposely trying

Claire's patience. I don't want to do that. I know she's trying to help in her own way, but I need a break from all her rules. "I think it's time for me to move to the penthouse," I say, floating the trial balloon. They both look at me, shocked. I expect them to argue and tell me I'm not ready to live on my own, but they don't.

I suspect that walking on eggshells and watching out for emotional outbursts has taken its toll, and three days later I'm living thirty-one floors above downtown Detroit. I had to talk to Doc Barb first, and she said as long as I keep my appointments and check-ins, and with my parents living about twenty minutes away, I should be fine. I never imagined a few days ago that moving out would be so easy. My clothes are here, Magnus is hiding from me in one of the three bedrooms or the home gym upstairs. The kitchen is stocked with stuff like pastries, bumpy cake, and Vernors ginger ale.

That's the good thing about having an assistant. Mimi arranged for everything and made the move easy. The bad thing is that she thinks Ro-Tel is the same as Del Monte, and she tells me a party store is where you buy booze. She says it's like a convenience store but sells hard liquor and kegs of beer. I think it's safe to say that outside Michigan, folks think a party store is somewhere you get crepe paper and balloons.

Life at the Westin Book Cadillac hotel is as different from Marfa as night and day. There are four penthouses on top, and three of them take up different corners of the building. From outside they look the same. The roofs resemble those Mayan temples where they used to kill people and throw them down the stairs—or something close to that. They're lit up at night like Broadway and take some getting used to.

Inside, the penthouses are all different. Edie's is ultramodern and the lights turn on as you walk around. Not surprisingly, most everything is light blue or white, with the exception of the neon bar down the hall. The ceiling is thirty-five feet high in some places, and two tall palm trees bookend the enormous windows. Any time of the day or night, the views of the city and river are just crazy.

For the first few days, I keep myself busy arranging the closet that is every bit as enormous and over-the-top as the one at Hawthorne. I fill Edie's walk-in safe with jewelry and change the combination to my old birth date.

I investigate the whole two thousand five hundred square feet, and I know there are still things I haven't discovered. I know Edie was supposed to be an art expert, but some of the paintings are horrible. I'm thinking about replacing them with painted skulls.

The night of my first cocktail party, when Claire will see if I pass or fail her etiquette classes, Mimi stops by to help me choose a dress. I suspect that maybe Claire has sent her to make sure I don't embarrass the family in something socially unacceptable like the shiny rubber minidress and studded collar I found in Magnus's bedroom closet. There's a matching studded doggie collar and a little leather jacket, too. I'm not one to judge, but I wonder if this is a Halloween getup or fetish attire. I'd ask Magnus, but he's not talking to me.

"That's from Zac's collection last year. You wore it to the Save the Whales event," Mimi tells me when I try on a deep blue cashmere dress with long sleeves that fits me like I'm sewn into it.

"Did I only wear it once?"

She hands me something sleeveless with a sassy full skirt. "Everyone's seen it."

They've probably seen the sparkly Cinderella pumps I plan to wear, too, but I don't care. I pick out dangly sapphires that shine in my hair and an elephant-shaped clutch covered in deep blue jewels that hangs from a gold chain.

Claire sends over three women to style my hair and do my makeup. Now I'm convinced she's worried that I'll show up in blue eye shadow and a Dolly Parton wig. When they finish, my makeup is subdued and fresh looking. I like it, but my hair is flat. After they leave, I add curl and bounce and a bit of volume on top, and before I stick my phone in my sparkly clutch, I hold my breath and call my momma. I hope I don't get sent to voicemail, or that she recognizes my number and connects me with Publishers Clearing House. But it's worse than voicemail or the prize patrol: Daddy answers and threatens to call the FBI.

Now I'm blocked.

"Welcome to UMC El Paso," I tell the teenage boy standing next to an emergency room doctor and watching a tube get shoved down his own throat. His black hair is buzzed short on the sides while the top looks like a hedgehog. He's wearing a long-sleeved Henley, jeans, and one tennis shoe, and if I had to guess, I'd say he was fifteen.

He turns toward me, as shocked and confused as all the other spirits when they first arrive. "Where am I?"

Like I didn't just tell him. I glance at the clock and begin my five thirty squats. I've been working out since I got here, but I haven't lost an inch. "UMC El Paso emergency room." I put my feet shoulders' width apart and blow out a breath as I slowly lower and begin the first five-by-five repetitions. One . . . two . . . three . . . hold . . . two . . . three . . . I suck in air and rise. . . . One . . . two . . . three . . . I'm not giving up. The weight has to start coming off at some point.

"Why am I here, ma'am?"

I take a deep breath and slowly lower myself again . . . two . . . two . . . three . . . hold . . . "You thought it'd be smart to hit a wasp's nest like a piñata." He returns his gaze to the red lumps covering his body. "Not too bright, Ace."

"Am I dead?"

I let out my breath and rise. "Not yet."

"Am I gonna die?"

"Questions of life or death do not fall within my purview. I'm just the apprentice concierge." I pause my workout to point to his face, so swollen he looks like the Elephant Man. *"But if I looked like that, I wouldn't want to stick around."*

"Who are you?"

Three . . . two . . . three . . . . *"Marfa."* I still cringe every time I say her name. *"Apprentice concierge."* I cringe every time I have to announce my job title, too. Not only have I never been anyone's apprentice, but a concierge . . . horrifying . . . two . . . three.

"Are you a ghost?"

"No." I put in a request with Raymundo to have signs placed around the trauma unit that answer the same questions the newbies always ask.

"It's our duty to greet new arrivals and explain their circumstances," he'd said. *"We keep track of all incomin' and outgoin', calm fears and answer questions. Not post impersonal signs."*

. . . four . . . two . . . three . . . hold . . . *"The rules are rules,"* he'd added, not even bothering to mention my idea to Director Ingrid. A few needed changes would improve morale and working conditions around here. Mainly mine. I hate the *"Don't Mess with a Texas Girl"* T-shirt and fat-girl jeans that I'm forced to wear 24/7 . . . four . . . two . . . three . . .

"Poltergeist?"

. . . five . . . two . . . three . . . hold . . . *"No."*

"Then what is—"

"Shh . . ." . . . five . . . two . . . three . . . The kid is interrupting my workout, so I temporarily suspend the remaining four sets of five until I can get back to it. It's not like I'm pressed for time.

"*Are you dead?*"

"*Yes.*" But I don't go into the boring details like Raymundo and Ingrid seem fond of doing. I shake out one chubby leg and then the other.

"*Are my folks here?*"

"*Not yet.*" But I have implemented a few rule changes on my own that make my existence a bit more tolerable. "*Follow me, Ace.*" We walk from the emergency room into an invisible tube that I call the coma pipeline.

Raymundo insists that I remain in the trauma unit, calming fears, until the patient is stabilized, but I prefer to avoid emotional outbursts and inappropriate displays of weeping. It is not in my nature to calm anyone, and I avoid it at all costs.

"*Is your hair blue?*"

"*Unfortunately.*" When I was first thrown into this hell, I'd stalk the surgeons' locker room and slip into the shower with them in an attempt to rinse the blue from my hair. I might be dead and look like a hillbilly, but I have my standards, and most surgeons— especially orthopedic surgeons—take better care of themselves than the hospital's general population.

Ace and I step from the pipeline and into the coma unit. Unfortunately, every time I entered a shower my energy repelled water away from me, charged water particles, and shocked the doctor's wet skin. They got all jumpy and not one part of me got in the least bit damp.

We continue down the hall toward the Limbo Lounge and I begin, "*You're in a coma. From the time of birth, your spirit creates energy to fuel your physical body. When you die, your spirit leaves the earth plane, and without fuel your physical body is returned to earth.*" Blah blah.

"'*Energy is always conserved but cannot be created or destroyed.*'" I stop and turn to him. He looks like he's still in shock. "*The first law of thermodynamics." In shock or not, Ace isn't as stupid as his wasp's nest behavior suggests.*

Raymundo catches my attention as he moves toward us. His mustache is pulled downward at each side of his mouth, which is never a good sign, but I go in with a preemptive smile and some fast talking. "This is our newest guest," I tell him. "Ace was stung by over a hundred wasps and suffered anaphylactic shock. I couldn't leave him standing there, staring at his gruesome condition." I put a hand on my chest. "As an apprentice concierge, a PORC participant trying to earn my wings, I had to ask myself, 'What would Jesus do?'"

He sets his golf club on one shoulder. "You need to be more concerned with, 'What will Raymundo do?' We don't make the rules. We don't bend the rules. You best get hooty right quick before you get sent back to Ingrid for a different assignment. Ingrid doesn't like to look bad to her judicator, and there will be hell to pay if you make her mad."

Ingrid is my ticket out of here. "What kind of hell?"

"I hear Connie at Vista Hills is clamoring for an apprentice. You'd love her. She's as cuddly as a shithouse rat."

"Charming."

He stands up a little straighter and turns to our newest visitor, all business. "Welcome to UMC El Paso, Ace."

"My name is Maynard Motley, sir."

"Ace has a nicer ring. Don't you think, Ace?"

Raymundo turns his angry brown eyes on me. "You don't learn, and I'm glad I ain't you right now." He lowers the head of his club. "If Ingrid loses her temper"—he pauses to shake his head—"she has six ways to Sunday of making you pay."

19
61

I stand in the residents' lobby of the Book Cadillac and a
long maroon car with shiny hubcaps and whitewalls pulls
beside the curb. It looks like something out of an old Hollywood movie, and Donovan gets out and moves to the back passenger door. I step from the relative quiet of the lobby and into
the sounds of downtown Detroit. A rush of cool night air lifts a
curl from the shoulder of my gray wrap coat.

I haven't seen Marv and Claire since I moved, and I give
them a pleasant smile and a polite greeting. "Father, you look
handsome, and you're as beautiful as always, Mother," I say, and
don't trip over the words.

"Thank you, dear. You look lovely."

As Donovan pulls away from the curb, we make small talk
like Claire has taught me, and I ask about the car.

"This is your grandfather's 'thirty-nine Packard limousine. It
was custom-built at the old plant on Grand Boulevard," Marv
tells me. "It's a shame to see what's become of the factory now."

I was in a limo once, but it had runway lights on the ceiling,
a bar for shots, and smelled of mold and last night's party. This

limo is more impressive than Charles's Classic Limousine, better known as the Chuck Bucket.

Donovan drops Marv, Claire, and me off at the historic Hickory's at 7:30 p.m. I'm told it's the perfect time to arrive for a party that starts at seven. The restaurant has closed its doors to the public in order to host this private cocktail party for Chester Chadwick's eightieth birthday. I don't know anything about Chester, other than that he's eighty, but I suspect the party will be filled with people like Old Edie and Harold. Pushing walkers and saying, "What? I can't hear you. Speak up," even as you're shouting in their ears.

Hickory's is exactly what the name implies. Aged wood floors, heavy high-top tables, wainscoting, rich velvet seating, and one of the longest, most elaborate bars I've ever seen.

I'm surprised to see people my age. I take a glass of red wine from a passing tray and hold the shiny clutch in my left hand. My ring and pinky fingers are as numb as always, but my first appointment with the orthopedic surgeon is next week. I'm optimistic he can repair my hand and make the ugly scars just a thin white line that will diminish with time. I hope I can wear short sleeves by the summer.

Marv wanders off as if he's afraid I'll have "emotional outbursts" or "display inappropriate coping mechanisms." He leaves Claire on "social norms" duty and she begins to discreetly point people out to me. "There's Sloane Palmer and her brother Mitch, talking to the Sternbachers next to the hanging fern. Your father is speaking with the Hunts, Tom and Ann."

"Oliver's folks?"

"And Meredith's. They've been our friends and neighbors since you were a baby. Look, Jack and Alda Schwartz are here, and I'm sure their daughter Margot is here somewhere, too. Yes, there she is." Claire points her wineglass toward a cluster of women who look to be my age. They're standing next to a high tabletop filled with cocktail glasses.

"Do they know me?"

Claire gives a slight nod as she takes a sip of wine.

I raise my glass and look at them over the rim. From where I'm standing, they all have the same look about them. Slender, pale socialites with hair that is either pulled back in severe buns or blunt cut with a razor-sharp edge. Minimal makeup, maximum wealth. Most are blonde like me, but no one has the bounce and curl I do. I'm not like them.

I'm from Texas, where a girl wouldn't be caught dead with flat hair. If she didn't come by a pile of hair naturally, you best trust and believe she'd reach for hairpieces and back-comb a glorious creation. Then she'd spray it down with super-hold so it wouldn't move if her dance partner got wild and swung her around the bar.

One by one the socialites notice me from across the room and give little waves. I wonder if they've heard that I fell on my head during a storm on the Amalfi Coast and have amnesia.

"Oh, there are the Digbys. We should avoid them for just a bit longer."

"Why?"

"You were engaged to their son."

"Was that Blake?"

"No, Roland. But I imagine the Ellsworths are here too." She stands on tippy-toe and scans the crowd. "I don't see them."

"How many times was I engaged, for cryin' out loud?"

"Just the two. We don't count the proposals you turned down."

"Of course not." I wonder if Oliver was one of those proposals and that's why he hates me.

"Edie!" I turn as a woman in a red silk capelet dress walks toward me. "You're back."

"Yes."

She leans forward and air-kisses my cheek. "I heard you have amnesia. Poor dear."

"I'm sorry, but I didn't catch your name."

"Sloane. You've done something new to your hair."

After Sloane is Margot. "If there is anything I can do, give me a call."

I think she might actually mean it.

Next is Royce. "I'm so happy to see you," she gushes, pressing her cheek to mine. "Love the accent."

I don't know her or what she means, but I'm going to add her to my list of people who think I'm faking. Right beneath Royce I'm definitely adding Greer, too. "So clever of you to reinvent yourself just when you were getting stale like some of us." She leans back to give a laugh like she's joking, but she's not.

"Bless your heart," I say through a smile.

I do have to say that more than half the socialites seem nice enough. They chat about their charitable work and foundations and tell me they don't like to be called socialites because they have jobs. Mostly in the fashion industry.

I grab a little sandwich from a roaming tray and hang my clutch from the crook of my elbow. I'd like to grab about three more, but Claire takes me to meet the birthday boy. Eighty-year-old Chester doesn't look a day over ninety-five, but everyone keeps telling him how young he looks for his age. I usually have no problem embellishing, but I can't get the lie out, so I just wish him happy birthday.

"Well, at least you're not one of those girls with a skirt so short it might as well be a belt."

I recognize that voice and turn to look into the steely eyes of Old Edie. "No, ma'am." If it wasn't for her hunched shoulders, she'd be my height. If it wasn't for Harold caving in on himself, he might be half her height.

"Hello, sir." He might be old as dirt, but he looks very distinguished in his dark brown suit. "You look quite handsome tonight."

He turns to Old Edie. "What'd she say?"

"You look handsome," she says, loud enough to be heard halfway across the room.

"What?" He puts a hand to his ear.

"She's flirting with you, Harold!"

Now it's my turn to ask, "What?"

"I'm quite taken, young lady."

Old Edie cackles. "Don't let him fool you. He loves women fighting over him."

"Find a man your own age," he adds.

I feel my cheeks burn. I don't think finding a man my own age will be a problem—when I get around to looking. Which I think will be soon. My body might be thirty, but I'm twenty-five and in the prime of my sexuality. "You've come off your spool. Both of you," I say, and head to the bar. I need tequila.

Halfway across the room I spot a familiar face. He's too big and dark to blend with the cookie-cutter Thoroughbreds in this room.

"Edie!"

A woman steps in front of me.

"Everyone's heard about your little accident." She leans in and does the air-kiss. "You poor thing."

My gaze returns to the bar and the back of Oliver's suit jacket. The last time I saw him, he couldn't get away from me fast enough.

"I can't imagine."

"Bless your heart." I step around her and continue toward my target.

I slide between Oliver and another man at the bar. "Miss me?"

He looks at me out of the corner of his eye. "Like a three-day hangover," he says, and his gaze continues down to my backside, which I must say looks amazing in this dress.

"You don't appear all that unhappy to see me."

"You don't know how I appear when I'm unhappy. You have amnesia."

"Margarita," I tell the bartender, and hand over my empty wineglass. "Amnesia doesn't have anythin' to do with my eyesight, and I see you checkin' me out."

"What do you want, Edie?"

I'm young and feeling sexy and he's mighty fine in his navy-blue suit, white shirt, and blue-and-red-striped tie. We don't get a lot of men dressed like this in Marfa. He looks good and smells better, and it's been a long time since I flirted with a man. I set my elephant-shaped clutch on the bar and say, "Take a guess, cowboy."

His green eyes stare into mine with cool detachment. "Like everyone else in your life, you want me to kiss your ass."

"No." I pick up my margarita and take a sip. Feeling sexy is something new to me and I like it. "Unless you're insistin' on it."

"I've never kissed your ass before; why would I insist on it now?"

"Curiosity?"

"I'm not curious." He takes a drink of some sort of brown alcohol over ice and I'm thinking up a real flirty comeback when he looks over his other shoulder and says, "Hello, Sarah. How's your mother?"

"Better. Thank you."

Oliver takes a step back to include a woman in a dark green dress with beaded flowers and little hummingbirds. "You remember Edie."

She sets an empty wineglass on the bar. "Yes." She doesn't air-kiss my cheek and she isn't smiling. Like Oliver, she isn't a cookie cutter like the rest of us. She's full-figured.

"Edie, this is Sarah Worthington."

"Hello." Her dress sparkles in the light, and the good Lord knows I love sparkles. "Are you related to Chester?"

"Yes." She looks up at Oliver and they share a smile when she says, "That's what Mother tells me."

"Is he your grandfather?"

"Chester is my father." Her smile falls and she returns her attention to me. "I'm sure your parents are glad to have you back."

"Oh, the jury's still out on that." I take a drink, and by her scowl, I doubt we were friends.

"Your socialite crowd must be thrilled."

I shrug and set my glass on the bar. "They don't want to be called socialites. They said they prefer purse or athletic-wear designers."

That gets a hoot of laughter out of Oliver and a smile out of Sarah. I only wish I knew what amused them.

"I like your dress, Sarah. The little hummin'birds are real cute."

Her smile flatlines. "I'm not falling for it, Edie."

"What?"

"You've never been nice to me unless you want something."

I'm right. We were never friends. Edie was probably evil to her because she's a full-size girl. I flash back on my childhood and—she's Tubby Toast. Sarah was Edie's Tubby Toast! That makes me— I gasp. I'm Dingleberry. "I don't remember the past, but I must have hurt you. I apologize."

"Right." She shakes her head. "Good night, Oliver," she says, and walks away.

I guess I didn't expect her to accept my apology, but it would have been nice. I return my attention to Oliver, and he is looking at me like I have horns growing out of my head. "What?"

He doesn't answer and signals for his check.

"Are you runnin' away from me again?"

"I'm not running. I'm leaving."

I don't know why I'm bothering with him. There are plenty of good-looking men in the room, and Harold is more talkative. "What are you afraid of?" I take a sip of my drink and catch a man staring at me from a high table across the room. His gaze is so intense I turn away.

"Flying pigs. Hell freezing over."

"You're such a drama queen."

Oliver lifts a brow. "That's rich."

I can't help but look out of the corner of my eye at the man who's still staring. Even when I turn to face the bar, I can feel his eyes on the back of my head. "There's a man across the room starin' a hole through me," I tell Oliver.

He glances over his shoulder. "Who?"

"He has a red tie and he's standin' next to a woman in a shiny silver dress."

After a few moments Oliver says, "That's Troy Wickerson and his wife, Janette."

"I don't like the way he looks at me."

Oliver returns his attention to the bar and signs his tab. "Wicky's not a bad guy."

My stomach gets tight. "Did you say Wicky?"

"Yeah. Troy Wickerson. He graduated from Yale the year before your brother and me." He puts down the pen and picks up his copy of the bill. "As you put it the other night, 'It's been a hoot and a half.'"

Edie's married lover is standing next to *his* wife and picturing *me* naked. I hate him. I hate him for the way he's looking at me, and I feel sick and panicky, pinned by Wicky's eyes. Oliver starts to turn away and I grab the sleeve of his jacket. "Don't leave me here." And I hate him for the way he treated Edie the last night of her life.

Oliver puts a finger beneath my chin and lifts my gaze to his. "What's wrong with you?"

Wicky's "you make me hard" texts race through my head. He hadn't killed her, but he'd pushed her to the edge. I suck in a breath like I'm coming up for oxygen. "I have to go." I uncurl my fingers from his sleeve. "Where's my coat?" I step around Oliver and take off toward the entrance. I swear Wicky's stare follows me, and a shudder runs up my spine.

My private cell phone and coat-check ticket are in my clutch. I stop. I don't have it. I left it on the bar. I don't want to go back in there, but I can't leave.

"Lose something?"

I look up at Oliver moving toward me, holding my sparkly elephant clutch. "Thank you." My hands shake as I take it from him. "Somebody should punch his face." If he hadn't driven Edie to the edge, maybe she'd still be here and I'd be in heaven.

"What's going on, Edie?" He grabs my wrist.

"I'm leavin'." I pull away hard and open the little purse. "I'm not stayin' here. He makes me sick."

"What the fuck did you do?" My sleeve is pushed up and he's staring at my bare wrist.

"None of your business." I push the sleeve down to cover the ugly scar. "You don't like me, remember?" I get my ticket and move to the men standing at the entrance. "We'll get that right to you," one of them says, and walks a short distance to a locked door.

Oliver joins me and asks, "What are your plans?"

"Call a cab." I pull out my phone. "I just moved to the Book Cadillac. Maybe I'm close enough to walk."

"Not in those shoes."

"I'll get an Uber."

He takes my shoulders and makes me look at him. "I'll bring my car around for you."

"That's real sweet and all, but I don't want to drive your car."

"That's good, because I wasn't offering. I'll take you to the Book."

"You?"

"Marvin and Clarice need to be told."

Yeah, that would be the right thing to do. "I'm not goin' back in there." I pull out my phone. "I'll text."

He swears under his breath, then says, "I'll find them and slip out the back." He pulls out his phone and asks for my number so he can text me when he's out front. I give it to him, and he raises his face to the ceiling. "God, you've always been more trouble than you're worth. I can't believe I volunteered for this." He returns his gaze to mine. "Give me ten minutes."

20

"I'm starvin'." I toss my coat and clutch on a white velvet lounge chair.

"You must be feeling better."

"I am." Once I got in Oliver's car and he shut the gull-wing door behind me, I stopped shaking. The closer we got to the penthouse, the easier I could breathe. Stepping through the front door, I'm safe.

"Are you hungry?"

"No." Oliver takes in the open floor plan and the stairs leading to the bedrooms and asks, "How long have you lived here?"

"I don't know." I step out of my shoes. "Ahhh . . ." I sigh as the floor tiles warm my toes. The good thing about living above a hotel is room service. The bad thing is . . . I'll have to think on it.

I pick up the phone and order roast chicken and Caesar salad. It's kind of like living at Hawthorne, only smaller and with fewer bathrooms.

Oliver moves to the windows, and I call out to him across the kitchen and living room, "Are you sure you don't want anything?" Lately, I've been craving roasted chicken and Caesar salad for no apparent reason. Back home chicken is fried, and there are generally three kinds of salad: cowboy, potato, and baked bean.

"I won't be here that long," he answers without turning from the view.

Once I finish ordering dinner, I join him. Tonight is the second time Oliver has rescued me. First when I got lost jogging and now when I raced from the cocktail party. I'm grateful. He's too rude to be my knight in shining armor, too stubborn to be a saint, but he makes me feel like I can count on him. "It's a great view," I say, and he makes a sound of agreement. "The palm trees are a pain in the backside, though. The arborists said they're not getting enough direct light, like I control the sun." I shrug. "There are special lights in the ceiling that are supposed to kick on, but I was gone and the timers got turned off." I like him. Despite what he says, he must like me, too. He followed me into the penthouse without being asked, but he hasn't said much. If he doesn't want to talk, why'd he come inside? "I know you promised Marv and Claire that you'd make sure I got home all right, like I can't ride a dang elevator by myself, but why are you still here?"

"Curiosity is clouding my better judgment."

"Havin' second thoughts about kissin' my behind?"

"I've never thought of kissing your ass a first time, let alone a second." He turns to face me, framed by a checkerboard of brightly lit windows next to patches of black frames. The glow of Detroit skyscrapers seems to reach up and touch the stars, while the Broadway lights just outside make Oliver Hunt look like he's a leading man at a movie premiere. "I'm curious why you ran out of the Hickory's like your tail was on fire."

"It was just time to go."

He shakes his head. "Try again."

"I don't want to talk about it." Or even think about it.

"Why?"

"Oh, now you want to get all chatty when you acted like talkin' gave you pains before."

"Like putting socks on a duck?"

"Close. Rooster." I do give him points for trying and, let's face it, for being so handsome.

He brushes his suit jacket aside and shoves a hand in the pocket of his trousers. "Why do you want to punch Troy Wickerson in the face?"

"Why do you care?"

"Why don't you want to answer?"

"Are you a CIA interrogator?"

"No."

"Lawyer?"

"In my past life."

In my past life I was a cosmetologist. "What are you now?"

"I invest in real estate. What's the problem with Troy?"

"You're like a tick." I give in and answer his question with one of my own. "Did you see the way he was lookin' at me?"

He nods. "I saw him."

I fold my arms beneath my breasts and look down at my toes and Tutu Pink nail polish. "Your friend is a really bad person."

"How do you know that?"

"I just do."

"Not if you can't remember him."

I look up. "Oh, I get it now. You think you can trip me up and prove to yourself and everyone else that I'm lyin' about amnesia." The doorbell rings and I say over my shoulder as I walk away, "You might think you're smarter than me, but you can't mess me up with 'gotcha' questions. It won't work." Right before I answer the door, I yell across at him, "Not even if you are a member of Mensa." I let in the same waiter who's brought me dinner the past several nights.

"Hello, Tony." He's carrying the same tray and wearing the same spotless tuxedo.

"Hello, Miss Chatsworth-Jones. How are you this evening?"

"Dandy, thank you, sir. How are you?"

"I'm just fine, thank you. Will you be eating in the kitchen or dining room?"

"Kitchen." I put a hand to my throat and gasp. "Is that a Dr Pepper?"

"Coke isn't on your order, but I know how you like your Dr Pepper at night."

"You're a man after my own heart." I pat the sides of my dress like I have pockets, then remember my clutch on the couch. "Not everyone knows that Coke means Dr Pepper." I don't have to sign a bill or anything, but I like to tip him anyway. I grab the little purse and give him a twenty, toss the clutch on the kitchen island and tell Tony good night. The island is stainless steel and some sort of white-and-gray stone, and the stools are clear like glass and more comfortable than they look, but cold. "If you change your mind, you can have some of my chicken," I tell Oliver as I pour my Dr Pepper.

He shakes his head. "I'll take some water, though."

I point my fork at the refrigerator and turn my attention to my salad. I don't think I ever had Caesar salad before the accident. Don't know why, just one of life's mysteries. Like the pyramids and fish falling from the sky.

I can feel Oliver's green eyes on me and look up as he un-screws the silver top of the glass bottle. He takes a drink, then sucks a drop of water from his bottom lip. "When did you cut your wrists?"

"I don't know." Which is technically true, though I can guess. "And before you ask, I don't know why, either. And even if I did, it's not your business."

"True, but I'm asking anyway." I ignore him and eat my salad. He finally gets the hint and says, "Meredith said you fell and hit your head somewhere in Italy."

"Amalfi Coast, so I'm told."

"That's the story, at any rate."

I look at him. "Are you callin' my parents liars?"

He folds his arms across his broad chest and shoves a hip into the stone island. "Why did you run when you saw Troy?"

He's not going to let it go, and I give in because he rescued me from Wicky. I'm appreciative, and I figure he deserves an explanation. "Fine, he's a coward," I say between bites. "He's a liar. He cheats on his wife." I raise my fork with a piece of chicken on it. "If you're so curious, you go ask him, but I doubt he'll tell you." I eat my chicken, then add, "While you're there, I'll pay you to open a can of whup-ass on him."

"I'd have to know why I need to open 'whup-ass.'"

Because he should pay for what he did to Edie. "Fine." I grab my clutch and pull out my phone. "I found this the other day in a purse." I pull up the old texts and hand it to him. "Start at the top."

I watch him raise one brow and then the other and then they smash together in the middle. I suspect that's the part about Meredith. "For the record, I like your sister. She and Georgie and Rowan came to visit me just yesterday. She gave me a nice flower arrangement and I gave her Magnus for the week. I think she got the short end of that deal." He looks at the phone like he might say something, but I head him off at the pass. "I don't want to talk about him. I don't want to think about him. When I do, I feel sick thinkin' that he touched me." I take a breath and continue. "I don't remember anything about tryin' to kill myself, but I suspect it had somethin' to do with callin' off my weddin' at the last minute and Wicky bein' an asshat."

He nods and sets the phone down. "If you feel that way, why haven't you deleted the text?"

"I ask myself that same question. Half the time I think I should, but the other half thinks his wife should know."

He takes a couple of swigs of water and watches me over the bottle. When he's done, he says, "Troy cheats just to cheat. I'm sure she knows."

I'd never cheat with a married man, and I'd never put up with a cheating man. I'd kick him to the curb like Momma did, and . . . she went on a cruise with her cheating man, my daddy. I know because I stalked Momma and found some pictures she posted online the other day. They were lying on a sandy beach somewhere, umbrella drinks in hand, laughing and smiling, and it's too much for my brain to process.

I pick up my plate and move past Oliver on my way to the sink. "But just because Wicky's wife puts up with it doesn't mean she deserves it." I rinse it off and turn on the quietest garbage disposal I've ever heard in my life. Momma's vibrates the counter and floor. I turn it off and say, "Should I apologize to the wife?"

He shakes his head. "You should stay out of other people's relationships, especially married people."

That sounds as if Edie had affairs with more than one married man. Like Troy Wickerson wasn't the first. If that's the case, I'd rather not know. "I'm assumin' you're not married."

"No, and you should stay as far away from *that* subject as you can."

Really? "We can talk about my life but not yours?"

"That's right." He lifts the water to his lips and drains the bottle. "Friendship works two ways."

"We're not friends." He sets the bottle on the island.

I don't know why he's so stubborn. If he didn't care for me at all, he wouldn't be here, standing in front of me, after he made sure I got home safe and sound—again. "I think we are."

"You also think Coke is Dr Pepper and talk with a Southern twang when you were born in Detroit and graduated from the same college as Hillary Clinton and Pamela Melroy."

Whoa. "Are you insultin' my accent?"

He digs his keys out of his suit pocket and says, "It's like country-and-western music: painful and drawls on forever."

He just insulted my accent *and* my music, and I'm no longer feeling flirty. Now I'm riled. "I might have a drawl, but I'm not dumb."

"You got lost five blocks from your house."

His words hit close to my heart and spread across my chest. I feel as dumb as he believes I am—not for getting lost, but for thinking he cares about me. I'm more hurt than I want to admit to myself, but I don't want to fly off the handle in front of him. "You're right. We aren't friends. Cute only gets you so far." I feel like I used to when I liked a guy, and I thought he felt the same, but he never did. "I'd never be friends with someone like you. You're cruel."

"It's a cruel world, Sunshine."

He looks slightly amused, which only makes me so angry I lose my temper and now I don't care. "Enough of this happy horseshit." I march toward the front entrance and get angrier with each step. "You said we hadn't talked in over ten years, and now I know why," I say over my shoulder. "It's not me. I'm a nice person. It's you."

He walks toward me and looks more amused than before. "Why are you so angry?"

I yank open the door. "Get out of my house."

"I haven't seen you this mad since the *Calypso* swamped your pink dinghy," he says as he moves past me and steps into the hall.

"Oliver." He turns and looks at me with one brow cocked. "You're an asshole!" I slam the door in his face, and yes, it feels good to get the final word.

"Don't forget to lock the door."

I was just about to do that, but I look out the peephole and wait until he's gone to twist the bolt.

I'm steaming as I head upstairs to get ready for bed. Normally, I like to turn on the fireplace and look out the windows at the stars or soak in the big marble tub and steam up the glass and mirrors. I like to contemplate deep thoughts, like where the first Edie ended up after she stole my path, how long I'll be stuck here in Detroit, and why I can't find a decent fish taco.

Tonight isn't normal. Still fuming, I pull my composition notebook from the bedside table and start an Oliver-inspired song on the first clean page.

You said we have an aversion, and knowing what I know, I thought it was me. I tried to start over. Tried to be friends. Now I know what I know, it's you and I'm free.

Cute only gets you so far. Yeah, cute only goes so far. It doesn't make up for a heart as black as tar. We'll never be friends—you have a bitter soul. We'll never be friends—you're a huge asshole.

21

The good news is that the orthopedic surgeon thinks I can get back all feeling in both my hands. Ninety percent movement will return to my left hand and the scars will fade to a thin line that can be removed with lasers. My surgery is scheduled for the day before Thanksgiving, and I'll have to spend only one night in the hospital.

The bad news is that I have to wear a splint for six to eight weeks followed by physical therapy. I'll stick around for a few sessions because I figure I should know all the hand and wrist exercises, but that means I'm stuck here until at least mid-January. I'd wanted to be home for the holidays, in Marfa, carefully hanging Christmas lights on the yucca tree in our front yard.

I've been in Detroit for almost a month, and it's been two weeks since I ran out of the cocktail party. As I learned later, Oliver had made the excuse to my parents that I was suddenly nauseated, which was the truth.

Oliver. That night, he insulted my accent, intelligence, and taste in music, and I still get mad thinking about it. I feel stupid for believing he helped me because we were friends, but that's my fault, not his. I don't know how many times he told me he didn't like me and we weren't friends, but I didn't believe him.

I do now.

I haven't seen Marv and Claire either. I know they're concerned about me so I've invited them to the penthouse for dinner. When I told Claire I'd cook, there'd been a long, silent pause before she said, "Are you sure? We can have dinner in the restaurant downstairs. I hear it's nice."

I chuckle thinking about it now as I set three green wicker place mats at the table that seats twelve. I've never set a fancy table before, but Marv and Claire live in high style, and I want them to see that I remember boot-camp etiquette.

I find a box of tapered beeswax candles in just about every color. My theme is Southwestern, so I fashion two green ones into a saguaro cactus by cutting one into pieces for arms and melting it back together. I want them to see that I am okay. I want them to see *me*. The new and improved Edie.

I have a short centerpiece of sunflowers and daisies and stick the candle in the middle. I'm happy with it, and I carefully place the right utensils in the right places. Just to make sure, I grab my phone and look it up on the internet one more time.

Even when it's just the two of them, I know that Marv and Claire dress for dinner. I dress with my theme in mind, and I find a white jean skirt and red blouse in the closet. From the row of boots, I'm surprised to see a pair of American flag cowgirl boots similar to the ones I have at home in Marfa. I look at the soles and am even more surprised to see they've actually been worn.

By the time the parents arrive, I'm even more nervous than I usually am around them. Marv is wearing a suit jacket and

Claire is in one of her flowy dresses. This one is white and green striped.

"You're wearing your Fourth of July boots," Claire says without a pained expression, which I take as approval. I didn't think I cared until now, and I'm not sure what has changed.

I serve them sangria made with red wine and cherry brandy, sliced peaches, oranges, and blueberries. They look a bit perplexed, but if they were surprised by the sangria, they're downright dumbfounded when we sit down to Frito pie, cowboy salad tossed with Momma's smoky dressing that I serve on a bed of romaine, and hot cornbread with honey butter—which I confess I ordered from the kitchen.

"Marvin, I think it's a casserole."

"The secret to Frito pie is waitin' to put the chips on top of each individual servin'. Some folks just cover the whole pie and stick it in the oven, but I like to hold off and top individual servings. That way the Fritos don't get soggy. Nothin's worse than a soggy corn chip." I take a bite and sigh. "Damn if that isn't a fiesta in your mouth." I swallow and take a drink of sangria, which I admit is heavy on the brandy. "This red chili won an award in a Texas cook-off." It's Daddy's own secret recipe, and he won back-to-back blue ribbons at the Presidio County cook-off in 2010 and 2011. "I read that some folks like beans in their chili, but I left them out. There's pinto and black beans in the salad, and let's face it, too many beans can cause a problem."

"Charming." Claire grabs onto Marv's wrist and picks up her fork. They both take a bite at the same time and I can hear the crunch of Fritos as they chew. They don't choke or gag, so I guess that's a good sign.

I slather my cornbread with honey butter before I remember

that people don't slather anything in this family. I take a bite and sigh. Yummy.

"Is the green candle an abstract piece?" Marv asks.

I look at the flames on the top of the cactus and its two arms. "No. It's a saguaro. It goes with my theme."

"Marv, it's a theme, and Edie made it herself," Claire says, like she's cheering on the slow kid at school.

"The salad is called Cowboy Caviar. I found the recipes on the internet," I lie. I offer more sangria, but Marv says he has to drive, and Claire doesn't want to get too full. They give me a toast while we have coffee and vanilla ice cream from the deli around the corner. Lately, I've been getting out of the house on my own and walking around to fill up my days. I've discovered two nice parks within blocks of the Book Cadillac. Both have fountains and manicured gardens, places to sit and people watch, and cafés. I walk Magnus there and we usually get coffee and a dog treat. He doesn't snarl at me these days, and we've come to a new understanding: we tolerate each other. When he wanders from his bedroom, he still gives me the evil eye, but if I shake his leash, he allows me to snap it on his collar. Magnus and I are quite the pair. He sits on his side of the bench while I sit on mine. He crunches his organic cookie while I drink espresso and watch the world go by without me.

"I need somethin' to do," I say after a pause, because believe it or not, trying on designer clothes and shoes has started to get old. With nothing else to do, I've started to run on the treadmill while watching ships on the Detroit River. Tony told me there's even drug-smuggling submarines out there. I don't believe him but I admire his *bool-sheet*.

"You're helping with the New Year's Eve party," Claire tells me, and turns to Marv. "Edie and I will cohost. We haven't shared hostess honors since she debuted in Paris at Le Bal. Remember her exquisite Giambattista Valli gown?"

"Of course, dear," he says, but I think he's tuned us out. I guess I've found one thing that Marv and I have in common.

As far as I can tell, I have two roles: I'm to make the guests feel welcome with polite chitchat and make sure the hors d'oeuvres are served on time and the booze never runs out.

"You'll need a new cocktail dress. Mimi can help you."

Mimi is more Claire's assistant now and I'm fine with that. "No, Mimi and I don't have the same taste. I'll find somethin' in the closet."

"Oh." She doesn't look as worried as she did before the cocktail party, but she adds, "We can shop together. It'll be fun. I'll have Mimi look at my calendar and find a free day."

A whole day that probably includes some sort of etiquette lesson, like the language of a thoughtful hemline. I'd rather pass on Claire's idea of "fun," but she smiles and it reaches clear to her blue eyes. "Okay. Just let me know. I'm always free. I don't have anything else to do." I give a long-suffering sigh. "That's why I have to find something to do before I go crazy as a sprayed roach." They both look at me with wide eyes and I reassure them, "I didn't mean that literally."

Marv places his ice cream spoon in the position that tells me he's done. "Do you have something in mind?" I shrug because I don't want to say, but he's persistent and adds, "Well, where do you see yourself in five years?"

I guess he'll eventually find out anyway, so I tell him, "I'd like to open a salon and spa like Chantal," I answer, but I don't say where.

They look at me like I said I want to become a bird and fly.

"An LLC?" Marv clasps his hands on the table.

"Yes. I don't want to put my personal assets at risk." I just looked that up the other day.

"The beauty industry?" Claire has a frozen little smile on her face. I don't think she shares my vision.

"Personal-care services fall into NAICS category 8121," I tell Marv.

He seems to take me a bit more seriously and leans forward. "Why a salon and spa?"

"I'm interested in hair and makeup and facials. I believe that if you look good, you feel good about yourself. I gave the girls at Livingston custom hairstyles and they were in high cotton afterward."

When they put on their coats to leave, Marv is still contemplating my dream and asking about a business plan. "Since you've lost your memory, no one expects you to have the same intellectual capabilities as you did before, but we have a number of attorneys who can assist you."

I don't think he means to insult me, so I spare him the torture of my most painful kid joke. "How did the beautician win the race?" I ask as we walk toward the entrance.

Marv gives a heavy sigh. "Not this again."

"By shear willpower," Claire says, quite pleased with herself. "Get it?"

"That's a good one." I'm surprised she's playing along. "But no. She took a shortcut."

Claire chuckles but Marv doesn't even bother with a pity laugh. He's not frowning, though, which I figure is progress. I think we've come a long way since our first meeting in El Paso. They aren't the monsters I once thought, and I'm not as crazy as they thought—or at least I like to believe so.

In the entrance, I thank them and give them each a hug. Marv pats me on the back as if to say, "Okay, we're done for the night." Claire is less stiff, and I think she teared up before she turned away and walked out the door.

All in all, I count my first dinner party as a success. They even toasted the meal, and Claire took part in my lame joke. Marv still acts like I might be prone to emotional outbursts and my jokes give him a migraine, but I think he likes me.

I put tinfoil on the chili and throw it in the refrigerator for tomorrow. The parents didn't finish their Frito pie, but I guess not everyone has as finely tuned a palate for Tex-Mex as I do. I rinse the plates and my company phone rings. I don't recognize the number but I answer anyway. "Hello?"

"I'm out."

"What? Who is this?"

"Katrina. You told me to give you a holler when I got out of Livingston."

I didn't think she would or could, but she did say a person could find anyone if they knew where to look on the internet. I guess she knew where to look. "It's nice to hear from you."

"I know, it's been a while. I'm living in Sterling Heights. Not far from the Golden Butthole," she adds.

I've never heard of Sterling Heights, but I *have* heard of the Golden Butthole. It's actually a big gold ring sculpture somewhere.

"Where are you?" she asks.

"I'm in Detroit."

"Oh, I'm only twenty minutes away. Livingston sucked after you left."

"Livingston sucked *before* I left."

She laughs and tells me about a new girl in the group and her plans to take some classes at Wayne State University next semester. She says she needs to pick up foreign-language and literature credits, and her future plans sound more solid than mine.

Katrina's bubble is a little short of plumb and the wheels might fall off her wagon, but she's my only friend in the world. We make plans to meet for coffee soon.

Two days after dinner with the parents is October thirty-first and Meredith picks me up for Halloween in the Park. It's nice to breathe clean autumn air and get out of the city. It's nice to be with faces I know. Rowan and Magnus are in matching cat costumes, and Georgie's stuffed into a padded dog costume that he's fussing about. I came prepared with eyeliner and lipstick, so I draw cat whiskers on Rowan and give Georgie a pink puppy nose to complete their looks. Meredith and I are wearing witch hats, and we take turns pulling a red wagon filled with blankets, the kids, and a dog in a cat costume.

The slight autumn breeze carries the scent of crushed leaves, cornstalks, and caramel apples. The park is filled with kids in every costume imaginable. My favorite is the boy inside an inflatable T. rex. The big dino head sags to one side, but the kid doesn't seem to notice that he's suffered a blowout as he runs around gathering little pumpkins.

Meredith introduces me to other mothers she knows, and I'm a little reluctant to say more than a polite hello. I don't know if these women knew me before, if they liked me, or if I slept with their husbands.

"Did Marvin and Claire tell you about the dinner I made for them?" I ask Meredith while we watch Rowan run around the patch with Magnus in search of the perfect little pumpkins for herself and Georgie. Her red hair catches fire in the afternoon sun, and her cat ears slide down the back of her head.

"They mentioned it."

"I don't think they liked it."

Meredith adjusts the hat atop her auburn hair and says, "They said it was interesting."

"Which means they didn't like it." Spider-Man and Batman run screaming past us like maniacs on a mission. Super Mario is close on their heels.

"They're trying."

"I know they're tryin'. I'm tryin', too, but I'm never goin' to be the daughter they raised. That has to be devastatin'. I understand, but I don't know what to do."

"Just be yourself."

I look at her cute face and freckles. I swear, she's such a good person. All the time. I try to live as Jesus did, but I'm too quick to anger. "I *am* bein' myself, and that's what horrifies them!"

"Not always."

We catch each other's eyes and start laughing.

"Can we go in the corn now?" Rowan dumps three pumpkins in the wagon, but her mother tells her to take one back for the other children. "Magnus needs one," she argues. Her lips and tongue are red from a cherry sucker she shares with Magnus when her mother isn't watching.

Meredith makes a turnaround motion with her finger, then points to the patch.

"I think Burton is horrified," I say, but to be fair, I can count the number of times we've been in the same room on one hand.

"He'll come around. He's still having a hard time with your memory loss."

And holding fast to his position on my ELAA list. "Do you believe me?"

"I believed you the first night when you were so kind and gentle to Rowan. The old you never would have been able to pull that off."

"Was I horrible?"

Rowan jumps in the wagon, and Meredith being her diplomatic self says, "No. Not horrible."

The wagon takes up too much room in the corn maze, and I volunteer to stay and guard it with Georgie. "We'll get to know each other." I pick him up in his big, padded costume with floppy brown ears. His blue eyes get huge as if he's trying to figure out if I'm okay or if he needs to start bawling. I've never really been around kids, so I don't know what to expect.

This time last year, I was winching myself into a wench costume before Lida and I made the rounds, starting with the Drunken Buzzard's costume contest and ending at Shorty's One Shot's Halloween Booooze Bash.

"Hey, young man." His eyes get even bigger, and I sing so maybe he won't cry. "The stars at night, are big and bright . . . deep in the heart of Texas." I don't cringe anymore when I hear Edie's pitchy singing voice, but I'm not exactly thrilled. Instead of crying, he puts his chubby little hand over my mouth. "Don't judge," I mutter beneath his palm. He gives me a drooling grin and shoves his fingers in my mouth, gets a good grip on my bottom lip, and pulls. "Owwwch!" He laughs like my pain is hysterical, and the more I say "owwwch," the funnier it gets for him.

Last year I was knocking back Fireballs and having a good ol' time. This year, I'm letting a small child rip my face off because it's keeping him happy.

Just as Georgie and I come to an understanding about where he can put his hands, Meredith, Rowan, and Magnus exit the corn maze. No, make that Meredith, Rowan, Magnus, and Oliver. They walk toward Georgie and me, laughing like happy campers, and my day takes a left turn toward unhappy camper. Since I saw him I've written two more songs in Oliver's honor. One is titled "Diablo."

"Uncle Oliver found us." Rowan holds the dog leash in one hand and Oliver's hand with the other.

"Hello, Edie." He's still as handsome as ever, but I am now immune to his green eyes and enviable lashes.

"Oliver," I say like his name leaves a bad taste in my mouth.

"How are you?"

He's being pleasant enough, but I'm not falling for it again. He thinks I'm dumb and my accent is annoying, and so I say just for him, "Happy as a dead pig in sunshine." Folks born and raised in Texas know that means "very happy," but I'm not sure why.

His brows pull together, and I turn to Meredith, who I can tell is trying to make sense of my response. Everyone knows that you can't overthink Texas sayings or you'll get a brain freeze, like if you drink a Slurpee too fast. "If you don't mind, Georgie and I have a date with a baby goat in the pettin' zoo."

"Can I come, Aunt Edie?"

Funny how quick she dumps Oliver for a goat. "If it's all right with your mother."

"Oh. Okay."

"Perhaps you want to leave Magnus with Uncle Oliver. He might act up around other animals."

"Okay." And as quick as that, she shoves the leash at Oliver and takes my hand.

Fortunately, I don't see Oliver for the rest of the day. I know

Meredith picked up on my hostility toward her brother and is dying to ask me what's going on. She gets her chance on the drive to the Book Cadillac.

"I thought you and my brother were on friendlier terms these days."

"I tried to be his friend, but he's ornery as a two-headed snake," I say, apparently not done with my Texas sayings for the day.

"What did he do?" she asks, but she doesn't sound surprised.

"I don't want to speak bad about your brother." Although, I guess I just did. "I know you love him. I'm sure he has good qualities somewhere in his bitter heart."

"Oliver is three years older than I am. He's always looked out for me and we're close. I do love him and he does have some good qualities, but he's stubborn. He can be quite rude, too."

"Tell me about it. He insults me every time I talk to him. I'm too good a person to put up with someone calling me names."

By the time I'm dropped off at my penthouse, I'm exhausted. I still want to have kids but, after today, I definitely want to put that off for a few more years. A pile of paperwork from one of Marv's business attorneys waits for me on the dining room table, but I decide to try to absorb it later.

I take a long hot shower and don't bother to get dressed up after I leave the bathroom. It's 6 p.m. and I pull on a pink-and-white-striped pajama top and matching shorts.

I ate so much junk at Halloween in the Park that I can't think about food. I flop down on the blue couch and reach for the control touch pad similar to the one at Hawthorne. Within moments, the television rises up out of the floor and I'm kicked back, pink velvet slippers propped up on the coffee table, watching old *Housewives* reunions.

Just about the time it appears like Teresa might kick Danielle's butt, the touch pad beeps, and the concierge icon lights up. "Good evening, Ms. Chatsworth-Jones. This is Ryan at the concierge desk. There is a Mr. Oliver Hunt who requests your approval. He says he's a friend of the family. Should I send him up?"

"He's not my friend."

"I can hear you, Edie," Oliver calls out.

"Good!"

"What would you like me to do, Ms. Chatsworth-Jones?"

"I don't have friends like you, Oliver."

"Do you want to have this conversation in the residents' lobby?"

"Go away."

"That's not going to happen."

He thinks he can push me around some more. He's wrong. "Stalker! Stalker alert!"

The connection drops and the icon goes away. The nerve of that guy, just naturally assuming I'll let him come on up so he can push me around and insult me some more. I settle into my spot and try to get cozy again. I can't believe he had the guts to show up out of the blue.

My iPhone rings. I don't recognize the number, but I answer anyway.

"Are you insane! Security just escorted me out of the building."

"Seriously?"

"Do you want to get me arrested?"

"Is that a trick question?"

"The security guys take stalking seriously." I can picture him pacing the street. "You need to tell them that I'm not here to stalk you."

"Why are you here?"

He chuckles without humor. "For some reason my sister is under the impression that I'm mean to you. She's extremely angry and won't cool down until you tell her we're friends."

"I can't imagine Meredith gettin' angry."

"She doesn't have red hair for nothing."

22

"My sister, who is rarely angry with anyone, ordered me out of her house," Oliver says as he tosses the wool jacket he'd been wearing earlier onto the couch. "I'm almost cuffed and taken in for stalking, and you are the common denominator in both events." He's wearing an old green T-shirt tucked into what looks like a pair of even older jeans. "I forgot how vindictive you can be."

"First of all, I only have your word on why Meredith's mad at you. Second, I'm not vindictive." Edie might have been, but I'm done apologizing for her. "I'm just not goin' to let you push me around and call me names."

"I never called you names."

"You made fun of my accent. Insinuated that I'm dumb."

He walks toward me and doesn't bother to deny it. "You called me an asshole."

I fold my arms beneath my breasts and don't bother to deny it either.

"I don't think you're dumb." He raises his hands palms up, then drops them to his sides. "Anymore."

"Well, I still think you're an a-hole." I'm not riled enough to say the real word. "I don't know why you're here, but I don't have all day."

His brows come together over his green eyes. "I'm here because your family and mine have visions of us being in the same room without wanting to kill each other."

I shrug. "It's not my fault. I tried to get along with you, but you're too bitter over something in the past." I walk to the couch and turn off *Housewives*. "You're holdin' on to memories and carryin' a grudge for somethin' that I know nothin' about. I don't share your memories." I toss the control pad onto a shaggy white throw. "I don't have a grudge."

"What do you call yelling 'stalker alert' with security ten feet away from me?"

That's not a grudge. "I call that the consequence of you bein' born in a barn. Everyone knows you don't just show up uninvited or, at the very least, that you call first."

He moves to the refrigerator and pulls out a bottle of water like he owns the place. Like I didn't accuse him of having the manners of a barn animal. He unscrews the top and asks, "What's it going to take?" before raising the bottle.

I walk to the kitchen, push him out of the way, and grab a Jones soda. Water spills down his T-shirt, and I guess I should apologize, but apparently I'm holding a grudge after all. "What's it goin' to take for what?"

"For you to get past it and move on." He wipes water off his chin with the back of his hand.

My jaw drops a little. "Well, don't that beat all with a stick." I pop the top and take a drink of berry lemonade. "Tell me somethin'. Why am I bein' blamed for what happened—what, how long ago?"

"Seventeen years, but it started years before that when I got invited to skipper the *Whirlwind* for the Neptune's Revenge Regatta, and you didn't."

"How old were we?"

"You were thirteen. I was sixteen."

That makes him thirty-three, which makes Meredith my age. "Was I a better skipper?"

"You thought you were."

He looks at me and I motion with my hand for him to keep going. "Don't make me put socks on a rooster."

He gives a slight shrug. "Positions were open to crew from thirteen to eighteen, but you had to weigh at least a hundred pounds and you didn't qualify." He takes a drink, and I watch his Adam's apple as he swallows. "You blamed me for your not leveling up. I probably could have put in a word for you, but I don't know if that would have made a difference and, the truth is, Sunshine, I wasn't about to replace a solid trimmer for a temperamental string bean." He points the bottle in my direction. "You pushed me in the lake and stomped off. We never got along after that."

I don't get why Edie got worked up over a sailboat, but I imagine she's not the only person who's felt an urge to push him in the water. "What's next?"

"Stupid shit that made you mad." He shuts up like he's done talking for the day.

"If you're not goin' to tell me everythin' right now, I'm goin' back to watchin' *Real Housewives*."

He turns to open several high cupboards. "Do you have Maker's Mark around here?"

"That bad, huh? There's a bar down the hall." He follows me through the combined space, down a short hall, and into a room set up for entertaining. "I don't really hang out in here."

Oliver moves behind a stainless-steel-and-epoxy bar with multicolored veins running through it. It's cool to the touch and has a weird glowing pulse that lights one color and then another. It reminds me of an art installation, which is probably why it appealed to Edie. There are some contemporary paintings, too, the kind that look like someone threw buckets of paint on a canvas.

"I'm surprised this room isn't blue and white like the rest of the penthouse." Oliver disappears behind the bar and sets Maker's Mark and two square tumblers on top before popping back up again.

"Me too. I don't really like all the white and blue. It's cold."

"Hire a decorator and get rid of it." He dumps two balls of ice in each glass and fills them a quarter full of whiskey.

No point in redecorating since I'm not going to be here past the first of the year. Maybe mid-January at the latest. "I don't like whiskey." I'll have to come back for appointments with Dr. Barb. I'm not sure how I'll work out the details, but I'll have to be careful. I don't want her to find out I'm back in Texas. The last thing I want is to get tossed back into Livingston because someone thinks I'm returning to finish the job Edie started in El Paso.

Oliver adds a splash of water to one glass before he comes from behind the bar and hands it to me. "If you weren't born in a barn, you'd know that a hostess never lets a guest drink alone."

"Do you remember everything I say?"

"Not everything." He lifts a finger from his tumbler and points to his head. "It's not the size of your storage locker, but your recall." He takes a sip and doesn't grimace.

I take a sip and do. "Like Arnold Schwarzenegger?" Lida and I used to argue over which *Total Recall* was better. She liked the remake, but the original was my favorite.

"No. Not like that." Oliver shakes his head, and glowing blue light filters through his hair.

I lean on the bar and try another sip. Ick. "You were sayin' something about 'stupid shit' that made me mad when I was thirteen. What's next?"

"I really didn't pay much attention to you until the summer you turned eighteen." He swirls whiskey in his glass and watches it wash over the ice balls. "I'd just finished my junior year at Yale and was home on summer break, working behind the bar at the yacht club three nights a week." He pauses to take a drink; then he's back to swirling. "Margaret Rose was serving drinks that summer, and she looked especially fine in her little shorts. We'd dated off and on for about three years. When either of us was away, it was off. When we were both home, it was definitely on. She was smart and pretty and our families thought we'd get married after we graduated."

He takes a drink and I ask him, "Did you love her?"

"Yes." He nods. "I never had to guess with her. I knew she loved me, and it wasn't complicated." He lifts his gaze from his glass. "That summer, you and Margaret Rose got very close. I tried to warn her that you didn't always play well with others, but she said you were like a little sister. I admit, you even had me fooled."

At UMC El Paso, Edie fooled me for a minute, too. I take a sip and control my grimace.

"At the end of July, I was closing the bar by myself and you slipped into the empty clubhouse. You were barely eighteen but walked in like you owned the place. You had on a little white dress and shoes that made your legs look amazingly long. You'd grown when I wasn't paying attention and you'd filled out. . . . You've always been beautiful, Edie.

"I knew I should kick you out, but you smiled and laughed like you used to before the Neptune's Revenge Regatta, so I let you keep me company while I sat at the bar adding receipts." He drains what's left in the glass and says, "Then one thing led to another."

He sets his glass on the bar like he's done talking, but he's left out the whole middle of the story. I feel like I've read the first and last page of a book. "Well? Did we kiss?"

"Yes."

He has my attention now more than ever. "How long?"

"Long enough."

"Five minutes? Ten minutes? Did we have sex?"

"Almost."

I lower my gaze to his mouth. "We must have kissed longer than ten minutes." I'm getting a little flushed just thinking about it. "Did I stop you?"

"Hardly, but before the dew dried on the grass the next morning, you ran to Margaret Rose and said we had sex on the bar." He pours another two fingers of Maker's Mark. "I don't know who you were trying to hurt more, me or her. In the end it didn't matter. You were the only one to walk away happy."

"If you two loved each other, why'd she believe me?"

"She said a guy was more likely to lie about having sex than a girl. And I guess dating other people when we were a thousand miles apart bothered her more than she let on. She said I was a cheater, and nothing I said or did changed her mind."

"Where is she now?"

"She lives in Grosse Pointe Woods with her husband and children."

"Do you still love her?" I take a sip and cough into my free hand.

"No, but it took a while." He shoves the cork into the bottle. "Her family quit speaking to my family. My family believed me, and yours believed you, so they didn't speak for a few years, either. It was quite a scandal. Oliver Hunt takes advantage of eighteen-year-old Edie Randolph Chatsworth-Jones. Yes, *the* Randolph Chatsworth-Jones. I was the villain and you got to be the victim."

I know why Edie tried to fool and manipulate me at the hospital. I can believe what he's saying, but still I ask, "Why would I lie about something like that?"

"Who knows what motivated you to do anything. It took Burton dating my little sister to repair all the damage. Your brother never believed you, and by that time, Marvin and Clarice didn't either."

If all of this is true, it would explain my first meeting with the parents at UMC El Paso. "What happened to make them believe you and not me?"

He shrugs. "I didn't ask, and they didn't volunteer an explanation. I can only speculate that some of your lies caught up to you, and they started to question everything you ever did or said. Their apology to me enraged you."

It seems a lot of the things that enraged Edie don't bother me at all. She was ruthless when she stole my sparkly path, and I'm not shocked that she took things so far with Oliver. I'm not shocked that she wanted to get naked with Oliver, either. When I thought we were friends, I had sin in my heart for him, too. Even now I want to talk about those blank pages, starting with the first time we kiss. I set my glass on the bar. "You skipped over a whole lot of the story. How far did 'one thing led to another' get before you stopped?"

"Why?"

Because I'm curious and getting even more flushed just thinking about it. Lucky for him I'm not the Brittany Lynn Snider who would have jumped on him before he got away, but I still have the same feelings and needs for love and affection. I'm not the Edie who broke hearts and carried on with married men, but I still want to be swept away by somebody special. I want to know what that feels like for the first time in my life. I'm neither Brittany Lynn nor Edie. I'm me. I want to know what it feels like to be *me*. "I don't remember that night. I only have your word on what happened, and you could be embellishin'."

"Why would I do that?"

"So you can blame me."

"I don't blame you for what happened between us that night. Only for what happened after."

I take a sip of whiskey and only choke a little this time. "You're hangin' on to the past."

"That's why I'm here. To put the past to bed." His voice drops a notch. "So to speak."

"As long as you look at me and see somebody else, someone I'm not and don't remember, that can't happen."

"I don't know what I see when I look at you. You're two people in the same body."

"No." I'm one person in a different body. "Think about it like identical twins, and I'm the good one you never met before."

He raises a brow and one corner of his mouth turns up. "How good?"

"Can't say. I haven't had the chance to be bad." I clink my glass to his and flip my hair like I'm wearing my sassy pants. "Not yet."

He chuckles and raises the glass to his lips.

"I'm a born-again virgin."

Now it's his turn to choke. "A what?"

"I don't remember havin' sex, and I don't know if I'm sup-posed to miss it," I lie, and set my glass on the bar. I miss being close to a man. I miss a man's arms around me and his breath in my hair. I miss the anticipation of skin on skin, and the fire-flash when it finally happens. "I don't even know what it's like to kiss."

He clears his throat. "And you want me to show you?"

If I have to drive him in the direction of the chute, I guess we're not going to rodeo. Which is probably for the best, since we're not friends, I have to remind myself. "No, I'll find some-one else to teach me. I'm a fast learner." But I'm still annoyed that he's not interested in my virginal self. "I've watched movies with kissin' and such."

"What's 'and such'?"

The movie *365 Days* on Netflix comes to mind. "Naked stuff."

"You watched porn?"

I'd go to hell for watching porn, but I rock back on my heels and look at him all innocent. "What's porn?" I ask, because I have amnesia.

He opens his mouth, then closes it. His neck looks like he's turning red. "Sex on film."

He's back to giving short answers to things he doesn't want to talk about. "Do you watch porn?"

He sets his glass on the bar next to mine and turns to the doorway. "It's time for me to leave."

And he should know by now that I'd never let him off that easy. "Do you?" I hurry to follow him down the hall, having way too much fun. "Do you watch people have sex?"

He reaches for his coat but I grab a sleeve before he can

put it on. His cheeks are turning red now, too. I can't tell if he's embarrassed or burning up inside with the same feeling burning me up, too.

I laugh. "You said you'd tell me everything."

He tugs on his coat and pulls me into his chest. Suddenly I'm not laughing as I look up into his green eyes. "Not everything," he says, his voice a little raw from whiskey and testosterone. He puts his hands on my shoulders to push me away or pull me closer, but he does neither.

The old me wouldn't be standing here, pressed against a man's hard chest, the heat of his skin warming me up through our clothes. The old me would slide my hand to the back of his head and bring his mouth down to mine. The new me looks up into Oliver's face, his eyes turning a deeper green and his jaw set as he wrestles with what he knows he should do and what he wants to do.

The new me takes a step back. For the first time in my life, I do not give into feelings and desires or the old voice in my head telling me that sex will make him like me. If we'd never met, if I'd never seen his face before tonight, I might go ahead. A one-nighter with a handsome stranger sounds good, and I might just do that sooner rather than later, but not with him. "Are we good now?" I ask. I'm certain that sex with Oliver would not disappoint, but no matter how good the sex was today, it won't make him like me tomorrow or ever. "Are you goin' to wake up in the mornin' still hatin' me and my drawl?"

"I haven't hated you for some time. I've avoided you." He gives me a crooked smile and shoves his arms into the sleeves of his coat. "God knows that if we'd ever been alone in the same room, we would have killed each other."

"What about now?"

"We probably wouldn't end up dead, but it's still not a good idea." He looks down to take his keys from his pocket, then back up at me. "For different reasons this time. I think you know what I mean," he says, and I know exactly what he means. It's in his eyes and the depth of his voice, but just in case it's not clear, he adds, "If we're ever alone in the same room and I shove my hand up your dress like when you were eighteen, it's on you to stop before things go too far."

I don't point out that *I* did just stop before things went too far, or that until tonight, he'd made it clear that he didn't want his hands anywhere near me, let alone up my dress.

I've been demoted to janitorial duty at UMC El Paso. That's Ingrid's "six ways to Sunday" punishment for my bending rule 5.5.10. by bringing Ace to the Limbo Lounge before his prognosis, and for my disregard for Patient Identification Protocol 9.9.5. in the PORC manual. What they call an act of disregard, I call an act of mercy. What Ingrid calls a possible misidentification of incoming souls, I call doing Maynard a solid.

One thing I've learned around here is that logic takes second place to the rules. "You don't have to understand the rules. You have to follow them. Period," is Raymundo's favorite saying.

Another thing I've learned: exercising is pointless, and no matter how often or how many ways I try to change my hair, it remains blue. Now, I have a fondness for blue, but not in my hair. I am the image of Brittany Lynn Snider before her accident, and there's no changing it, and that, in itself, is a special kind of hell.

Now that I've been busted to the rank of janitor, I can't go to the emergency room, introduce new patients, or tell them what to do. My job is to clean up after them, which means put away the playing cards and bingo chips they've left out and fluff pillows in *the Limbo Lounge. I can only talk to the patients if my conversation is uplifting and hopeful. I was raised on polite conversation and fed etiquette at every meal, but souls are selfish and just want to talk about themselves. If I wasn't already dead, I'd die from boredom.*

At the moment, there are only three coma patients at UMC El Paso, but they're not here in the lounge. I don't know where Raymundo is either. I'm by myself and don't know which is worse: being alone or listening to Ruby talk about her ailments. She's eighty-one and the list is long.

It's quiet except for the screams from the aquarium. Lot's wife turns into a pillar of salt as Sodom and Gomorrah burn in the background. I move to the doorway and stick my head out. The hall is empty, and I quickly walk to the big tank. I discovered the hologram has uses beyond projecting 3D Bible scenes when I caught Raymundo watching the CJ Cup at Shadow Creek not too long ago. He says that projecting outside the hospital is how they track the occasional soul who manages to leave the grounds with a family member or chase after boyfriends suspected of cheating. It's never supposed to be used for personal reasons, but when I caught him watching golf in Las Vegas and breaking the rules I blackmailed him into showing me.

"This is only for a concierge to use, and that ain't you," he'd said as he demonstrated how it works. "The tank operates on two electrical frequencies. When it detects high energy from livin' spirits, it projects 3D holographic imagery. You and me are different. The tank recognizes our lower frequency and engages Omni Sight, a real-time view of anywhere on the planet."

I check behind me one last time and pass my hand over the top of the tank. Sodom and Gomorrah change into an image of the earth. It shows the date, October thirty-first. Halloween. Last year

I dressed up as a dominatrix and Magnus as a dom for Sloane's party at a bar in Bricktown.

"Find Edie Chatsworth-Jones." It doesn't move, but I know it's voice-activated. I frown and bite my lip. I try, "Brittany Lynn Snider," and just like that the image opens at a park. Little kids are running around in costumes, and I see myself holding a baby dressed as a dog. I don't recognize the child, but Meredith is beside me with Rowan and Magnus—both dressed as cats! Magnus hates cats and kids.

Brittany, the impostor, has curled and teased my hair like a Texas rodeo queen. If I didn't know better, I'd think she was wearing a Halloween wig. She's making me a laughingstock and ruining my reputation with the people who count. My friends must be horrified. My parents must be confused and horrified, but not surprised.

At different times in my life, I've been the cause of their horror and confusion—and pain. Sometimes on purpose for the way they treated me. Sometimes indirectly for the way I treated others. That last night at the Plaza in El Paso was the latter, but no less painful for them, I'm sure.

My parents weren't perfect. They sent me to an exclusive boarding school at the age of nine, despite the fact that I begged not to go. I felt as if I was ripped away like Velcro, and I soon learned that life wasn't about what I wanted; it was about what was best. Best manners, best appearance, best people, and best causes. Although I hated it at the time, my parents were right to send me off to Connecticut. I was a needy child who would have become a needy woman—God forbid. I know my parents are as loving as they know how to be. They don't say it often, but they love me as much as I love them.

My parents raised me as their parents had raised them, with the expectation that an excellent education would lead to an excellent job. An excellent place in society would lead to an excellent fiancé, and it did. Two of them.

Both Roland and Blake come from the same social background, old family money and excellent breeding. They're both handsome, and I was attracted to their drive. We suited each other, but I never should have accepted their marriage proposals. Each time I said yes, I was in love and excited about the future. Each time, I loved picking out wedding dresses and over-the-top venues. Each time, I got carried away with planning the society wedding of the year—but when it came to walking down the aisle, I had the same realization each time: I never want to be a wife. Wives are needy and, believe me, I should know. All my married lovers had one thing in common, a needy wife.

Dr. Barbara Ware told me that I have attachment issues and have self-sabotaged my relationships, whether it be an inappropriate relationship with a man I met at work or a secret affair. That was certainly the case with Troy Wickerson. He'd just moved back to Detroit and I was facing an impending wedding. He was new and exciting and I had to have him. He fell in love with me and planned to leave Janette. I fell in love with him and canceled my wedding. I was high on love—until that night at the Plaza in El Paso when my world caved in on me again. I was taken back to my first engagement to Roland Digby and the affair with Porter Reese, Sarah Worthington's husband. Sarah was fat and Porter was a Cabanel painting come to life. A dark, broody fallen angel. The affair was wild and consuming. I wanted him forever, right up to the moment people found out and it turned dirty. The tawdry details almost ruined me and my family. I was excoriated in public and in private, and the humiliation in my parents' eyes as they tried to hold their heads high was pure agony.

I tried to kill myself in the guest cottage at Hawthorne to escape the pain, but my parents found me. It was covered up, and I left the country until the gossip turned to something else and the scandal became old news.

This latest affair with Troy, I knew there would be no escaping the scandal this time. I broke off my engagement to one of the most eligible men in the world for another seedy affair with a married man. I couldn't live through that again. My heart was broken and the pain ran so deep in my veins, I tried to carve it out with a razor blade. If I had to do it over again, there's one thing I'd do different. I'd hang a DO NOT DISTURB *sign on the hotel door. If I'd succeeded, I'd be in heaven, and Brittany Lynn Snider wouldn't be wearing my clothes, ruining my hair, and dressing my dog like a cat.*

I watch the baby in my impostor's arms shove its hand in her mouth, and I almost gag. I hate baby drool and I look for Magnus. He's on his leash and . . . speaking of a dark angel fallen from paradise, Oliver is with them. It's been a while since I've seen his smile.

Oliver was my first crush. I was eight years old, and he'd complimented my felt antlers at his family's Christmas party. That's all it took, and I spent years trying to get his attention, but he never noticed me until the night I walked into the yacht club where he worked that summer I turned eighteen. I wore a short sundress and four-inch heels, and it finally worked. I laid myself on the bar like a dessert tray, offering him whatever he wanted. He sampled a bit here and there, but he wasn't interested in more. He was interested in someone else. I was in love with him, but he was in love with his girlfriend.

I lashed out and told a lie. I never imagined the lie would get so big that there was no going back to the truth. I never thought my family would start to doubt me, but they did. I blamed Oliver and Burton and I still do. I hate them for the questions my parents had in their eyes after that.

If not for me, Oliver would have married his girlfriend. I don't remember her name, but I saw her with a bunch of kids in Trader Joe's recently. She was wearing a Pittsburgh sweatshirt in Red Wings territory. That's like wearing Gaga's meat dress to a dogfight: both are ghastly and a health hazard. She looked like a pudgy soccer mom, and Oliver should thank me.

I look closer at the little gathering in Grosse Pointe Park. Shockingly, Oliver is speaking to my impostor. He's smiling, but she is not. I'm sure he's being his rude self, because she doesn't look happy. Good, maybe she isn't as dumb as she sounds.

I think I hear footsteps and wave my hand over the aquarium before I'm caught and demoted to . . . what? I don't know nor do I want to find out. The image fades as my impostor walks away and the hologram returns to Lot's wife.

Raymundo walks into the lounge with a teenage girl and I can feel her attitude halfway across the room. He thumps his golf club on the floor like usual and says as if there's anyone else in the room, "Can I have all y'all's attention? This is our newest guest, Hannah."

Her attitude isn't the worst thing about her. Her short green hair has been shaved bald down the middle and pulled into pigtails, making her look like a demented clown. She's wearing a Ramones T-shirt, black pants, and a nose ring. Her skinny arms are crossed over her chest, and she's frowning about something. I don't know why anyone would purposely make themselves look like a mental patient, but at least she doesn't have fifty piercings in her face.

I move toward the wannabe rebel and her angry gaze meets mine. Great. I smile and remind myself that I'm an uplifting and hopeful janitor. "Welcome, Hannah."

"My name isn't Hannah. I self-identify as Jello. My pronouns are ze/zir," she says, like changing her patient name is an option around here.

Raymundo shifts his weight to one hip and shakes his head. "You can identify as a baboon's red ass, but around here, you're Hannah."

"Charming."

She unfolds her arms and looks me up and down. "Nice sparkles," *she says in that special way reserved for snooty teenagers.*

I laugh like I mean it and look down at my shirt. "Thank you."

"I didn't know they sold five-X at GapKids."

No one has ever mentioned my weight, and I raise my gaze to Raymundo. "If I wasn't a janitor, I'd identify her as 'Clown Show.'"

Raymundo smiles and says, "I'm promotin' you to apprentice concierge again."

"What? You can promote me? Is that in the PORC guidebook?"

"Concierge Powers: 1.1.1.12." *He grins like the devil.* "This young lady is all yours. Congratulations."

I watch him walk away and raise a fist in the air. Yes! I'm back and I don't have to be nice and uplifting all the time anymore.

"Is a pork handbook like rules for fatties?"

Nor have I ever been called a fatty. I turn to her and say, "You don't want to mess with me, kid. I'll cut you to the bone with a smile." *I gesture to the room and am going to forget she said the f-word, because I'm trying to work my way to heaven one good deed at a time.* "This is the Limbo Lounge. Comatose patients come here to relax and socialize with others."

"I'm not socializin' with you fat people."

This has got to be a test. God knows my weight is a sore subject right now. "Television programming is provided by Paradise Inc. The drop-down menu shows dates and times for each listing."

"Did you hear me or are you slow?"

I'll work on a good deed later. "Did someone accidentally run over your head with a lawn mower, or did you eat one too many Tide Pods?"

Hannah smiles with one side of her mouth and gives a slight nod as if acknowledging a worthy opponent.

She's rude and exploits weakness. We're going to get along just fine, and I return her nod. I'd rather trade insults with Hannah all day than listen to the details of Ruby's cataract surgery.

23

November starts off with a double dose of crazy.

It gets crazy cold, and I learn the hard way about windchill when I grab my trench coat and take Magnus for a walk in the park. I start to shake standing in line to get Magnus his snack. People around me are wearing light jackets and acting like freezing wind gusts are normal.

It gets crazy weird when I have cappuccino and crepes with Katrina at a café within walking distance of the Book Cadillac.

She looks good and healthy and her hazel eyes look clear, but then she starts talking about *The Time Traveler's Wife*. I never read the book or watched the movie, but about five minutes in, I figure I don't need to now. She goes on and on about a guy name Henry traveling through time and turning up naked, and I tune her out for my own sanity and think about someone more interesting, like Oliver. I haven't seen or heard from him since Halloween. I'm not surprised since it's only been a few days, but I've been thinking about him. I've been thinking about his and Edie's past and wondering if he's let it go. I've been thinking a lot about the look in his eyes when I was pressed against his chest. I'm proud of myself for taking a step back instead of going horizontal, but there's still that old part me of that thinks I blew it and he'll never like me now.

"The book reminds me of you."

I look up from my crepe. I don't know what the heck Katrina is talking about. I have a feeling I don't want to know, either.

"I come from a family of mystics and clairvoyants. I'm not as gifted as my mom and gramma, but I see a person's aura and read energy." She shrugs as if what she said is perfectly normal. "You're metaphysical."

I don't know what in tarnation that means, so I use some of the polite manners I learned in boot camp to say, "That's fascinatin'," and change the subject. Later, I look it up, and I gather it means a reality that exists beyond understanding. Like my life.

I really don't think Katrina knows anything about my reality. I think she's confused and trying to make sense of my amnesia, and I add her to the ELAA list under Jury's Still Out.

Not that the list is going to matter after January. My plans to return home have been delayed, not forgotten. I hadn't tried to call Momma since Daddy blocked me on her phone. I decided to give it a few weeks before I changed my phone number and tried again. This time I had a plan. I play on my momma's love of God and gab, and I tell her I'm Tara Sue from Dalhart, the daughter of her third cousin, twice removed. She says she doesn't recall a third cousin twice removed from Dalhart, but I have so many details about our family, it doesn't take much to convince her.

"I'm a good Christian woman," I tell her. "Reachin' out to kin in turbulent times."

She quotes Bible verses that I've heard a thousand times before, but it's so good to hear her voice, I just listen. "The

Bible tells us to prepare for the great turmoil and such. I pray you're ready for the rapture, Tara Sue. I'd sure hate to see you left behind."

"Praise the Lord and his mercy," I say as I lie on my bed and stare up at the swirly patterns on the ceiling. I swear Momma never tires of the rapture. Since she and Daddy are vacationing together these days—which is still disturbing—I wonder who she is going to wave at when she floats away on her cloud. I guess there's still Floozy Face.

"It was the most romantic thing that's ever happened to me," she says. "He even got down on one knee."

"What?" I sit up. "Who?"

"Pudge. We was at Caesar's Palace, pluggin' money in the Lucky Seven slots for about an hour, when he looks at me and says . . ." She pauses for dramatic effect. "He says, 'Carla Jean, we should have Elvis marry us right here and now.' I about died right there on that ugly carpet. All a sudden I hit it big at Lucky Seven and the lights were flashin', there was such a ruckus. I took it as a sign, and I agreed on the spot. I know winnin' that hundred dollars was my sweet Brittany Lynn's way of givin' her approval from heaven."

What? No, it wasn't.

"I know she's happy that me and her daddy are back together. Sometimes I feel her spirit sittin' right next to me in church. She loved singin' for Jesus, and Johnny J. says he can hear her voice in heaven's holy choir."

I open my mouth, but I have no words. She and Daddy are married? By an Elvis impersonator? Johnny J. hears my voice in "heaven's holy choir"?

I'm as shocked as a mosquito in a bug zapper. My brain goes blank and I sit on the edge of my bed and stare at the wall.

Maybe I need to wait a while before Tara Sue from Dalhart makes another call.

I'm still in shock but trying not to think about it a week later when I have tea with Claire. She has me fill out a style questionnaire and says our "stylist," Arianna (no last name), needs to learn my fashion preferences that reflect my new personal style. That's great and all, but I don't have a personal style. Before the accident, my biggest concern was finding the right size. If I had to guess, I'd say tight and sparkly. These days my style is whatever is in the closet.

Claire has decided we're now calling the New Year's Eve party we're cohosting "New Beginnings." She worries that some people might dismiss our theme as unimaginative, as if "Golden Years" was so much more creative.

"To this family, it means optimism." She gets a tear in her eye as we study photos of decorations and swaths of linen. She turns her head as if crying is a bad thing, and I put an arm around her shoulders. "It's perfect, Momma," I say, and I don't know who's more shocked. "I mean Mother."

"When you were a baby, you called me MomMom and then just Mom, but I've become quite used to Claire."

"What about Marv?"

"Best not." She shakes her head. "My dear father used to call him Marv and they detested each other. He prefers Father, or Papa."

Stiff, all-business, no-nonsense Marvin never mentioned that he'd prefer that I not call him Marv. I feel bad and resolve to work on it. But I guess I don't feel so bad that I resolve to stop telling stupid jokes. I think he secretly loves it when I do, especially corny riddles.

The day of my wrist surgery, I open my eyes and see him and

Claire standing at the end of my hospital bed. I'm groggy and whisper, "Déjà vu," and for the first time, I hear him chuckle. I like the sound of it and ask, "What did the buffalo say when his son left?"

"Close the gate," Claire answers.

"Good try." I shake my head. "Do you know the answer, Marv?" Then I remember he doesn't like being called that. "Sorry I called you Marv. Should I call you Father or Papa?"

"I won't know you're talking to me if you don't call me Marv." Then he says without cracking a smile, "Bison. The buffalo said, 'Bison.'"

The next afternoon Donovan drives me to Hawthorne and helps me from the car and into the house. It's Thanksgiving and the whole family is there. Old Edie wants to know what happened to my arms and why my hair isn't brushed. Claire and Marv are as formal as always, and it's actually Burton who is the first to ask how I'm feeling.

My left forearm and hand are bandaged and held in a metal splint. The right is wrapped with gauze and tape; both hurt like heck. "Like a robot," I say, and hold my arms straight out in front. Rowan is the only one who laughs, and I think maybe the pain pills might be to blame for how funny we think I am. When the medication wears off, nothing is funny and the pain is worse than when I woke up in El Paso. By the time I leave Hawthorne two days later, I can manage with my right hand and wrist. The hardest part is wrapping my arms in cellophane to take a shower.

Magnus doesn't seem to care about my pain or limitations; he still needs a bush and a dog treat. I've learned my lesson about winter survival, and carefully dress in a wool coat, furry boots, a hat, and a scarf. The hardest part is getting Magnus into his blue parka. As we leave the Book Cadillac, I catch my reflection in the glass doors and sigh. There's no way to look cute in a blizzard. I know people around here say there can't be a blizzard without snow, but the wind seeping into my bones feels like a blizzard to me.

It's a Sunday and the park is filled with people and dogs. Magnus picks his favorite bush, and I watch skaters in a rink set up in the middle. Lots of kids and laughter, and I wonder if Edie ever stood in this same place, watching people in the same rink. I wonder what she thought of it all. I wonder if, like me, she saw families and wanted that for herself someday.

"If it wasn't for your dog, I wouldn't have recognized you."

I don't have to look across my shoulder to know who's standing beside me. I recognize that voice, even in a crowd of people. "It's freezin' out here."

"Wait until January," Oliver says. "Your lungs freeze in January."

"Great."

"Didn't you just have some kind of surgery?"

Now I look at him. He's wearing a dark blue parka the same color as Magnus's. It's not even zipped all the way. His cheeks look chilled, but I don't think he notices. "Are you checkin' up on me?"

"I'm meeting friends." He lowers his gaze to my coat sleeves. "I don't live far from here, on Griswold. How're your wrists?"

"Good. Better, I think. I had a vein graft and my tendons worked on, so hopefully I can use my left hand again. My right wrist was mostly cosmetic." Magnus finishes his business and sits on my feet instead of the cold concrete. "It's been a few days, and I'm feelin' better."

Oliver turns his attention to the huge Christmas tree at the end of the rink and casually asks, "Have you found someone to teach you to kiss?"

"Not yet." He's not fooling me. He's a lot more interested in my answer than he lets on. "But I'm hopin' to find someone real good at it before Christmas."

He looks at me out of the corner of his eye. "Why Christmas?"

I carefully pick up Magnus with my right arm. "I'll need practice." As I turn to leave, I add, "For when you kiss me under the mistletoe." I can practically feel his eyes watching me as I walk away. He might not have been thinking about kissing me on Christmas, but he is now.

Both Oliver and I are wrong about blizzards. They actually start December 5.

The first time I see Michigan snow is when Meredith and the kids and I are leaving Santa's Magic Forest. It rarely snows in Marfa, and is more like a dusting that usually melts by noon. The only Blizzards come from the DQ and have Oreos or toffee chunks. I've never seen the fat flakes drifting toward my upturned face and resting on my cheeks and forehead. Rowan shows me how she runs to catch flakes on her tongue, and I am enchanted.

Despite jolly music and wreaths hanging from lampposts, it doesn't feel like Christmas to me without the Glorious Way Evangelical holiday bazaar, sweet baby Jesus's Nativity in Momma's front yard, or lighted antlers on pickup trucks. I try to get in the holiday spirit and liven up the penthouse. I buy a real tree and make some ornaments out of colored paper and tissue and put a big tinfoil star on top. The tree is only three feet high, but it makes the place smell like Christmas and puts me in a festive mood. Then Magnus ruins my holiday joy because he won't quit hiking his leg on it. He doesn't pee on the palm trees in front of the windows. Just the one tree that lift my spirits, and I have to have it dragged out to the dumpster.

By Christmas, any enchantment has worn off. Michigan is

frozen. The snow is piling up, and the sleet is like needles in your face. People's eyebrows freeze. Overcast skies block any hint of sunshine and, on the rare occasion the sun does pop out of the clouds, it might warm up a degree or two.

Being away from my family for the first time during the holidays is rough. I want to send Momma a really nice anonymous gift. Nothing like a Crockpot or Chia Pet. More like a ruby necklace because it's her birthstone, but I'm afraid Daddy might get suspicious and turn it over to the FBI. I can't send it from "Tara Sue," because Momma will want to return the favor, and "Tara Sue" doesn't have an address anywhere near Dalhart. I'd like to buy Daddy something for his truck, but why would the girl of Momma's third cousin twice removed send a gift to a man she's never met? I remind myself that it won't be long now until I see them in person and that that will be better than a Crockpot and jumper cables.

I spend Christmas day at Hawthorne, and the place is decorated beyond belief. It's like every rich house in every Christmas movie all rolled into one. The usual suspects come, and we all toast each other. Old Edie peppers me with questions I can't answer, and Harold looks even shorter.

I keep expecting Oliver to walk through the door, but after Claire's fabulously planned dinner, he's still a no-show. I guess he hasn't been thinking about kissing me under the mistletoe.

We gather around a huge tree that looks like Martha Stewart decorated it herself. Claire and Marv give me a gift of online business classes. At first, I'm a bit surprised. I was going to get my cosmetology license first, but I realize it's their sign of approval. It's not the type of sign I'm used to. Not a celebration at the Dairy Queen, or a big bear hug, but they're not Momma or Daddy. I can't judge them by what I'm used to.

I can go to cosmetology school and take online classes at the same time. I hadn't thought of doing that, but it means I can open Shear Elegance earlier than I'd hoped.

Meredith and Burton give me books on pet care, Michigan scenery, and Southern poems. Burton even thanks me for being a good aunt. Out of everything, I'm most grateful for that.

What do you buy for people who have so much money that they have everything? Rowan and Georgie are easy, but just thinking of the others is stressful. In the end, I don't buy them anything. I give them art from the penthouse. Edie's tastes aren't mine, and I might as well start getting rid of the stuff. I'll come back for my monthly appointments for a while yet. My left hand is still in the metal splint and the occupational therapist tells me I'm showing progress, although even when I'm 100 percent, I'll want to come back to Michigan for special occasions. I'll bring cow skulls to brighten up the penthouse, although I don't know how much I can be here once I start beauty school.

I pulled the contemporary painting from the wall in the entertainment room and wrapped it up for Burton and Meredith. It suits them more than me, but they say they can't accept a thirty-thousand-dollar piece of art.

"That thing is thirty thousand?" I point to the canvas of dripping paint and burst out laughing.

For Claire and Marv, I wrap up a vase made of bronze that has two headless men on each side. The artist hadn't bothered with arms either, but he did give painstaking detail to each penis. It's ugly as all git-out.

Marv and Claire react the same as Burton and Meredith. They say it's too extravagant, which is funny given that they basically live in an extravagant museum. "I don't like it, and I know you like flower vases in about every room," I say.

Later when I'm back at the penthouse, all alone and looking downward at the city wrapped in snow and Christmas lights, I think about Oliver. I know I shouldn't be disappointed that he didn't show. He never said he'd meet me under the mistletoe. He didn't live up to my expectations, but it's my fault for always thinking people feel the same things I feel.

I'm young. I'm lonely. I need to get out. I've focused too much of my pent-up lust on Oliver when that is the exact opposite of what I should be doing. For one, an affair with him could blow up and make things worse between us. Two, I don't want to start something if I'm not going to be around enough to enjoy it.

I spend the week between Christmas and New Year's looking hot and going out. There is no shortage of bars and good-looking men, and I flirt and smile and size them up as they look me over at the same time. I don't have time for a boyfriend, but I can make time for a one-nighter. It's been a long time since I've felt a man's hands and mouth on me. This time I'm not looking for love or a commitment past sunrise.

I let a few men kiss me and am reminded of how much I like it. Desire tugs at my insides, but I always go home alone. One night I drink too much tequila and follow a handsome bartender when he takes a break. He makes me feel good, and I think I want a quick orgasm to take the edge off, but once his hands tug at my skirt, I discover that it isn't what I want. I'm not looking for love, but I don't want a wham-bam on a beer keg, either.

I don't know what I want. I'm physically in Michigan but my heart is in Texas. I can't stay as long as I'd like, but I can't wait to go home. I figure I'll leave the day after my appointment with Doc Barb on January fourth and be back in Detroit for an appointment with Dr. Graham on the fourteenth, when I can hopefully trade in the metal splint for a wrist support made of neoprene and Velcro.

I book a round-trip flight to Midland for January sixth through the twelfth. I'm staying in the Rock Hudson suite at the Paisano hotel in Marfa, because it's bigger than the Elizabeth Taylor suite, and less like a regular room like the James Dean. Then I call the Do or Dye and make an appointment with Carla Jean for Friday the seventh.

No one will know who I am in Marfa, either. I'd originally thought I'd turn up as Tara Sue. It sounded like such a good plan in November, but if a third cousin twice removed shows up from Dalhart, Momma will want to introduce me to the rest of my long-lost kin.

I have a new plan now. Since I can't show up as a relative without the whole family picking apart my story, I'll go as myself, Edie Chatsworth-Jones. I'll charm the pants off Momma and Daddy and they'll fall in love with me. I'll have to fly back and forth for a while, and it'll take longer to win them over. I figure we'll start out as friends, but Momma's heart will recognize mine, and she and Daddy will come to think of me as family.

Marv and Claire are leaving for Florida the day after the big New Year's Eve party. No one will even know I'm gone before I'm back. I like this new plan.

When I arrive at Hawthorne on New Year's Eve night, the whole place is bedazzled in gold.

It sparkles and shines both inside and out and reminds me of the movie *Crazy Rich Asians*. Everything from the little petit fours with *New Beginnings* written on them to the floral arrangements are amazing. I fit right in with my flashy gold sequin dress. For the first time, I'm wearing little spaghetti straps instead of long sleeves. If anyone asks about my splint, Claire has advised me to say I had surgery for carpal tunnel.

At first glance, my dress looks a bit risqué. It's not the neckline or the length. It's that I can be mistaken for naked. The 3D floral sequins are sewn to fine mesh and the backing is the same color as my skin. It was one of the dresses that Arianna brought to the penthouse for me to choose from, and we paired it with beige Prada pumps. My hair is brushed into a classic French twist on the back of my head.

Throughout the evening, I perform my cohostess duties without incident, but I know that most of the guests are puzzled by my accent and lack of memory. I'm introduced to people I'm supposed to know, but I'm used to it now and just smile. Except for Burton and Meredith and a few trophy wives, most of the guests are Marv and Claire's age. Like any good hostess, I chat about the weather and entertain with tales of living in downtown Detroit. I talk about people slipping and sliding all over the place like they don't know what to do in snow.

"The wind started wrappin' that scarf around her face tight as a mummy," I tell a middle-aged tycoon and his much younger wife. "And she walked right into a lamppost, bless her heart." She talks about the 2014 blizzard, and just as he's telling me of record-high snowfalls, I raise my gaze and notice Oliver standing by the marble fireplace, where his parents are chatting with mine. I don't know when he arrived, but the last time I looked up, he wasn't standing there. He's wearing a blue dress shirt and khaki pants and his tie is pulled loose around his neck like he's been out having fun somewhere else. It's about ten minutes until midnight and I wonder why he's bothered to come at all.

I met Tom and Ann Hunt earlier, and they seem nice enough, but a little apprehensive, as if waiting for the old me to pop out like a demon. I don't blame them, given the past, but someday people need to relax.

I excuse myself and move toward our latest guest. I am the cohostess and it's part of my duties, but as I get closer, I can see both sets of parents get stiff like they're holding their breath in nervous anticipation. I guess that someday isn't today.

"Hello, Oliver." I lean in and give his cheek an air-kiss. He smells like crisp air and man soap.

"Sunshine." His green gaze takes me in with one quick glance. "How was your Christmas?"

"Wonderful." I smile like I found someone else to kiss me under the mistletoe. "Better than two dead pigs in sunshine," I add, just because I know how much he enjoys my Texas sayings.

"I thought it was one dead pig," he says through a quiet laugh.

"Two doubles your happy."

He shakes his head. "I don't have any idea what you're talking about."

Now it's my turn to laugh along with him. "I know."

The parents visibly relax, as if they hadn't quite trusted that Oliver and I had buried our aversion to one another. That's progress.

Close to midnight I hand out poppers and cardboard horns and start counting down the seconds. Last year I partied in Alpine with Lida. The tequila shots flowed like a fountain, and DJ Randy Randy spun country and western till the break of dawn. For the most part, I'm partying with the sixty-and-older crowd this year. Surprisingly, I don't think the world has ended. I don't know if it's because I'm not going to miss the hangover or because I know I'll be partying in Marfa this time next week.

At the stroke of midnight, the lights in the house go off and fireworks explode from the beach. People blow their horns and fire their poppers, and beneath a hail of streamers and confetti, I turn to Oliver standing beside me. "Happy New Year." I grab his tie and plant a friendly kiss on his lips. That's all it takes for tingles to run up my spine and my heart to beat harder in my chest. I pull back as streaks of red, white, and blue burst in the night sky and flash across his face. He looks at me for several long moments before he says something that I can't hear over the *boom boom boom* outside the window and inside my chest.

"What?"

He puts his hand on my back and brings me closer. "Get your coat," he says, next to my ear. "We're leaving."

"Why?"

"Because when I kiss you, I don't want my mother in the room."

I'm shocked and not sure I heard right. "You're goin' to kiss me?"

"That's why I'm here."

I've only been sinning in my heart with Oliver for months. The old me doesn't have to be told twice, and I slip my right hand into his warm palm. The new me moves with him through the crowd and halfway down the gallery to a sitting room where no one ever sits, and where I'd tossed my coat because I was too lazy to take it to the closet. The old me turns to him in the dimly lit room. The new me raises my mouth as he pulls me against him. His lips brush mine, and all of me responds to his hot kiss, wet and hungry and so good I never want to stop. The strap of my dress falls from my shoulder and Oliver's hand follows it down my arm. "I've been picturing you in your short little pajamas since that night in your penthouse," he says against my throat. "I've been thinking of you against my chest, looking up at me, your mouth just below mine."

"Why didn't you come for Christmas?"

"Because I knew I'd do this," he says just above a whisper as he closes the door and backs me against it. "I knew I'd pick up where we left off eighteen years ago. This time I'm going to finish what we started. I'm going to give you something worth remembering."

I'm supposed to have amnesia. I'm not supposed to know what the fire heating up my stomach means or recall tingles whirling across my skin, but I want more. I want him to give me something worth remembering, and I want to give him something to remember when I'm gone.

He looks at me and his warm breath brushes my cheek. "If you're planning to stop me, now's a good time," he says, even as he raises my knee to his waist.

"You said I should stop you when you shove your hand up my dress." He does just that, and I tear at his shirt and belt instead of stopping him. He pushes my panties to one side and we have sex against a closed door, in a house filled with people. It's definitely worth remembering. So good that he takes me to his apartment and it gets better.

Oliver knows things. He knows a woman's body and has moves the likes of which I've never experienced. I'm supposed to have amnesia, but I know a few things myself. Thankfully he never asks how a mental virgin knows where to touch and kiss and how to work him over.

He makes me breakfast at noon and takes me home. We spend the day in and out of bed, and he joins me and Magnus on our walk in the park. He tells me he's leaving that night for Saint Thomas and is playing golf on a course he's thinking about buying. He doesn't say when he'll be back and I don't ask. He kisses me goodbye near Magnus's favorite shop, and I wave with the big mitten covering my splint as he walks away.

It's too bad I'm leaving just when things are starting to get good.

24

A hundred miles from nothing and on the way to nowhere, Marfa is exactly how I left it. Clear blue sky and desert monotony. Sun-bleached houses and cactus gardens. Abandoned buildings and questionable food trucks. Dust always kicking up somewhere, and the relentless battle to keep it from settling on everything. Even in January.

I'm home. Finally. I drive through the town as slow as possible, taking it all in. I've missed every building and tumbleweed. I've missed the ease of living and knowing my place in the world, and I raise my sunglasses long enough to wipe a tear from my eye.

Warm air flows through the vents of my brand-new Rapid Red F-150 while Toby Keith sings to me from eighteen speakers. I tap my thumbs on the steering wheel and join him, belting out "How Do You Like Me Now?!"

I still can't believe I walked into a dealership yesterday, pointed to the shiniest vehicle on the lot, and handed over Edie's black American Express. I expected the salesman to laugh his ass off or call the cops or kick me out of the showroom. Instead, he gave me the keys and I drove away from Rogers Ford in a Limited SuperCrew.

I flew into Midland yesterday and bought jeans with rhinestone wings on the back pockets, sparkly inlay boots, and a truck. I spent the night at the DoubleTree and headed out for Marfa this morning. I've always wanted a big truck and this one is everything I've ever dreamed of and more. It has leather seats and a moonroof and options that I've never heard of and don't understand. It's big and powerful and a far cry from the minivan I used to drive through town.

The Do or Dye is on Austin Street, not far from the little coffee shop where I used to get my morning horchata latte—cinnamon milk, please—and settle on the patio to watch Elliot Franco lift weights on the porch of his double-wide. I called him El Fuego on account of him being so hot. He never called me anything on account of him not knowing I was alive. I bet this truck will get his and everyone else's attention.

I pull the F-150 into one of the parking slots in front of the salon and my heart starts to pound. It gets louder as I climb down from the truck and shut the door behind me. I breathe in the desert for the first time since I left that Sunday so long ago. The air smells of cumin from the Food Shark a few blocks away. I never knew that broken concrete and cracked stucco had any sort of scent at all, but it does. It smells like hard mud that's baked in the sun for decades. It smells like home.

Ramon Campos's old green Bronco rolls past, tailpipe hitting the road every few feet, but I'm struck by the silence. No sound of traffic or voices or crush of snow. Was it always this quiet? My breath doesn't freeze in front of my face and I unzip my quilted coat and leave it in the truck. Is Marfa having a heat wave or have I gotten used to living in a blizzard?

I hit the lock on the key fob, the truck chirps, and the lights flash as I stare at the WALK-INS WELCOME sign and the logo of a bottle of hair dye painted on the door. I've waited for this for so long. Wanted it since my spirit roamed UMC El Paso, yet I'm afraid, and it feels like my boots weigh twenty pounds each. I force one foot in front of the other. The front door is as heavy as I remember, but the cowbell hanging on the handle sounds louder.

I take everything in all at once: the smell of hair solutions, shampoo and super-hold, the sight of Lorna wrapping Rosita Ortega's hair on pink rods, and the sound of Astrid Rojas under a dryer with a *People* magazine. I worked here for five years, and it feels different and familiar at the same time.

I look at my old station, and it's like I never left. After I got my cosmetology license, I painted BIG DREAMS DESERVE BIG HAIR in big purple letters above my mirror. It's still there along with my styling tools and shears. Everything is the same—except there's a big stuffed unicorn sitting in my chair.

"Can I help you?" Lorna asks.

I turn my attention to her and place a hand on my stomach. "I have a two o'clock appointment with Carla Jean."

She gives my hair a once-over, and I recognize the pity lowering her brows. The kind of pity reserved for abandoned dogs, train wrecks, and straight hair. "Carla Jean," she hollers, and I hear my momma talking to herself like she's always done. My pounding heart beats against my ribs and my breath whooshes from my lungs a moment before she appears. "You must be Edie."

Then everything stops. Heart, lungs, time. That's my momma's

voice, but about the only thing I recognize is her hair. It's still rat-
ted like a tumbleweed, but she's lost so much weight, I can't say
that I'd know her if we passed on the street. Her face is thinner,
her crow's feet are deeper around her eyes, and her jawline is a bit
slack without a double chin to fill it out.

"Come on over."

My insides are stuck on pause, and I feel light-headed as I
follow her across the small room and sit in her salon chair. She
looks good, but she doesn't look like herself. I guess that makes
two of us.

"Well, you're just pretty as a picture." She runs her fingers
through my hair and gets a feel for the volume and texture.
"What can I do for you today?"

All my life, Momma's been big. In her and Daddy's wedding
picture she was pregnant with me. There hasn't been a time
since I was born when she's been under 210, and it isn't as if
she's a tall woman. She's so changed, it's like I don't know her,
but then I smell her Yardley English Rose perfume and tears fill
my eyes. I want to fall on her neck and tell her I love her and cry
until I'm out of tears. Astrid's hair dryer shuts off, and I choke
and snort trying to hold back.

"Man troubles?" Momma asks.

I don't have a man. I have someone who makes me laugh
and gives me orgasms, but Oliver is not my man. I wipe my eyes
and nod because I can't tell her the truth.

"Men are the worst kinda trouble," Lorna chimes in.

"Can't live with 'em, can't shoot 'em," Rosita adds.

Astrid looks up from her magazine. "Not unless there's a life
insurance policy."

Momma hands me a tissue box and I put it in my lap. "We've

all had our share." She does that *tsk-tsk* thing she's always done and then says, "Well, sugar, there's nothin' that can't be made better with an updated look."

I blow my nose and almost smile. Momma hasn't had an updated hairdo since she visited Dollywood in 1994.

"Oh honey, what happened to your hand?"

I'm wearing the neoprene splint with the Velcro wrapped around my pinky and ring fingers. "Boatin' accident," I lie, but it could have happened that way. The orthopedic surgeon is happy with my progress and gave me new hand exercises, but it's going to take a while before I don't have to wear any sort of brace. "My dinghy collided with the *Neptune* at the Revenge Regatta." Or something like that. "I would have been skipper if it wasn't for the weight restriction."

Momma just looks at me and nods her head up and down. "Well, if that don't beat all. You thinkin' about goin' platinum?"

I shake my head. No way am I going to let Momma strip my hair.

I watch her through the mirror as she grabs a salon towel and pins it around my neck. "A perm would give you some volume. I just got new spiral rods and such."

Not a chance. "I think I need a shampoo and blowout." She looks so disappointed that I didn't take her suggestions, I add, "And curled with your hot wand and fluffed some."

Momma's eyes light up. "I just got a three-barrel curlin' crimper I've been dyin' to try out on someone."

That makes me a little nervous, but it's better than a perm.

"I'll have you lookin' so fine, your man will come runnin' back faster than a chicken on a Cheeto."

Momma spins me around and lifts the top of her station, and

I lay my head back in the bowl. She washes my hair like she did when I was a kid and I can't help but shiver.

"You wantin' more crimp than wave, or more wave than crimp?" she asks when she sits me back up.

"Wave." I study Momma's face through the mirror. Her eyes are the same, blue as the endless Texas sky. She brushes my wet hair and glances over at my old station.

"What brings a big-city girl like you to Marfa?"

This is the first time anyone has mistaken me for big-city. "I'm here workin' on a book." I came up with this new story on the flight to Midland. It's the perfect cover. Artistic musing explains why I'll be in and out of Marfa, and it's something that people believe in around here.

"Did you hear that, Lorna?" Momma pumps up the chair. "We got a new writer in town."

"What are you writin' about?" Lorna wants to know.

I thought of that, too. "Heaven," I answer, because talking religion is the fastest way to become Momma's friend. I know I shouldn't keep lying to her, but my other lies didn't work out. Daddy ruined the Publishers Clearing House fabrication, and most of my relatives who live within fifty miles would love to call *bool-sheet* on Tara Sue.

"Well, you're in the right place. God made Texas with his own hands, but he gave Marfa his heart." She gets her pink comb and runs it through my tangles. "My daughter's with the Lord, so I know a thing or two about heaven."

She points her comb to the chair next to us. "She worked right there."

I take a good look at my old workstation and notice a stuffed doll sitting next to a bottle of hair protector. It has a beard and goatee and looks like . . . "Is that Jesus?"

"Sure enough is. It's a plush Jesus that someone left on my daughter's grave." She sprays a handful of whipped mousse in her hand and combs it through my hair with her fingers. "I just couldn't leave my Lord and Savior to the elements." Momma dries her hands and fires up her blow-dryer.

I can't think of anyone who'd stick a stuffed Jesus on my grave. *My grave*. I don't want to think about that. I *can't* think about it without my brain twisting in my head.

Mom shuts off the blower and picks up where she left off. "Most everyone in town turned out for her funeral at Glorious Way Evangelical. We made sure she had the best of everything. Her daddy went into debt on the flowers alone."

I can make sure he doesn't have to go into debt for anything ever again.

"It was beautiful, and I know Brittany went straight to heaven."

No, she didn't. "I'm sorry for your loss."

"It's a tragedy." Momma's eyes start to water, and I hand her a tissue. "Thank you." She dabs at her tears. "She was too good for this world."

I was?

"Just a good person," Lorna adds.

That's true enough.

"Her smile lit up a room and everyone just loved her."

They did?

"There isn't one person who's ever said a bad word against her."

I can think of a few.

"She was the perfect child."

Someone's been sniffing peroxide.

"I'll see her again after the rapture."

"I'm sorry I never got to meet her." I'm smiling on the inside as Momma turns the salon chair and I notice something at my workstation better than plush Jesus: my old cell phone. It's scratched and the screen is cracked and I want it in the worst way.

"You should write about her in your book."

No one would believe me, and I'd get sent back to Livingston. "We can talk about that and other things, too."

I think she's going to ask me what other things, but she gives me a hard look through her mirror and says, "Have we met? I don't recognize your face but there's somethin' familiar about you."

Yes! Momma recognizes me in her heart. I knew she would, but I didn't think it would happen so fast.

"Maybe it's your voice."

Dang Tara Sue. Her heart doesn't recognize me. I think fast and say like a Michigander, "My maahm says I *ki*-nah have one of those voices."

"I guess that's not it." Momma sections my hair and clips it to my head. She's already mentioned the rapture, and I don't have to wait long before she brings up her second-favorite subject.

"We were at Caesar's Palace, and we'd been pluggin' money in the slots when I hit it big at the Lucky Seven. Pudge looks at me and says, 'Carla Jean, we should have Elvis marry us right here and now.' I about died right there. Pudge and me, we've had our share of problems, but I agreed on the spot, because I knew winnin' that hundred dollars was my sweet Brittany Lynn's way of givin' her approval from heaven." Momma weaves my hair through the barrel crimper, and I keep a close eye on it just in case it starts smoking. "I know she's happy that me and her daddy are back together. Sometimes I feel her spirit sittin' right next to me in church. She loved singin' for Jesus, and Johnny J. says he can hear her voice in heaven's holy choir."

She opens the crimper and a perfect curly wave falls out. She pins it to my head and adds, "That Paula Abdul was jealous of her voice and voted her off *American Idol.*"

That's a big old whopper.

Momma keeps talking about how perfect I am as she piles up my hair, and I keep an eye on my phone. I lived on that iPhone, and I can't help but think it has the answers to some of my questions about the car wreck. I need it. It's mine and I want it back. I get my opportunity when Momma takes the cap from my shoulders and moves behind the front counter. Lorna is busy with Rosita's perm, and I slip the phone into my leather tote. Maybe because I'm home and around my momma, I pause for a second and ask myself, What would Jesus do? I shrug on my way to the front. If Jesus had paid for the upgrade and his name was on the contract, I'm pretty sure he'd say that you can't steal something that belongs to you.

I walk out of the Do or Dye and a cool afternoon breeze rebounds off my "custom do." If it was warmer, I'd be walking bug bait for sure.

Yes, I still give my hair a fluff bump, but I have so many clip-ins right now, my head feels heavier. Momma transformed her signature "halfway to heaven" style into her first-ever "Loretta Lynn at the Grand Ole Opry" custom do. Don't get me wrong, I love Loretta, but I don't want to look like the coal miner's daughter.

Everyone in the salon oohed and aahed, and Momma was so proud of herself, she took a photo for her portfolio. Of course, I smiled and said I love it, but I can't wait to wash out the gravity-defying super-hold and gel molding compound. I've only been gone eight months, but my definition of hair dos and don'ts has changed. This heavy "Loretta Lynn at the Grand Ole Opry" custom do is a HELL NO YOU DON'T!

Still, I make another appointment for Monday.

I jump in the F-150 and plug my old cell phone into the car charger. It doesn't light up right away and I wonder if that's because it's really dead or broken. I head to the Hotel Paisano to check in, but I only get a block down Dallas and stop. Elliot Franco is out of his home gym and walking into the coffee shop across the street. It's been a while since I had my favorite horchata latte with cinnamon milk, please, and I make an unscheduled stop.

The coffee shop is the same as I remember, except they don't offer cinnamon milk these days, so I order an espresso. I find a little bistro table where El Fuego is available for my viewing pleasure. He's as handsome and buff as ever, but he's nowhere near as hot as Oliver. His hands probably aren't nearly as good as Oliver's either, but for the first time in my life, he notices me. He does one of those head-jerk acknowledgments that men give when they think they're God's gift. He's got the smooth, sexy Latino look to him, and eight months ago, I would have been thrilled with a head-jerk.

I guess since I don't look away, he takes it as a sign to join me. "You're new around here."

So he does talk. "How did you guess?"

His perfect lips turn up at the corners and a dimple dents one cheek as he slides into the chair across from me. "I'd remember you." So he can smile, too.

"Yep, this is my first time." I've dreamed of flirting with this man, but I blow on my espresso instead and say, "I planned on visitin' a good friend of mine, but I just found out she died eight months ago. I'm all choked up." I take a sip before I set down my cup. "Her name was Brittany Lynn Snider. Did you know her?"

He gives it some thought, and I think he's going to say no and get me aggravated. "Big girl? Two and a half axe handles?"

He did not just say that! He couldn't just leave it at two axe handles? "She was full-figured."

"She used to drink coffee here most days."

So he *did* know I was alive.

"She used to stare at me."

I prefer "admired from afar," thank you.

"I'd look out my window, and she'd be sittin' over here watchin' me. She had a screw loose."

My screws were never loose! "How dare you? She was a beautiful person. Inside and out." I grab my tote bag and stand before I give into my impulses and dump coffee on his head. "You weren't raised right." All those years I thought I was a faithful admirer, and he thought I was a crazy fat stalker. Heat flushes my neck and cheeks, and I can't get out of the shop fast enough. I hold it together long enough to climb inside my truck before my vision blurs. I'm as hurt today as I would have been eight months ago. As embarrassed too.

You can get used to a lot of things, but being called fat isn't one of them. You can smile and pretend it doesn't bother you, but it always will. Being called stupid gets me riled, but I can fight back. There was nothing I could say or do when someone called me fat. Momma always said it didn't matter what ornery folks thought, but a little part of my heart died each time.

"You can pretend that you still live with your momma because she needs you, but deep inside you know that's not true," a little voice in my head says to me. "You stay because you know what to expect. You stay because home is a safe place to hide when the world gets too ugly."

I thought of myself as a strong woman because I finally got the nerve to flip off Dingleberry. I thought sex was a way to get a man. I thought a Little Debbie Oatmeal Creme was a healthy snack because it had oatmeal. I used to think a lot of things about myself that weren't true. I'm almost afraid of what I'll discover next.

25

If you're trying to watch your family from a distance, a Rapid Red F-150 with the chrome package and dual exhaust isn't the best plan. It's like driving around with a neon arrow pointing at you. The day after I arrive in Marfa, I drive to Alpine and rent a banged-up Sienna. I know all too well that no one notices a silver minivan. I rent a storage unit big enough to store the truck and head to the Dollar General where Lida works. At least that's where she was working, but the manager tells me Lida moved to Fort Hood with her husband.

Lida's married?

I'm gone less than a year and my parents get remarried and Lida gets a husband and moves to an army base. A whole lot has changed since I died, and I can't help but feel like everyone has moved on without me.

It's Saturday, and that means Daddy's barbecuing something. I drive incognito to Momma's house, but another family is living there. I just stare at the new blue paint and white trim. There's a new porch and carport, and the raised prickly-pear garden me and Momma started when I was ten has been torn out. I lived in that house for twenty-five years, and now every trace of my life has vanished.

I leave feeling as gutted as my old house and drive to Daddy's, but they're not living at his trailer either. I know this because Floozy Face wouldn't be sweeping the front porch if Momma lived there.

I drive around Marfa looking for a barbecue smoke signal, but the only smoke I see is coming from Jorge Espinoza's taco truck. I'm hungry but I'm going to pass on Jorge's Especiales. Instead I opt for a cold beer and fish tacos. I'm wearing my new jeans, sparkly boots, and a jean jacket, and fit right in at Boogie's Tex-Mex. My hair survived Momma's Loretta Lynn custom do, but it does feel a little dry from all the heat and gel. Not dry enough to keep me from my Monday appointment, and nothing that won't benefit from a nourishing treatment at Chantal.

Only I'm not going to be there next week for my standing appointment, and I need to cancel. I left my Hawthorne Corporation Samsung in Detroit so I can't be traced to Marfa. The last thing I want to do is answer questions about why I returned to Texas, and I pull out my personal phone and look at my calendar. I have an appointment with the Aveda Institute in San Antonio in two weeks. I filled out the initial paperwork, but it's so far away I want to see the school before I commit.

I forgot to tell Meredith that I can't make Rowan's "About Me" program at her preschool academy after all. She taught Magnus to crawl on his belly for the "I Love . . ." part of the performance. I'm sorry that I won't be there to see it.

I fire off a text to Chantal but hesitate over what to write Meredith. She and the kids are a big part of my life in Michigan, and I'm going to miss them. A little part of me will miss Magnus, too, but I doubt he'll miss me at all.

I think about Marv and Claire. We don't always understand each other, but I think we're more accepting of our differences now. Burton was just getting to the point where he would talk to me without scowling. I don't want to hurt any of them, but this is my home. Besides, it's not like I'm never going to return to Michigan.

I think about Oliver, and I don't know if he'll miss me. I don't know what he thinks of me—other than that he's gone from hating me to wanting me in just three months. I don't know what I think of him either—other than that I've felt a connection to him from the first time I saw him walk toward me on the dark patio at Hawthorne. Then again, I thought I had a connection to Elliot El Fuego, too.

I pick up my old cell phone still hooked to the charger, but it still isn't working. What a letdown, but thank the good Lord and baby Jesus, my favorite restaurant is still up and running. Boogie's Tex-Mex still smells of grease and fish and salsa, and the same Lone Star sign hangs behind the bar. The same twinkly lights are tangled in the horns of Boogie's eight-point buck, and his girls Sheila and Shana still wait tables.

The beer is just as cold as I remember, but there's no need for space panties, because I can only eat two fish tacos. Boogie's still makes the best Tex-Mex, but later, in the Rock Hudson suite, I pay the price for eating all that batter and grease.

The next morning, I check the old iPhone. The screen is black, but I'm not giving up. There has to be a way to get it open. I grab a piece of toast and head out for Glorious Way Evangelical. No need for GPS. I know the way.

I sit in the back and scrunch down, hoping no one notices me and wants to know if I'm saved or if they can pray for me. Momma is in her regular spot, and if I wasn't seeing it with my own eyes, I wouldn't believe Daddy was sitting right next to her. I can't see his face, but he has the same permanent dent in the back of his head from wearing the cowboy hat he outgrew when he was seventeen.

I expected to feel funny about seeing them together, but it warms a place in my heart that I didn't know needed warming. A little piece of a child's heart that always longed to live under the same roof with both her parents. I'm glad I came prepared with my own Kleenex.

Johnny J. is at his fire-and-brimstone best as he smacks his Bible on the pulpit and preaches about God and sin and the path to redemption.

"Second Corinthians five-seventeen. 'Therefore, if any man be in Christ, he is a new creature: old things are passed away; behold all things are become new.' Praise Jesus."

"Praise Jesus," I say along with everyone else. My faith journey has changed along with everything else in my life. I guess coming so close to seeing God, I don't think the same as I used to. I believe in him more than ever, and I've come to think God cares more about what's in a person's heart than where he or she sits on Sundays.

"Ladies and gentlemen, when you accept Christ in your heart, all things become new. No one knows this better than our newly baptized brother Pudge Snider. Brother Pudge, would you come up and share your faith story?"

What? He not only goes to church now, but he was baptized and has a faith story? Am I in a prank video?

I can hear Momma bawling from all the way in the back as Daddy walks to the dais. I've never seen him dressed for church, and he never wore glasses before. "I'm a sinnin' man," he begins, and hearing his voice brings a flood of tears to my eyes. "Worldly and selfish, always puttin' my desires before God. I didn't believe I needed savin', and that ain't nothin' but the truth.

"When my baby girl died, I blamed God. He took my only child, and I wanted to crawl in that hole with her." He sniffs and clears his throat and my chin starts to quiver. "I started drankin' and skirtin' around more'n usual. One night I pert near died out on Highway Sixty-Seven, but God had different plans for me. He reached down and pulled me outta the darkness. He put my beautiful Carla Jean back in my life and set my feet on a godly path. I don't know why he saved this ol' sinner, but he did, and I don't take that lightly."

I've cried through five Kleenexes. I can still hear Momma, and I'd guess she's used up half a box.

"I wasn't a great daddy, but I live my life different now. I live for God, and for the chance to see my Brittany Lynn once more. If she ever gets to lookin' down from heaven, I think she'll be proud of her ol' daddy and the way I see to her momma." He clears the emotions from his throat and continues. "Me and Carla Jean are tryin' to get some money together for a park we wanna put over there near the fire station, 'cause Brittany Lynn wanted to grow up and be a singer or a volunteer firefighter. If any of y'all can spare a couple of dollars, we'd appreciate it."

I cover my mouth with my fingers and nod. That was so long ago, I forgot about my back-up plan if Brittany Wittany didn't work out. I'm surprised he remembers.

"And me and Carla Jean started a support group for grievin' families. I used to believe that bein' a man meant holdin' it all in, but it helps to talk it out. We're always on call and anyone sufferin' is welcome."

Daddy found God and started a support group? He must have switched bodies with someone else, too. He's a blur as the congregation stands and praises the Lord. I stay seated because I'm afraid if I get up, my legs won't support me.

Momma moves into the aisle and waits for Daddy. She's wearing a pink dress that I've never seen before, and the congregation praises Jesus when they hug each other tight.

The choir sings "Our God," and I take that as my cue to slip out the door. The minivan is near the same spot where I parked Momma's Town and Country eight months ago. I climb inside and stare out the window, seeing nothing.

This whole time, I thought I'd come back home and everything would be the same. Momma would live in our house and Daddy would live with Floozy Face and his dog, Scooter. I thought everything would be exactly as it was the day I left. Lida would work at the Dollar General, and I could get cinnamon milk in my horchata latte.

Folks might come and go around here, but the population always hovers around two thousand. Artists might put up new installations, and Hollywood might make movies just outside of town, but Marfa stays stuck in time.

Until now. I never thought my death would bond my folks together. I never thought it would change them so much. I never thought I'd be like the kid with her nose pressed against the window, watching everything from outside.

I knew some things were bound to be different. I don't look like my old self. Everyone thinks I'm dead and all, but I thought for sure Momma's heart would recognize me. It still might, but now she lives with Daddy and they have each other. They don't need anyone else. If there was ever a chance of getting her out of Marfa so she could help me with Shear Elegance, it's never going to happen now. I know that might have always been a pipe dream, but now it's not even that.

When Ingrid offered me a new life that day in her tulip office, I pictured me and Momma drinking Dr Pepper on the front porch of a brand-new ranch house. I'd come visit her, and she'd kick her feet up after her bunion surgery. I saw Daddy in a new truck and pull trailer, bagging wild boar with his pocketknife and sleeping in a deluxe camper at night.

I grab a Kleenex from my Chloé bag and blow my nose. My eyes are red and swollen from crying. I think about the last time I got a big hug from Daddy and a tight squeeze from my momma. I want to feel that kind of love again.

Someone raps on my driver's-side window and startles an "Aaahh!" out of me. It's Momma, and I wonder how she noticed me in my incognito van.

"I thought I recognized ya." She's wearing her same old quilted coat, and now it swallows her up.

"Yes, ma'am. I never miss church."

"You must have been raised right."

I smile. "Yes, ma'am."

"How'd that custom do work out for ya? Were ya happy with it?"

"Happier than a dead pig in sunshine. Thank you."

She nods her head, then suddenly stops. "Good God almighty, your eyes are cried out. No man is worth that kind of ugly."

I don't take offense because it's something I've heard all my life. "No man trouble today. I was moved by the spirit. Your husband's faith story touched my heart. I could have listened to more."

She puts her hands together like she's praying. "He's a changed man and a witness for Christ." She turns away and waves both hands over her head. "Pudge. Pudge! Get over here!" Then she turns back to me and says, "Ya might be interested in our Bible study meetin'. I'm the group leader, and we're studyin' the book of Matthew this month. Our goal is a better under-standin' of the Lord's teachin's and applyin' them in our daily lives. I'd introduce ya, but I won't be attendin' today's meetin' due to Pudge's baptism barbecue."

Baptism barbecue? What's Daddy bagged and tagged lately?

"What'er ya hollerin' about?" Daddy asks as he stands next to the van. He's wearing the same work coat he always wore to court, and he is a sight for my ugly eyes. My heart swells with love and joy and I struggle with a new flood of tears.

"This young woman came into the shop for a custom do on Friday. I showed you the picture. It took pert near three hours to pin and curl her hair, not to mention—"

"Is there a reason ya hollered at me?" Daddy interrupts Momma's flow.

"Your faith story moved Edie's heart and she's cryin' her eyes out."

He dips his head to look at me. "If I helped ya, that's God workin' through me."

I don't pay much attention to his words; I'm too busy looking at his face in my window. Except for the glasses, he's the same. Same blue eyes and crow's feet baked into his skin. "Yes, sir."

He pulls back. "Ya take care, now."

Don't go, Daddy! It's me. Your baby girl! "What do y'all grill for a baptism?" I ask so they won't leave me.

"Pudge's secret-rub brisket, secret-rub ribs, secret-rub pork, and beer-butt chicken. I'm makin' smashed taters and a Texas cake for dessert. The whole family's comin' and bringin' enough food to feed half of Marfa."

I'd love to see my relatives again. "You're makin' me hungry just listenin' to you." Especially Aunt Lavon and Sissy.

"Church is out, Carla Jean."

"Why don't ya come on out? You're too thin and need somethin' that sticks ta your ribs."

"Really?" There's hope yet.

"Edie's comin' for barbecue," she tells Daddy. He whispers something to her, then she replies, "You're right."

Daddy bends down and we look each other in the eyes. We haven't been this close in a long time, and my chest is so clogged with love for him that I can hardly breathe. "Carla Jean is a generous woman, and I know you'll understand when I tell ya the barbecue is just for family. My wife cried for seven months straight after we lost Brittany Lynn. She's still sufferin' but was doin' better until last Friday. Now she's cryin' again, and the last thing she needs is a big-city writer takin' advantage of her emotions for some book."

"I would never do that." I still believe there's a part of her that will recognize a part of me. Maybe she already does; she's not the kind of person to invite strangers to family barbecues. One, she doesn't trust anyone not born and raised in Marfa, and two, a family brawl could erupt at any given time and air dirty laundry. "You have to believe I would never upset her."

"I don't have to believe anything." His eyes turn hard, and I recognize the look. It's the same flash of anger he gets as he reaches for his pellet gun and aims at Skitter Brown's dog dumping on his lawn. "I'm askin' ya nice, leave Carla Jean be."

I keep quiet even as his words shred me, and I want to beg him to stop hurting me.

"Take care of yourself," he says, and wraps his arm around Momma, and they walk away from me. I feel like I've been hit in the chest with a wrecking ball. Each step takes them farther into the distance, and all I can do is watch.

If I have to listen to the intro music to 7th Heaven one more time, I'm going to throw a chair through the screen. At least that's what I want to do, but I don't, because I want to get promoted to concierge. I want Ingrid to recognize that I'm a good person now. Fighting the system doesn't change anything; it'll just get me demoted again. That's not the direction I need to head in. I've been in PORC long enough. I know how it works. I get promoted to concierge when Raymundo gets promoted to director and Ingrid gets promoted to Southwest District Five judge when Judge Judy gets promoted to heaven. There's no fast track. No work-around. No rules that I can bend and change. Edie Randolph Chatsworth-Jones has no more cachet than Brittany Lynn Snider. Hard to believe but true. She's ruined my hair, talked to my enemy, and banished my dog to a life with the girl who can't put her shoes on the right feet. If Rowan can't take care of herself, how can she take care of my smoochy, kissy-face Magnus?

I glance at the aquarium and am tempted to look in on my impostor. Raymundo isn't in the lounge right now, but there are four patients torturing me with Paradise Inc: Joey, John David, Clementine, and Remington. No, I did make up the last two. I learned my lesson with Ace.

Raymundo enters and does his usual. He bangs his club on the floor and says, "Can I have all y'all's attention. This is our newest guest, Blossom."

Good Lord, she looks more weed than Blossom. I guess that she's in her late teens, and if there is one good feature about her, I don't see it. Not her frizzy red hair, whiter-than-white skin, or orange freckles. Her jaw is set and her hands are clenched.

Oh boy. Hannah was a handful, but this girl is filled with rage. I move toward her and she looks up at me. Something in her brown eyes stops me.

"Blossom, this is my apprentice, Marfa."

"Good God, that's hideous," she says.

I open my mouth to tell her I've seen better clothes in leper colonies, but I don't. "Why are you at UMC?"

"You work here. Figure it out."

I know why she's here without checking with Raymundo. It's in the desperation in her eyes. The hopelessness and pain.

We've never met, but I know her. She and I have stood at the same crossroad. She and I took the same dark path. I know the same cycle of depression and despair. I know the same quagmire of pain and darkness and feeling that life will never get better. I've heard people say that suicide is the easy way out, but I beg to differ. The planning is easy, but the follow-through is damn hard—and I should know.

I stand at a different crossroad now. I can walk away from this girl. I don't have to tell her I know how she feels. I don't have to try to help her. That's not my job.

I'm just an apprentice concierge is all.

"Sometimes life really sucks," I say. "Just when things are going good, something happens. Sometimes it's the bad things people do to us. Sometimes it's the bad things we do to ourselves."

26

Life sucks.

I didn't stick around Marfa after Daddy told me to leave Momma alone. I drove that red truck all the way back to Midland and put it in a storage unit. If that didn't suck enough, I lost my old iPhone somewhere between the Paisano and the penthouse.

My first week back in Detroit, I don't get out of bed and I don't answer my phone. I curl up and pray to Jesus to make everything like it was before I went to Texas. I want a do-over. Just wipe away those two days in Marfa like they never happened. I pray like Momma did in the hospital. I plead and barter, but God doesn't answer and I cry until there's nothing left. I sleep for twelve hours at a time but wake up tired.

The second week, I stop praying and stand in front of the windows for hours, staring at the frozen world far below my feet. I don't belong anywhere. I'm just an insignificant speck in a window. I called Dr. Barb and told her I have the flu and couldn't make my last appointment. She believed me.

I add lying on the couch and watching movies and reruns

on TV to my routine. I move from bed to the windows to the couch, then I start over again. Meredith texts about Magnus. I tell her to drop him off in the lobby and have the concierge bring him to me. She wants to know if I'm okay. I tell her that I'm great but have a head cold.

She buys it and a few minutes later I open the door for Magnus. He heads to his bedroom and I head to mine.

Oliver doesn't buy it, though. After a few short back-and-forth texts, he shows up in the lobby. He tells me he wants to see me to make sure I'm doing okay. I tell him I'm fine and refuse to see him. On good days, I am empty and I have nothing to give or say to anyone. On bad days, I relive every excruciating detail of my time in Marfa. Thoughts of *I should have done this different* and *I shouldn't have done that* plague me. Momma and Daddy walking away in their old coats plays in my head like a painful film clip, and the pain doesn't end there, because I realize Daddy is right. Momma can't heal her grief if I'm there trying to fill my old place in her heart.

I don't want to cause Momma grief, but where does that leave me?

My daddy borrowed money for my funeral, and I can't financially provide for my parents. I live in a multimillion-dollar penthouse, have more designer clothes than should be allowed, and pay two hundred dollars to have my dog groomed like a sissy, and my mother's coat hangs off her. I am tortured by thoughts of Momma and Daddy having so little when I have so much, but there's nothing I can do now. There are no more plans. No more lies. Nothing.

Who am I? Without my home and my family, I don't know. I'm one woman's soul in a different woman's body. No one really knows me. I stand alone. Screaming in silence. A speck in a window. I pull out my composition notebook to write about my pain, to let it pour from my wounded soul onto the page, but the only word I get out is *lost.*

Every day I change from one pair of pajamas to another and crawl back into bed because I can't manage more. I stare at the ceiling and Magnus barks at me from the doorway. "Food's in your dish," I say without looking at him. He barks again and I roll my head toward the door. The concierge took him out not long ago, but I know what he wants by looking at him. "Pee on one of the trees downstairs." I don't care. They're a pain in the ass and belong outside anyway. He doesn't move, but his beady eyes drill holes into my brain. "Pick one. Pretend it's a Douglas fir and that I spent hours making paper ornaments. Pretend it's a Christmas tree that made me happy." I return my attention to the ceiling, but he barks two more times. "Good God almighty!" I could call downstairs again, but I don't, and I throw the covers back. "I just changed into clean pajamas."

He yips and spins around like he's got to go bad. "Fine! Why I bother with a hateful dog, I surely don't know." I brush my teeth and tuck my pajama legs into furry snow boots and my hair into a furry hat. By the time we walk to the elevator, Magnus is in his blue parka and I'm in a long wool coat and scarf. I put on big dark sunglasses and wear them through the residents' lobby and out into the overcast gloom of Detroit in January.

Magnus stops on the welcome mat and I have to carry him to the park so his paws won't get frostbite. The sidewalks are busy. Everyone has someplace to go. Their world hasn't stopped. I am surrounded by people, and I've never felt so alone. I look at them as they walk past, and I'm angry that they get to have good lives. I want to yell, "Y'all suck!"

I set Magnus down and he finds a patch of pristine snow and pees all over like he's writing his name.

"Dogs are not allowed to urinate in this part of the park."

I turn to look at a woman whose hair is brushed and who isn't wearing pajamas under her coat. If I had the energy, I'd hate her. "That's exactly what I told him, but he never listens to me." There isn't a bush or tree or planter in the entire park that hasn't been peed on by every dog in the area.

"You are the owner."

"I tell him that, too."

She raises a hand, pointing toward Magnus, who hasn't stopped peeing yet. He must have really had to go.

"Make him stop."

"There's no stoppin' once he gets started, but you're welcome to try."

"I bring my kids to this park!"

I couldn't care less. "Well, tell 'em not to eat the yellow snow."

Her mouth drops open and she makes a sound of indignation. "That's disgusting."

"You should have been here after my niece snuck him her tuna sandwich. *That* was disgustin'." Magnus finally shakes his leg. "You're a good boy," I gush, and pull my roll of poop bags from my pocket. "Do you have to go number two?" He answers by standing on the tops of my boots. I scoop him up like a baby, and he looks at me like I've lost my mind. He's right. I lost it days ago. "Yes, you are. Oh, yes you are." I shove the bags in my pocket. "Such a good boy, Momma's buyin' you a good-boy treat."

I walk away without looking back. If a dog peeing in the snow is that woman's biggest concern in life, then she doesn't have any real problems. I find just enough cash in my pocket to buy Magnus an organic treat with special dog icing. He gobbles down half by the time we're back home inside the penthouse. My coat is covered in dog-treat crumbs, and I drop it along with Magnus's parka inside the front door. Behind me I leave a trail of hat, scarf, and boots on the way to the couch.

I went outside. I got fresh air. I don't have to do that again. Tomorrow, I'll make arrangements for hotel staff to take Magnus to the park twice a day. Let one of *them* get harangued by a stranger.

An ASPCA commercial comes on; just like the kind that always made Momma's eyes get all watery. I used to turn the channel really quick so she didn't have to watch it. She'd always say, "Thank you, baby."

I curl up in a soft throw blanket and lay my cheek on a blue pillow with tassels. My life is pointless. I think of Edie and the decision she made at the Plaza hotel in El Paso. Feeling hollow yet filled with pain and wondering how she can be both. Lost in what went wrong and not knowing how she can face another day. Lost in despair, a pain so deep she tried to carve it out of her veins and just wanted it to be over.

I would never cut my wrists, but I understand getting lost in pain. There's no way out. No reason to believe it will ever change. Just a speck in a window.

I reach for my stash of Kleenex and blow my nose. I choke on my tears and cover my eyes with my forearm. I would never cut my wrists, but I think of drifting away to my sparkly pink path. No back-and-forth this time. Just a straight shot toward Jesus.

I've had one goal, one single purpose since the switcheroo and I was given a different life. That purpose is gone. The dream of being back with my family is over and done. I think I'm over and done, too.

Something wet and sharp licks my cheek. I lift my arm and Magnus licks a tear from the corner of my lips. "What do you want?" I roll onto my back and he takes that as an invitation to stand on my chest and stare at me. If I ride my path to heaven, who'd buy Magnus special dog treats with blue icing? Who'd take him to the groomer so he can get his sissy haircut and a new bow in his topknot?

Rowan would, but Meredith has her hands full even when he's just a part-time visitor. He lies down and we look into each other's eyes. "You want to be friends now?" He licks my chin. I ignore his dog breath. "You expect me to take care of you forever?" Which I guess is the difference between Edie and me. She didn't consider Magnus. "Who's got your back when you pee in the snow?" She just left him to fend for himself. "That's right. I do."

I don't know why the sudden change in him. He went from wanting to bite my face off, to hiding from me, to indifference, and now I can't go to the bathroom without him scratching to get in. Since he decided we're friends, he won't sleep in his room and jumps in bed with me instead. He lays pressed against me, and no matter how many times I scooch him away, he finds his way back.

During the day we follow a routine. We watch TV, stand in front of the windows, bundle up and go to the park. Come back, order food, start over. But I have made one improvement in our daily routine. I've decided to stop looking like a bag lady, and I get dressed before our daily walk. I've noticed that my clothes are a little loose from loss of appetite, so I add a nightly Dr Pepper float that I share with Magnus while we watch Netflix in bed.

I guess Oliver got tired of the cold shoulder. He's left me alone, and I don't feel great about how I treated him. I talk to

Marv and Claire, but not as often as they'd like to hear from me. I avoid Meredith and the kids. It's just me and Magnus. Two specks in a window.

February first, I pull myself together enough for my appointment with Dr. Barb. I call an Uber, and Magnus and I are picked up in a Ford Escape. She goes through the usual questions and does that thing where she looks at me and waits.

"I don't have a purpose," I finally tell her. "I don't know what to do with the rest of my life."

"We talked about your dream of owning your own salon and spa."

Thanks for picking a scab, Doc. "I don't have that dream anymore."

"What happened?"

If she only knew. "I'm just not excited about it now."

"You have your philanthropic causes."

I shake my head. "I might have before, but I don't have the same passion for art and whales. I don't know anythin' about those charitable organizations, but I'm happy to send them money."

"You suffer from acute memory loss and have only been back home for four months. Don't be hard on yourself. You'll figure it out."

I did once.

"Your life is a clean page in a book of clean pages."

"That's scary."

"Or optimistic and exciting."

I'll take the doc's word on that. Magnus and I make it home in a Prius and as we walk into the lobby, Oliver is walking out. We stand just inside the doors and he looks at me in that way he has of taking me all in at once. "Your dog is getting fat," he says.

Lately Magnus has packed on some weight. Probably because I carry him to and from the park and give him too many treats and Dr Pepper floats. "It's winter," I say in his defense. "He needs an extra layer."

"Your family is worried about you." He takes my elbow and ushers me into the elevator. I let him, but we don't say anything else until we enter the penthouse. I think he's going to ask me the obvious questions, but Oliver never does what I think he's going to do. "We spent a whole day in bed, and I think it's safe to say there were no complaints."

I unbutton my coat and, thinking about that night, I feel heat rise in my chest and throat.

He tosses his coat on the kitchen island. "I leave town and you brush me off when I get back." He's wound up so tight, I can see it in the way he walks toward me. "Tell me this isn't a game you're playing, Edie. Tell me you're not making a fool out of me again."

"I'm not." I never thought that my leaving would make him think I'm playing games like all those years ago. "I'm just—"

"Confused?" He stops in front of me and runs his fingers through his short dark hair. "Join the club."

"Lost."

His hands fall to his sides, all his pent-up energy flows away, and he simply looks at me.

"I just exist." I lift a hand and drop it to my side. "I don't know what I'm supposed to do or where I'm supposed to live now." I thought I did, but I don't.

He slides his warm palm to the side of my throat and lifts my chin with his thumb. "Where do you want to live?"

A few weeks ago, the answer was easy. I gesture around me. "I don't remember pickin' out one stick of furniture or paintin' or why there are palm trees in the livin' room. This is where I live, but I have no real attachment to this place."

"You can live anywhere."

"It's more than pickin' out a place." I shake my head. "It's . . . where do I belong? It's . . . who am I now? I look in a mirror and I don't know."

His thumb slides across my jaw. "Want to know what I see?"

I'm almost afraid of the answer, but I nod.

"I see a different Edie from the one I knew before you walked out onto the terrace that night at Hawthorne. You're better. Better to your family, especially a little red-haired girl who just wants to love your dog. You're much stronger than you think, and it doesn't come at the expense of making others feel weak. There aren't motives behind everything you do, and your generosity doesn't come with a price. You might feel lost right now, but you're smart and will figure out your life.

"When I look into your blue eyes, I see every emotion you're feeling. Nothing is hidden. Everything from lighting up when you think you're funny to squinting when you're annoyed. It's all there, anger and joy and lust. The last two are a real favorite of mine, especially at the same time.

"You're not the woman I knew; you're the woman I want to know. I want to take my time with you. I don't want to rush and miss anything." He pulls me close and presses his forehead to mine. "If any of that appeals to you, let me know."

I let him know by taking his hand and leading him upstairs. I have him spend the night so he can use his bedroom tricks to take my mind off my problems. It works until the next morning when he's gone and I'm back to racking my brain for a way to help with Momma and Daddy's debt. They borrowed money to bury me and I'm not even dead. I can't just send them a check or cash or wire money into their bank account. I can't even give them the red F-150 now sitting in a storage unit in Midland. I don't know what to do, and I don't have the energy to get dressed. I lie around in my pajamas feeling horrible and helpless to do anything.

The solution to my problem shows up later in the residents' lobby just as Magnus and I return from our walk. "Katrina," I say, taken aback. I didn't remember making plans with her or I would have changed out of my pajamas. I look like crap, but I've seen her look worse and I invite her up anyway.

She's dressed in black like always and takes her coat and knit hat off while she turns in a slow circle and looks around at the high ceilings and window. Magnus keeps an eye on her. He can spot when people aren't right like he did me. "Wow. I didn't know you were this rich."

"Neither did I." She laughs and I hang her coat with mine and Magnus's in the usual place. "Are you in school?"

"Yeah, but I'm on spring break until March seventh." She looks at me and I notice her eyes are clear like the last time I saw her, but I wouldn't say she looks totally sane, either. "Did you go out in pajamas or am I missing something here?" she asks.

I look down at my blue flannel pj's with pink sprinkle dough-nuts. "You caught me," I answer as I kick off my boots.

"It's three."

"So?"

"So that's not good."

"Are you here to judge me?"

"No. I came so you could braid my hair like you used to."

Of course she naturally assumes I'm dying to give her a cus-tom style. "Is this for a special occasion?"

"No. Does there have to be a special occasion?"

"No, but you know the rules and didn't make an appointment."

"There isn't anyone lined up outside your door."

I sigh, and she and Magnus follow me upstairs through my bedroom and into the bathroom.

"This is *fan-cy*. I've never seen chandeliers in a bathroom before."

"There's one in the closet, too."

While she's turning her head to look around, I look at the condition of her split ends. "The weather has dried out your hair. You need two inches trimmed off the bottom."

"Okay." She sits at the vanity, assuming I'm dying to give her a custom cut, too. I'm not, but I find a water bottle and the red zipper bag from Livingston. The scissors I find in a cupboard aren't cutting shears, but they're sharp and will do the job. As I fill the water bottle, Magnus stands on his back legs, scratching at a drawer like he's trying to climb. I lift him so he can sit on the top of the vanity like a gargoyle and stare at Katrina.

"Is he going to bite me?"

I screw on the top of the bottle and set it next to my watch-dog. "Well . . . probably not."

"Is he crazy?"

"No more than me or you." I secure a cape around her neck and spray her hair.

"I'm not as crazy now."

I comb her tangles and wish she was in a salon chair so I could raise her at least a foot. "Am I supposed to take your word on that?"

She laughs. "Not so crazy I walk my dog in my pajamas in the middle of the day."

She's got me there. I shrug and say, "Why bother to change clothes when I'm just goin' back to bed again?"

"Because you need to join the real world."

I wouldn't say Katrina herself lives in the real world. What did she say over coffee and crepes? That she reads auras? "I joined the real world. I went to Texas to see some people I know, but they didn't want to see me. Now I don't have anyone." I pull a section through my fingers and to the cut line. "I've lost every-thin'." I comb, looking for strays. "Nothin's left."

"I can't believe this."

"I know. My life is crap, and I'm stuck livin' it."

"No, you're being a crybaby."

My mouth falls open. "Me?"

"On the way here, I passed a man wearing grocery bags over his tennis shoes. You and I have boots, a warm place to live, and good food. Our teeth aren't falling out and we don't duct-tape our coats to keep the stuffing inside. I knew him once upon a time when he raised fine horses, had plenty of food and all his teeth."

That's the most I've ever heard her speak at one time. "There's different kinds of sufferin'. You can have money but still have nothin'."

"Tell that to the guy with the grocery bags on his feet."

I snip a few uneven hairs and put the scissors on the vanity to stop myself from cutting a chunk out of the back of her hair. "I lost the most important people in my life, and I can never see them again," I begin, and there's no stopping me once I start. "They had to borrow money to bury their only child. They don't duct-tape their coats, but it might come to that. I wanted to set them up so they never had to worry about money for the rest of their lives. I couldn't just hand them a check." Tears cloud my vision. "I have more money than I know what to do with, and theirs is half spent before they make it." I wipe my cheek on the arm of my pajamas. "It's killin' me inside." I pick up Magnus and bury my face in his topknot.

I expect Katrina to call me a crybaby again or ask why I was in Texas if I have amnesia. "What about a contest?" she asks.

I look up. "I tried the Publishers Clearin' House sweepstakes, but Pudge didn't believe me." I set Magnus on the floor and take the cape from around Katrina's neck.

"Hmm . . . Lottery won't work . . . You're not Oprah. Maybe a charitable organization."

"They won't take charity." I reach for a comb to part her hair into sections.

"How about a society? I got a thousand bucks from the Hip-Hop Society for outstanding achievement when I was ten. Every year a dance studio sends in one name to the society. The year I won, I didn't know my instructor sent in mine until I got the call."

My hands still and my gaze lifts to hers. She's half a bubble off plumb, but she's smarter than me. Why didn't I come up with that idea months ago?

27

Who knew that I could hop on a Chatsworth-Jones private jet and travel anywhere anytime I wanted? Not me.

I feel a little out of place at first, but like with the Phantom, you get used to traveling in style and comfort. Katrina gets so used to it, she passes out on champagne. I don't think she's supposed to drink on her medication, but she's in her mid-twenties and tough as a stewed skunk.

We fly into Midland and grab a taxi to the unit where the Ford truck has been stored this whole time. It starts right up, and on the drive to Marfa I notice that Katrina's smiling a lot. I don't know if it's a booze glow or if she's planning how to kill me. I ask her and she laughs but doesn't say which.

She loves the shocking-pink Airstream at El Cosmico just outside Marfa and thinks she wants to glamp in a yurt. "I know how to use flint and steel to build a campfire," she says. Unfortunately for her, I booked two rooms at the Saint George, where there's actual plumbing and restaurants within walking distance. Hotel Paisano is just up the street, but I don't want to take the chance of being recognized. It's not that I'm hiding this time. Momma and Daddy know my foundation has chosen them to receive our first grant, but I don't want to cause problems and make Momma cry again.

I'm a private foundation. The Chatsworth-Jones New Beginning Foundation, an organization with the goal of serving individuals, families, and communities in need. It falls under the broad category of a human services charity, which considers a recipient's life experiences and is so general I can choose to fund anything from food banks to substance abuse programs to community parks.

Katrina wanted to name it No Time Before You, but that's too long and requires an explanation that I'd rather keep to myself. The Brittany Lynn Foundation was dismissed for the same reason. It took me, two lawyers, and Marv three months to get the foundation registered and compliant and operational. I never knew there was so much paperwork and so many hoops to jump through. Oliver tried to help me understand it all, but I'm not going to lie, paperwork and hoops are not my forte. I have a new appreciation for Marv and his lawyers, but I insisted on choosing the first grant recipient. Lawrence and Carla Jean Snider of Marfa, Texas, were chosen for their charitable outreach to grieving families. They are granted a Ford Rapid Red F-150 Super-Crew truck and a check for fifty thousand dollars toward the first of four phases of the Brittany Lynn Memorial Park.

Last week, Momma and Daddy hired the only lawyer in Marfa to meet with one of the foundation attorneys. They signed contracts stating that over the next four years, they will be granted a total of two hundred thousand dollars to complete the park. There are some timetables for each phase and supplementary provisions for yearly maintenance after completion.

In addition to the grant, they will each receive a managerial salary of five thousand per month for the rest of their lives. And because I'm afraid they'll go broke in Vegas, buying everyone they know a hot tub, or Johnny J. a new church, I've provided a financial advisor out of El Paso for them.

The foundation (me) has arranged for Katrina and my parents to meet at 11 a.m. in front of the courthouse with a big prize check. It's the prettiest building in town and the grass is always green. The local newspaper, the *Sentinel*, will be there; a news station is coming in from Midland; and I hired the best professional photographer in town.

Katrina is on the board of directors and thinks she's a one-woman prize patrol—minus the balloons. She should be sober by tomorrow, and I am happy to fade into the background and watch. She heads up to her room, and before I lock up the F-150 one last time, I open the glove compartment to make sure all the other paperwork is in there and I pull out a charger cord attached to my old cracked iPhone.

I doubt it's going to turn on this time when it didn't before, but I plug it in first thing when I get inside my room. I wash my face and about jump out of my skin when I walk from the bathroom and the old iPhone pings and the face lights up. I snatch it up before it can turn back off. Lida and I smile from the home screen, and I put in my pin number. I look at the smashed selfie taken at the Lights Festival not too long before I died. That's my big smile and bigger sunglasses. I remember posing at the right angle for the shot, but it's like looking at a photo taken a long time ago. Like a high school yearbook picture. That's not me now.

I pull up my messages and tap HotGuyNate before the phone has a chance to die. The texts turn from natural conversation to sexting in no time at all. They're uncomfortable to read now. Him saying what he's going to do with my big breasts and me writing how much I'm going to love it. Him telling me to meet him at the Kitty Cat Lounge in El Paso and what he had planned for later at the motel across the street. Me saying I can't wait to ride him like a hobbyhorse. My chest burns with embarrassment, and through the cracked screen I read the last few texts:

HotGuyNate: *Are you there yet?*

Me: *I'm about sixty miles away.*

HotGuyNate: *I can't make it.*

Me: *Is this a joke?*

HotGuyNate: *Sorry.*

Me: *Why?*

HotGuyNate: *My wife found out.*

Wife? I drove two hundred miles to meet up with a cheating asshat? I *died* in El Paso because of a man?

I toss the phone on the bed and turn to look out a window at the night sky crammed with stars. I guess Edie and I have much more in common than I thought. We both ended up at UMC El Paso at the same time for the same reason—only I didn't *try* to kill myself. I'm still not exactly sure how it happened, but I rolled Momma's minivan and died from my injuries.

I hardly sleep that night, and the next morning my nerves are shot. I put Katrina's hair in a bun and give her camera-ready makeup. She dresses in my Marc Jacobs mint-green sheath and Ferragamo flats. She looks professional, and I watch her take her meds before we drive the few blocks to the courthouse and put HotGuyNate out of my mind for now.

The *Sentinel* reporter and Big 2 News wait with the photographer on the front steps of the courthouse. Katrina, with check and truck keys in hand, joins them while I stand beneath a big shade tree, close enough to see the event but far enough away not to be noticed.

I don't have to stand there long before Momma and Daddy roll up in Daddy's old truck, tools and dog in the back. They're wearing their Sunday clothes and hold hands as they walk up the sidewalk. Even before they make it all the way, I reach into my purse and pull out a tissue. I started a charitable foundation to make sure they are provided for as long as they live. I've never been prouder, but I wish things had turned out different and were easier between us.

The ceremony lasts five minutes. Five minutes that seem to pass in five seconds. Katrina answers questions and gets her picture taken with Momma and Daddy. I wish it was me, but I'm just happy to know they'll never have to wear old coats again.

Katrina joins me and we chuckle as Momma fires up the new Ford and follows behind Daddy and his dog in the old truck.

"That was fun," Katrina says as we walk to the Saint George. "Who gets the next check?"

"I'm still lookin'."

We cross the road and she says, "If you were born and raised in Michigan, why do you sound like the people around here?"

I shrug. "Read my aura."

"I did, but the answer isn't in your aura. I don't see past lives or otherworld connections."

Well, that's a relief. A horn blasts from the street beside us and we both jump out of our skin. The window on the F-150 slides down and Momma sticks her head out and says, "Pudge and me don't know why you've been so kind to us, but we want to thank you proper and invite you to supper."

One of the hardest things I've ever done is look at my momma and say, "Thank you, but we've got a plane to catch."

"Well, another time, then."

"I'd like that."

I watch her go, but my heart doesn't break as much this time. I love my folks and Marfa as much as ever, but I can't live with one foot in Texas and the other in Michigan. It's too hard and I don't belong here. Not because there's no place for me, but because this isn't my home anymore. While I was so focused on Texas, I didn't see that I'd planted my Louis Vuitton's squarely in Michigan and made a home for myself.

My home is where I walk my dog and buy him organic treats with blue icing. Home is where I found a beauty school I want to attend and where I'm working toward my dream of opening Shear Elegance. Home is where my sister-in-law, Meredith, and brother, Burton, live and where I love to watch their kids grow.

Home is where Marv and Claire live in a house as big as a museum. They'll never be my momma and daddy, but I don't want that of them. They're my parents, Marv and Claire Chatsworth-Jones, and I love them for their class and generosity. They still miss the old Edie, but they also love me for who I am today.

The who-I-am-today tells stupid jokes just to hear Marv sigh, although I think he secretly loves it when I do.

Home is where both my heart and soul live, with a man who loves me for me, and who looks forward to my return. Just the other night, he had me hitting high notes that inspired a brand-new song in his honor.

I am not Brittany Lynn Snider or Edie before El Paso. I'm me. My life is a book of blank pages, and I get to write the next chapter.

I think I'll title it "Macarons at Ladurée."